EMBERS OF ORIGINS

J du Preez

Embers of Origins

This is a work of fiction. Names, characters, businesses, places, events, locales, and incidents are either the products of the author's imagination or used in a fictitious manner.
Any resemblance to actual persons, living or dead,
or actual events is purely
coincidental.

First edition, 2025
ISBN: 978-1-0492-8408-8

Table of Contents

EMBERS OF ORIGINS

The first of the Clara Sing duology.

"Sometimes we just have to wait a bit for forever."

Written on a balcony overlooking Vala in the spring of 2025.

Author's Note:

Clara Sing started out as a minor character on the pages of **Embers of Orbit**. In **Embers of Iris** she all but jumped off the page. I knew she had more story to tell after that. The logical place to follow her was to Kepler after the story of Aten and Iris.

A new world, new culture, new dangers, and most importantly... new love interests. This new journey takes Clara from her irreverence on Earth to a misplaced woman, navigating Lyra—an alien world a thousand light years from Earth, abandoned by its previous inhabitants.

Embers of Origins has Cry-Fi at its heart and goes out to all those Read to Bleed fans. Where belonging is a luxury and love is a battle. Where what we desire clashes with what society demands.

I hope everyone who reads this will forget the world for a while and wander the rain-soaked streets of Lyra, sit on the moss fields staring at the moonless sky, or just stand on a balcony watching an alien sun rise over Vala, holding hands with their heart.

I also strongly recommend listening carefully to **I'm just a girl by No Doubt**, before or during your read of **Embers of Origins**.

-J

ↄ PROLOGUE ɕ

It was my last day on Earth. One way or another.

I stepped off the train with a drop, plunging back into the noise of the world from the liminal warmth inside. The beam, Daedalus, loomed wide above the world, bathing everything in chilled blue neon light. The icy glow above and the snow below, freezing my bones by sight alone.

Taking in the frigid, anxious air, I knew I had to start moving.

I scanned the thrum of the crowd for Aten and Iris.

My friends.

At least that's how we ended up. Everyone around me looked like shit. It likely had something to do with the apocalypse, but there's just no pleasing some people.

The old iron-clad machine stood hissing on the tracks as I wandered down the length of it. Beyond it, like a crouching mountain, was an exodus ship. A sleek sardine can of ominous hope. For many it was the last chance to get off planet, gambling on the void to be gentle as our world burns.

The ship knelt below the beam, almost as if watching it. Anticipating its journey through, to gods-only-knew-what, in the Kepler system. A colony and a new life, or death in the vacuum.

But, I wasn't boarding this ship. Aten and I had one last piece of code to run in a nearby site, to give the hopeless a chance. The code that meant the difference between a hell of a ride and being atomised for everyone traveling the beam.

We were to take an auxiliary ship to ride the blade of plasma. Or we would die equally as horribly if Aten's code didn't work. But he was always a clever boy—prodigious even. That's one of the things that drew me to him originally.

"Let's not get into that again, Clara," I said aloud to myself, receiving stares from bleak faces.

Finally, I spotted the pair. They both stood a head above the crowd, just as I was a head below. Their dark eyes were rimmed with red. Iris's long black curls were loose and messy. The last goodbyes must have been tough on them. As for me, my goodbyes had been done long before. All but two.

I looked the pair over as I strolled up to them. They didn't get time to fuss before I spoke.

"You know we can just remotely upload, right?" I said, trying to bring a warmer note to the iced gloom around us.

Aten shook his head. His infuriatingly beautiful hair didn't even wobble.

"No," he said. "For this we have to link to a secure site."

"Damn it," I huffed.

"Damn it," he agreed.

A brief look of hope on Iris's face fluttered and died quietly.

I led the way to the car our enigmatic leader Corrin had arranged for us. Corrin and I never got along. Call me old fashioned, but sentient governing AIs strolling around didn't strike a chord with me. He was too calm and too organised to pass as human. That and his unnaturally pasty face.

The car he sent was, at very least, a beast of a machine. The only drip of colour on the otherwise monotone scenery. It was almost as good looking as Aten. It, however, improved slightly on Aten's sandy brown skin, with a polished cherry red. The couple said their teary goodbyes. I could almost hear him tell her it'll be ok, like he always had. Imagining him telling her how she held his heart and that he would see her soon. Like he always had. Goodbyes had never been hard for him. But he always found his way back to her. Always her.

By the time I had loaded my bag into the car, Iris and Aten stood holding hands as if saying their vows. A glint of precious metal around a finger on each side, and fresh-baked goods tucked under Aten's arm. A smile tugged at my lips. How close Iris and I had come to blows when we met. Yet, I stood there grinning like a fool at my closest friend and roommate. She had snagged the boy after all. With a little help from me. This time hopefully it would stick.

They chatted seriously, before walking over. Their mood seemed improved, but I could still feel the grit in it. Some of my own luggage also wouldn't fit in a car. The type you carry forever. This time, there would be no second chances. We were leaving our home world, like a second-hand sci-fi story, with as many yellowed and dogeared pages.

"Don't be late," Iris said to him as they approached. "I mean it."

Iris turned to me.

"Take good care of him," she asked.

A year ago, that would have been the most absurd request from her. Now it was a given, and she knew it. I let her see a flicker of that old rivalry, long since smoothed into something softer.

"Of course," I replied, "he's such a hotty after all."

Grinning helped me ignore the way my vision blurred.

She wrapped me tight. It was love, wine in the snow, coffee-brown paints, and music on rooftops. It was the type of friendship that only enemies could forge.

As for Aten, she grabbed him by the collar. Their lips met in heat that could have melted the snow in the local district.

My head turned away in reflex. My chest clenched.

I loved Iris of course, but Aten...

He was like a donated rib. One I couldn't get back.

But the scar lingered.

With a final whispered goodbye and a lingering hand later, Aten and I sat in the car. The engine pounding, shaking the car like a dog waiting to be let off its leash. I stared into the snow ahead.

The road was a stark black line against the blue-tinted terrain.

"Ready?" I asked him, not sure myself.

"No," he admitted, not taking his eyes off the rearview mirror.

He sighed, slamming it into gear, and we hurtled away in red and rubber.

The road was deserted as it streaked by. Small hints of black or green marking our passing through the endless blue-white countryside. Aten had his window open a crack, a twist of cigarette smoke streaming out. My window was down more. I was enjoying the frigid air on my skin, knowing I'd never feel it again.

I was daydreaming, staring into the powder.

Without warning, the car lurched. It slid, wailing and kicking up frost. I braced for my life, pinching my eyes closed, holding my breath. Another hard shift and a tail wiggle later, we were running straight again. Far behind us a cow stood, barely even reacting to the event. A stark reminder that death didn't need a beam to end us.

My eyes were wide open, as my heart pushed blood to every corner of my body. I sat upright, grabbing at the seatbelt and clipping it in with shaky hands, hoping that was the last surprise we would run into.

Aten shot me a self-satisfied glance, but said nothing. Something as stupid as a cow ending our journey after all we've been through would have been ironic. I slowly released my grip on the seatbelt, trying to relax.

Less than an hour later, a small town appeared in the distance. In the centre of it stood a giant white cube of a building—a titanic sugar cube. I felt a grin forming. Salvation was in sight.

The plan was laid out in my head. As much as I hated to admit it, I wanted off Earth. Sooner suited me better than later.

"So we run in, load the code, hit send, and fly?" I asked.

"Not exactly," Aten replied, as if that explained anything.

"What did I miss?"

"Me, getting suspended."

My entire face went slack. If Aten wasn't a councillor anymore...

"Were you planning on telling me?" I asked, annoyed at his stupid handsome face.

"Sure, ten seconds ago," he quipped.

I gave him the finger as my brow tried to fold in on itself.

"So, what's the plan genius," I asked, less than happy.

"Well *I* have to drive back, but there's time."

His plan, whatever it was, didn't involve me then. He was committing treason but leaving me out of it. At best, he would be denied a seat on the science ship. If they didn't shoot him outright.

Not like him at all. He'd have to double back, and he would be cutting it close. Even with the beast we drove, getting back to the exodus ship would be...

I shook my head.

I didn't have time to think about that. We had to get in the hard way. Bypassing security would be easy. Access to the systems after, would not.

"So, here's what we need to do..." Aten started, as if reading my mind.

Turns out our planning was a monumental waste of energy. Corrin, the smug metal bastard, had sent ahead and the facility practically rolled out the red carpet for us. He always did have a soft spot for Aten. Apparently convincing a team that disobeying orders to save their own skin was less complicated than we thought.

The facility was open to us.

We got to work.

Code integration only took minutes, but the upload dragged ass far too long. I was starting to doze off by the terminal, while Aten spun his wheels behind me. Each second ticking away on time he already didn't have. While Corrin had secured our entry, there was still no seat for Aten on the science vessel. Corrin's influence could reach only so far.

I swung my chair around.

"You go, sexy boy," I said, teeth and lashes doing the work. "I'll finish this and be on the ship."

"Clara I can-"

I shooed him. "You have driving to do. I've always been better at this anyway," I lied. I didn't want him to go, but I wanted him to live.

He dropped his head in defeat with a small chuckle.

"Alright, Clara, you win this time."

It wasn't as much of a win for me as he thought.

I stood hugging him tightly. His arms could make me forget about judgment day. Stepping back, my eyes found his lips. My hand drifted up, brushing against them. But I'd never be the one those lips were promised to. I'd never be the one that baked for him and he'd never lie to me about liking it.

"Cookie crumbs," I said, as my face heated.

I shook myself. This was not the time to rehash old battles.

"Don't take forever, boss," I said instead.

"Thank you, Clara," he said, punctuating it with a painful kiss on my cheek. "For everything."

He turned and ran. Thankfully the tear waited to fall until he was gone. I hoped I would see him again.

That we'd come out the other end in one piece. Then looking at the untested code, I hoped we would come out the other end at all.

Ten long minutes later, with the upload completed, I walked through the ozone and new car smell of the science ship. I strapped in, ready as I would ever be. My view was of the town and white hills beyond. A black line drawn across it all. Aten's artery to salvation. The atmosphere was filled with tense conversations. Then the rumbling started. Low at first, but rising in tempo like a mad drummer. My bones shook, then the sound exploded into a roar. I sank into the seat, every inch of me straining against the pleather.

The town started sinking from my view, then the hills, and soon the Earth itself seemed to set behind the window frame. All the while the vibration and roar continued as an assault on every sense.

Then it just stopped. I floated forward, the seatbelt holding me with a lover's embrace.

My inner nerd was freaking out. I was in space. Earth and the beam hung together outside of my window. A steady blue stream of solar fire, siphoned from the sun, and streaming into the void beside the muted blue of the world.

Kepler should have a fairly decent colony set up, but it would be hard work. Or it would be a failed world. A grave for humanity. I prepared myself for either.

My hands tightened around the arm rests. There was no use in worrying about the destination. I shook my head, banishing the thoughts. The journey still lay ahead, and whatever new normal that entailed.

The blue consumed the ship interior.

We were ready to enter a funeral pyre for all that was Earth. Everything we knew fading in the light.

Everything shook and rattled.

A hum of a thousand bees bled through my soles and up my spine.

Then the alien beam swallowed us.

ↄ ONE ɕ

The cabin flashed white, fading to blue. The hallway stretched into an endless tunnel. The seat in front of me pulled away as if on a rail, followed by angular veins of pale blue creeping along the floor. I became aware of my bones shifting under my muscles. My window yawned and elongated, gaping into open space. Stars flashed and popped outside in every colour like an astronomical sparkler. My eyes burned—the sensory overload forcing them to close. I'm not sure if I screamed, but my throat felt raw. I could see the beam even while my eyes were closed, as if the ship had become transparent. It formed a tube of rainbow plasma stabbing into infinity.

There was a loud pop, shoving me forward against the restraints. All the air was ejected from me, my stomach following soon after.

Every nerve bristled with static. My face was wet, and the taste of metal joined the bile on my tongue.

I swiped at my face and it came away crimson.

"Well that's not fucking promising," I groaned.

It felt wrong. A thousand lightyears in a few minutes. I had expected it to take days, but was thankful it hadn't. My body burned in too many ways as it was.

The cabin was chaos. Crying, retching, and even screams. Many passengers were injured, or bleeding from the nose or eyes. A smaller number were slumped over, suspiciously—no, eerily still. A sour copper smell consumed the interior.

We had made it through the beam, though in what condition I didn't know. I turned from the desperation in the cabin. Outside *Kepler b* lay ahead. In the last few decades, we had been sending ships over in a steady stream. Of those, the bulk, nearly ten million people, had Aten to thank for their survival. The planet should be a massive colony, or even a city.

Kepler's second world drifted into view, illuminated in the inky black. It was an immaculate view, leaving me breathless.

It was a whole new world hanging there.

My eyes followed the curve of the planet to the night-side. There were lights. Lakes of it larger than any colony could have been. Webs connecting them, woven in silver-blue. The night side of the planet was flooded with the illumination of vast cities. I was doing the math in my head. What would it take to build on that scale? Ten million, no. A hundred million. It would have taken hundreds of years for them to have expanded to that extent. I squinted, pressed against the window. Something was off. It was all wrong.

My eyes stayed locked on the pools of light, sinking into the impossibility of them. I took deep breaths forcing myself into calm.

The pilot's voice crackled into the cabin. The static of panic quieted but would never still. I gripped the arm rest, hoping for good news.

"Ladies and gentlemen, we'll apparently be docking at the space station in the next hour. Please remain seated."

The... space station? Did they repurpose some of the exodus ships? Anxious dread bubbled up in my stomach. The cabin filled with renewed nervous murmurs, mirroring my own trepidation.

"What the hell was going on?" I whispered to myself, as a massive floating structure started to come into view. Smaller lights could be seen hovering around it.

I kept myself pressed up against the window, as the station grew closer—larger. It hung in orbit. A city-sized impossibility.

"Someone's got a lot of explaining to do."

The ship rocked as it docked. I grabbed my bag, filtering out with the other passengers. Some remained in their seats crying. Others weren't moving at all. It felt horrid leaving them, but nobody could help them now.

I walked through the hatch—white light blinding me for a moment. Once my eyes adjusted, I was filled with disbelief. Ahead of me the interior of the space station stretched out like a mall. No, like a small city. Everything was smooth and white, punctuated with lines in that familiar blue.

The ambient light was coming from somewhere unseen, but was warm instead of sterile. There must have been thousands of people moving around from every demographic and background imaginable. Most impressively, artificial gravity. That certainly would not have been on my bingo card. Though how that was possible was a mystery, overshadowed by how sore my body was.

Above me the ceiling towered, multiple floors stretching out of view. The station held everything from structures like offices to food vendors. New smells of all types wafted through the air, more pleasant than the interior of the ship. My stomach latched on to what must have been a nearby food stall and bubbled. I hadn't eaten in a while.

I was stunned by it all. No matter how many people were shipped to the planet, I couldn't imagine that all of it could have been accomplished. At least not in the few years we'd been sending ships down the beam. Aten was going to love it when he arrived.

We were quietly shuffled into a number of queues, like cattle. Twenty minutes later, I had been identified, tested for pathogens, and handed an ID slip.

The identification was little more than a small burned-orange rectangular bit of plastic, with my photo and an indecipherable block of dots and dashes beside it. On the reverse was my name and a twenty-digit code. The technology was simple compared to the station surrounding me.

"If it ain't broke..." I grumbled to myself.

My working theory—we must have slipped further through time than anticipated. It was only a theory. I hoped we would have some answers soon.

Our group was funnelled into a sterile room with rows of seats and a large screen. Unlike the rest of the station, these rooms were beiger and showed their age from disuse. Everyone was quiet in anticipation and exhaustion. I hoped that Iris and Aten's ship wouldn't be far behind. A friendly face would have been a blessing.

A young woman walked in with small quick steps, dressed like a flight attendant. She looked more nervous than we were.

"Hello everyone, pleased to meet you. My name is Meradine. I'll be getting you... you fine folks up to speed."

But Meradine did not look as if she was pleased or believed that we were indeed fine folks.

"Don't do us any favours," I grumbled, drawing sniggers of agreement from around me.

She spoke too fast and didn't take questions, all the while holding a clipboard like a shield, barely looking up as she read each point. At least we got some basics and a pamphlet, no doubt printed years before. Kepler, or rather *Lyra,* was a bustling planet with a population of over two-billion people.

Confused murmurs from the back.

There was alien tech, but the aliens had buggered off at some point in the past. Knowing nods made the room sway. This wasn't news really. The beam was a known quantity. It seemed to be a forgotten road they started building but abandoned.

Lyra had very short years and longer days, which had the fun effect of making me almost fifty years old. Some light, but nervous chuckles bubbled from a group of younger women. Gravity and atmosphere were comparable to Earth at least.

Then Meradine dropped the other shoe, right on the room's toe.

The time dilation had shunted us forward, nearly four-hundred years.

I nodded, less shocked than the rest. But I've always been a bit faster than others. The hall, however, erupted into madness. Some wailed. Some shouted about it being a mistake. A woman beside me simply slipped off the chair to her knees.

We had come with the spirit of pioneers, only to find out we weren't the vanguard, but the leftovers. She patiently let everyone tire themselves into silence. Her face remained stoic throughout.

Afterward, we were each handed a small comm device, a food ration of sorts, and an address of some housing we were allocated. We would be contacted they claimed. Nobody made a fuss. The fight had gone out of them and me.

We were herded through the expansive interior to the space elevator, without so much as a wet cloth or a head pat. I smelled like sick and sweat. My head still throbbed.

The space elevator was a monumentally impressive construction. Any physicist worth their degree had nightmares about the forces involved. But there it was, without ceremony. The trip down took an hour, affording me phenomenal views of the planet below as it snuck closer. It could have been Earth if not for the landmasses. The pamphlet showed two large continents with a smaller one wedged in between the other two. With nothing but time, I ate the dry ration and studied the elevator. A new world was exciting. Settling in was not.

We entered the clouds and everything faded to mystery grey. The view of the ground itself was left to our most feral imaginations. At the bottom we were wished luck and then the doors closed behind us. I dragged my bag out into the gloomy day. Ahead of me lay the city of Vala. Towers of teal lancing the grim grey sky.

I was left alone at a space-port for the second time in two days.

ɔ TWO ɕ

A group of my fellow passengers wandered off as if they knew where they were going. I decided to follow them. They likely didn't know anything I didn't, but at least we had something in common. Soon it became obvious that they were as lost as I was. They bickered and hesitated. I slowed, and they didn't stop to wait for me. The people around me were dressed in T-shirts, suits, and overalls. No chrome or footlong mohawks in sight. The other refugees dissolved into the foot traffic.

"Thanks for nothing," I grumbled, my voice low.

"Hey!" someone said angrily, shoving past me. They fired off some more angry and foreign words. I could only make out something like "*High I'm Dew*", but I wasn't sure what it meant.

I scanned the crowd, hoping for some clue of what to do next.

A uniformed man stood nearby. He appeared to be an authority figure, kitted in a blue shirt and pants, with a hat that didn't fit into the apparent fashion. A golden metal ring hung on his chest. I pushed through the crowd towards him.

"I'm from Earth. Help me?" I asked, catching up to him and pointing at the infinite string that was the space elevator cable disappearing into the twilight sky.

He was younger than I was, with an attempt at a moustache staining his lip.

He scowled, following my finger. Then looked between me and the cable to space, realisation slowly colouring his expression. His demeanour shifted.

"Ugh," he said, shaking his head.

I showed him my apartment key and my ID.

"No," he grumbled, pushing my ID chip back to my pocket. He waggled his finger warning me.

I tucked the ID away and handed him the key.

He squinted at it. There were a few numbers printed on a tag attached.

He smiled, nodding knowingly.

"Mhm," he said, considering the tag. "Come," he commanded.

He started off towards the road, waving me with him. I huffed, preparing for where, or whatever, he was leading me to. My bag clattered behind me as I followed him.

We waited for some odd-looking cars to whisper by on the brick road. They were pure white, with the telltale glow peeking out from under them. There were no visible wheels. Street signs were worthless too. The letters used I mostly recognised, but the words were indecipherable. The... officer, weaved through the crowd on the sidewalk, then ducked into an alleyway. I stopped, clenching my fists before the dim passage, ready for trouble. Not that I knew much about fighting, but tired as I was, I still wouldn't go down without a fight. Dipping my head, I moved forward.

The alley smelled of rot and something metallic. It was coated in smears of black and what looked like dead plants. I followed the strange, almost wire-like branch system to its base as it crept along the dirty concrete. The plant-like thing sprouted from two small red shoes in a shape that looked uncannily like legs. The branches were moving—breathing. I leaned in, holding my own breath.

"Hallo. Come," the officer urged, making me jump.

I blinked myself back to Earth. Lyra, I suppose. Waving at the man, I continued following him. I looked back, at the strange image. The skin on my arms pulled tight, and I sped up my pace away from it.

After a few minutes of walking, I couldn't help but start to feel a might reassured. The city was alien, but I was no stranger to otherness. The foreign language, the styles, and the architecture, reminded me of my trip to old Earth cities. The abandoned locations were ruins, but carried the bones of being human. The walk on Lyra was like that. A strange place. But there was still laughing, honking in the distance, and people walking hand-in-hand. It wasn't Earth, but it was ultimately still human.

The officer stopped by a building and gestured to the door. I nearly walked into him.

"Ok?" he asked, then marched back the way we came without waiting for a response. He was clearly satisfied with his contribution.

"Thank you," I called after him, but he kept going without looking back. And once again, I was dumped in front of a door, with no direction.

The building wasn't large. I took a step back to get a better look and almost fell on my ass in surprise.

"The fuck... Is... Have I lost my mind?"

There on the front as big as a billboard was the face of Aten. It was as if he was following me through time and space, with that perfect damn jawline and smirk.

There was a sign below his face I could actually understand.

Receivers of The Gift

I wasn't sure if it was a cult or a fan club, but standing on the street wasn't doing me any good. I reached for the door, my hands trembling. I flexed my fingers a few times, then forced myself to enter.

The inside was bright and mild. The walls were decorated with faux pillars and the floor was covered in large red tiles designed to look like carpet.

A balding older man approached me. His outfit reminded me of a bishop. Red pomp with too many flaps.

He smiled a toothy smile at me and murmured something in the strange language of Lyra. The only part which I understood was Aten.

"I don't speak... Whatever that is," I interrupted him.

He looked stunned for a moment before his smile returned.

"Ah, you must be a new arrival," he said in perfect English.

"Oh thank the gods," I said, hands in the air.

He chuckled. "I imagine you have-"

"Miss Sing!" a voice boomed. The bishop-looking man appeared annoyed at being interrupted.

I turned to see a slightly younger man in an altogether plainer robe jogging up.

"Doctor Sing, it is you?" the younger man asked panting when he arrived. He was plain looking, with a pair of oval glasses being his most distinguishing feature, along with a single long earring that did not suit his appearance otherwise.

The two exchanged some words in the Lyran language. The newcomer kept smiling as the bishop's frown kept deepening. Then abruptly, the older man turned to leave without another word. He glared at me as he went.

"Sorry about that," the younger man said. "My name is Harry by the way. I recognise you from your photo."

"Oh, yeah," I said, not knowing what photo he was talking about.

"I'm sure you must have a million questions."

I looked around. Pictures of Aten, framed in gold were littered everywhere. The thick red curtains and vaulted ceiling gave the impression of old Earth churches.

"Look, Harry," I said in a flat tone. "I only want directions, not to join your cult."

Harry looked around then chuckled.

"I can see why you would think that. But the *Receivers of the Gift* are more of a community guide. We guide for moral and intellectual thinking."

I made a show of looking around.

"Could have fooled me, man," I said dryly.

"Granted we have our... stranger members," he smiled. "But Aten wasn't a god. Merely someone who's ideals we follow."

I nodded slowly, eyebrow raised. Aten was going to have a good chuckle when he arrived and shattered their world view. Harry shook himself. His cheery expression faltered.

"I've been here ten years, and I'll admit, some of it is still strange to me."

"This damn time dilation," I spat. Would it be a decade before I would see Iris and Aten again? Longer?

"Um... Look doc, English is the least of your worries. Only the elites still speak it. On the ground it's Lyrican, and alien oddness. Be happy everyone still has two arms and legs. But that's why I'm here. To help get you settled in."

"You knew I was coming?"

"Well, no," he admitted, sheepishly. "But you're hardly the first from Earth to end up at our doors."

"So, what's next?" I asked.

"Right, right," he said, hands smoothing his robe.

"Well, you knew Aten, right? You were his assistant. That counts for a lot here."

I rubbed my eyes.

"Fucking great. I travel a thousand lightyears so my relationship with a man can give me a leg up."

"Speaking of Aten. Will he be joining us soon?"

I narrowed my eyes at him. He held up his hands with a weak smile.

"Alright. Another time. What's your job allocation?"

"I got..." I said taking out the ID slip and my house key.

"Null huh?" he said as if that would mean something.

I tucked it away as a later concern.

"Tell you what. I'll get you to your residence, it should be quite nice," he said, guiding me to the door. "Take a few days to settle. I have a friend who can help you. Lyra can use all the physicists they can find."

I tabled my questions. Clearly, I was talking to the wrong man. I'd have to wait for Harry's contact. I didn't have the attention left to spar with him anyway.

We arrived at the road and he flagged down a cab as if it were a city back home. It was much like the cars I saw earlier, but altogether more run-down. Paint flaking and a clanking as it slowed. It had a driver, which surprised me. On Earth AI was common. Another mystery generously gifted by Lyra.

I nodded to him. "Thank you, Harry."

"Here," he said, grabbing my comm. "Contact me if you need anything."

I checked the screen. His contact details and picture listed. The picture making him look more interesting than he was in reality. I popped off a quick mock salute, then loaded my bag in the back while Harry talked to the driver for a moment. The driver shot me a glare that almost soured my milk. Then Harry nodded and stepped back as I got in.

"Oh and don't touch the blue plants," he yelled as the car pulled away.

I looked around to ask what he was talking about, but it was too late.

Small red shoes and breathing branches. I hoped it was less of a big deal than my knotted stomach thought it was.

The sun... Kepler's sun, hung low on the horizon as the car floated down the road silently. The cab itself smelled of old cigarettes and mud. I leaned on my arm and took in the strange vistas. We passed building after building that would have not been out of place in any Earth city. But that pervasive blue glow was all over. Even the run-down cab had some on the outside. Lyra tech or reversed alien tech perhaps. The car turned onto a motorway and I got my first real look at the city.

It faded into a distant orange haze. In the middle distance was the city centre, with the enormous teal towers. There were also huge domed buildings dotted about, that looked more opulent than even the tallest towers. Scattered throughout were large out of place triangular monoliths. The alien blue glow at the centre of their construction. I had seen the type before. Daedalus and the beam.

The city stretched beyond any of the ten cities back home. I hadn't just missed the colony phase. Instead, I had become an alien among my own species.

It was a short drive. The cabby kept looking back at me as if I was going to steal something out of his filthy car. Anything I would have taken I would have needed antibiotics to get rid of surely.

We stopped in an unremarkable street, and he pointed at a plain-looking, grey building. Graffiti gave it some personality, but not the type I liked on my living space.

I hopped out, thankful to be out of the smelly vehicle. I had barely grabbed my bags before he pulled away. He shouted something out of the window, but the only word I understood was "Terran". I didn't have to speak the language to know it wasn't meant academically.

"Thank you. Asshole!" I shouted after him.

I clipped out my travel handle and made my way to the apartment building. At least the numbers were still the same.

104.

It took me a moment to figure out the lock, but I managed to let myself in. It turned out to not be 'quite nice' as Harry had predicted.

The interior was dim and more beige than white. I squinted my eyes as they adjusted. It smelled of disuse and mould. If Lyra even had mould.

I clicked a button, turning the lights on.

"Practically a local already," I mocked.

The main room looked like a bedroom and study combo. The bed was a sad beaten thing, that clearly wasn't new. In fact, it wasn't even made.

Beyond that was a small spare room, a tiny but fully loaded bathroom. Next to the main room via an archway was a surprisingly substantial kitchen, with appliances I mostly recognised. On the bed was a small booklet in English, showing nearby points of interest.

"Very touristy. But there's no return flight for me."

I kicked off my shoes and dug out fresh clothes. Then I went to test out the shower. The water was hot, as hot as I could stand, washing off the trip, the landing. Earth.

I stepped out still drying my head, catching myself in the mirror. The fresh clothes helped, but my hair looked less pixie cut and more barber accident. I sighed. A thousand lightyears from Earth and bad hair.

"First days are always the hardest, Clara," I said, covering my face with the towel.

I threw it to one side and collapsed on the bed, thinking about home. A home that was erased. An entire planet wiped from the universe.

Iris... Aten.

I wondered when... If I'd ever see them again.

I relaxed, letting my tears fall as I did. Sleep found me soon after.

ↄ THREE ɕ

Something screeched, jolting me awake. The sun was already filtering in through the cloudy window. I walked to the kitchen, grabbing some water, hoping it was safe to drink. I needed something to eat, which meant wandering outside. I'd have to do it sometime. I paged through the booklet, hoping it would all make sense. It was clearly written by someone who was born on Lyra. I threw it back on the bed, then set off into the city. Something flew by. It looked as if someone had glued dragonfly wings onto a gecko—cooing as it went.

"That's fun," I remarked. At least the alien life was interesting.

I looked left and right at the road. There were no obvious signs of anything that looked like a café or restaurant. The top of one of the titanic teal towers stood out above the rooftops to my left. I opted to go the opposite way.

I walked for a while with little to see, keeping a mental note of each turn. I avoided alleyways, still seeing the tiny shoes with the breathing branches growing out in my mind.

The cold of the morning started breaking when I made it to a main road. Immediately the smell of food wafted over me.

"I hope it's not blue... or wriggling."

I was pleased to discover that the smell was burgers and fries. I nearly cried from excitement.

Pointing to order seemed to do the job. The vendor was friendly enough, and helped me pay. It involved swiping my orange tag over a small surface marked with a "L" crossed with two lines. How much it cost I didn't know, but I walked away with a juicy looking burger and two fistfuls of fries.

The meat on the burger remained a mystery to me. A mystery best left unsolved. I strolled down the road savouring my prize, feeling very satisfied with myself. The street was lined with shops of all kinds. It was a classic case of wherever you go there you are, on a humanity wide scale. Fruits, some human, some alien. Curio shops labelled *Authentic Earth* selling day-to-day tat from our home. I paused outside a pet store with odd sounds creeping from it, but decided not to go in. Turning on my heel and started my trek back to my apartment. Home, I suppose. I did stop briefly to grab another meal. It was nothing special. Just ramen, made from the same plastic they used on Earth undoubtedly.

Harry's contact would be a welcome sight, if they could explain even half of what I needed.

A few blocks from my place, I noticed two men following close behind me. I did not get the impression they were looking out for my wellbeing. Not spoiled for choice, I ducked into an alleyway as soon as I turned a corner. I snagged a can, throwing it down the path I would have taken.

There was muttering and then the two came jogging past.

"Hey, hide-on-two! We only talk, yes?" they called after me.

It's not the first time I've heard that word, and I was sure it wasn't a cute pet name.

I leaned back against the wall. It was cold enough to feel wet. I kept my eyes on the road I had been on, not daring to look behind me. I could hear something scuffling and hoped it was a rat.

I stayed as long as I could bear, before the goosebumps running up my spine reached my neck.

When peeking there was no sign of the men. For all I knew they could have been good Samaritans.

"Fucking, yeah right," I scoffed.

I hurried the rest of the way.

I would have to be more vigilant. A change of clothes at minimum.

My mental note of my next steps had formed:

- Figure out how money actually works
- Get new clothes.
- Learn Lyrican.

Though how I was supposed to do any of that was a mystery. I entered the house, actually appreciating the stale air in the safety. Picking up my comm, I selected the first, and only contact on the list. Harry's face appeared on my screen with a green and red button under it.

At least some things remained the same. I tapped the green button.

It made a rhythmic pinging sound a few times and then he answered smiling.

"Doc Sing. So nice to hear from you."

"Harry," I purred, "I need your advice."

He looked very pleased with himself.

"Oh sure, anything I can do to help."

I told him about my to-do list and the men who followed me.

"Oh dear. I'm sorry. For such a pretty woman, the area can be... dangerous."

Ugh.

He was one of those.

"The good news is..." he continued, "my friend will be there in two days."

"Day after tomorrow. And he'll be able to help?"

"Oh Ramsey. He'll fix you right up."

I smiled at him. "You are my hero, Harry," I sung, winking.

He blushed.

"I'll speak to you soon then, I hope," he hinted.

"Sure, sure. Thank you."

My third day was much like the second. I was more wary and made a point of looking vigilant. No trouble found me as I stocked up on as much food as I could carry. I even managed to buy some *Earth-Style Soda.* Better yet, I found smokes. Turns out that's something that survived the four hundred years.

I struggled to get to sleep. Being so idle was too far outside my norm. I went outside, standing with my back against the wall. I puffed out a satisfying cloud with a long exhale. Something skittered across the road the size of a rabbit. It moved like a spider then ran up a wall.

"Fuck that entirely," I said as I flicked the bud away and fled inside, locking the door firmly behind me.

On the fourth day I was reading on my comm from Earth when someone knocked.

"Hello? Clara Sing?" they asked. A man's voice, huskier and smoother than Harry's.

I leapt up to my feet, grabbing a pipe I had 'acquired' from the dumpster outside.

"Can I help you?" I shouted through the door.

"I'm Harry's friend. Name's Ramsey."

My knuckles tightened around the metal in my hand, then I placed it down again.

I opened the door a crack, my foot blocking the swing. He raised an eyebrow.

"You alright?" he asked, his accent thick with vowels.

Ramsey looked like an action hero. Square jaw with some rough stubble. Broad nose and brow with dark piercing eyes. His hair was all but shaved off.

His lips were curvy for a man, and they were curled into a marble smile.

"Oh, hi," I said blushing despite myself.

"You busy?" he asked, brow furrowed.

"Oh shit, no. Sorry."

I swung the door open wide. He peered into the apartment.

"Null housing, huh? For a doctor. Fucking disgusting *Highonblues*, I tell you what."

"Some of that was English," I drawled.

He smiled broadly.

"Ah, yes. I'm gonna like you," he said waggling a finger in the air. He pulled a box of smokes out, tapped it on his wrist, and offered me one. I took it with a nod. He lit it for me, our eyes on each other.

"You're not assigned to work. That makes you Null, see?"

"That's not encouraging."

"It ain't, no," he said, shrugging. "You won't starve or nothin', just be bored as arse."

"What about *hide-and-dew*?"

He chuckled. It was as dark as his eyes and deep to match his voice.

"High-on-blue," he said, emphasising each syllable. "The elites, royals, or governors. Whatever the hell they call themselves. Down here we stick to Lyrican, if you don't want to be lumped in with their like."

"Alright," I said apprehensively. "What the hell am I supposed to do with myself?"

He winked, making my chest tighten.

"What indeed. Would you like a drink?"

"Yes," I said far too quickly.

He nodded his head over his shoulder and we walked up the road, the opposite way of the main street.

We walked for a few minutes. Ramsey had his hands in his pockets, his eyes scanning constantly.

"Is the area that dangerous?" I asked.

"Oh, nah," he laughed. "Old habits, is all."

"I think I was almost mugged on my first day out."

"Opportunists," he shrugged. "Must've heard you speaking English."

"Like you are?" I poked.

He pulled in a sharp breath through his teeth. "Ouch. In the jewels for helping a girl out."

"I didn't mean it in that way."

He smirked at me. "No worries. We'll get you sounding like a local in no time, I tell you."

I didn't know if that should have made me feel better, but it didn't.

A handful of silent minutes later he gestured to a small stall built into a wall. It had a single row of seats. The smell of spices and coffee spilled from the back with steam.

"Cozy," I said sitting.

He pulled up the chair next to me, sitting half turned, one leg still standing. The old man behind the counter saw him and forced a smile.

"Cutter!" the man said, jovially with a curl on his *"R"*.

"Gus, this is Clara," Ramsey said, making sure to use slow English.

I waved politely.

He ordered through some banter and then turned back to me.

"The way Harry says it, you're in the weeds a bit," Ramsey smirked.

"That's an understatement. I don't understand how anything works."

He nodded knowingly.

"I get that. Well, here's the rundown if you want it..."

He explained about the money slip that doubled as ID. Food and housing was covered as long as I maintained my 'Null' status. But they'd always be sub-par. He gave me a rundown of some of the cultural beats and norms. My temples throbbed, overloaded.

We stopped only to receive the food and drinks.

"Watch out this one, Clara. He a real *clipper*," the old man chuckled with a wink.

"A what?"

"Nothing," Ramsey interjected holding his hand up, "he's making fun of me is all."

"No sir. Not meaning offense."

Ramsey smiled at the man, who ducked back into the kitchen looking nervous. It gave me the chills, and I felt really home sick suddenly. But I had that feeling since I landed. Between language barriers and culture, I didn't understand, I decided to ignore it.

We ate what turned out to be good pasta and an even better beer.

"You busy tomorrow?" Ramsey asked, leaning on the counter.

I looked at him, eyebrow cocked through a swig of beer.

"So busy. I have ceiling staring scheduled from twelve."

"Sounds like you have the morning free for language lessons then," he said smiling with all teeth.

I rolled my eyes.

"You know I'm fifty years old right. A new language is going to be hard."

He laughed. "That means I'll pick you up at thirteen for lunch, yeah?"

My internal clock groaned.

"Sure," I said neutrally, "I'll still get the hang of the twenty-eight-hour days... Eventually."

He gave me a few phrases to practice while we finished our drinks, then walked me home. We joked and even teased a bit. He was pleasant and definitely easy on the eyes. But once I was inside my own place, I let out a long sigh collapsing on the bed. The quiet, relaxed interior a welcome change.

I looked around the dim apartment, taking stock.

"Guess I better settle in then," I said to the room.

"Looks as if I'm going to be here a while."

FOUR

Ramsey was there at thirteen sharp as promised to start my 'lived in' experience of Lyra. He was smoother than I liked to admit. I found myself drawn to him with each missed consonant. Even though I had some reservations, he wasn't hard to stare at. There were the ways others reacted to him. It put me on edge sometimes. Regardless, it was easy to be very open around him. Having someone to talk to was a welcome change.

He'd ask about Earth, and the work I did there. Soon, he was the closest thing to a friend since I had arrived. Potentially a bit more than that. It was shocking to find myself having a good time. I started to feel almost normal. Slowly my Earther skin began to shed.

I picked up Lyrican quick enough. For all the fuss about the language divide, it was barely more than hyper-slang English. And I had nothing but time. I spent it learning what I could. Reading Lyrican books and watching their shows. In only a few weeks, Ramsey's friends had become mine too. It made me feel more and more like a local.

We were sitting around a table in a Japanese style diner a few weeks in. The tables were low and we sat on small pillows on the floor. The kitchen was filled with the sounds of frying and cooks shouting orders. The diner itself was as rowdy—drinks flowing freely. I was leaning with my back against Ramsey. A local lemonade-type drink in my hand that could run a power plant. His leather jacket was draped over my shoulders to keep the cool night air at bay. It cloaked me in his scent. New upholstery mixed with fireworks. I tucked deeper into the jacket, and him.

The conversation was fully in Lyrican, and I was keeping up better each day.

Towny was cracking a joke, likely a dirty one knowing him. I didn't quite get the punchline as the others laughed. Keela narrowed his eyes at me.

"Too fast for you, Sing?" he asked, then burst into a grin.

"I'll get there. It's just... tricky," I defended, raising my drink high.

"Still a Terran, aye?" Keela joked.

Ramsey moved fast, not warning me. I was still leaning back on him and barely caught myself. He wrapped his fist in Keela's collar, faces close together. I huffed, annoyed with another display of macho shit.

"Call her that again and you'll be eating your sushi without teeth, you *rotlick*," he growled.

"I meant Earther," Keela whimpered. "Sorry, Cutter. Shit!"

Ramsey pushed him away.

"Apologise to Clara, fuckwit."

"I'm sorry, Sing," Keela grovelled. "I didn't mean nothin' by it, I swear."

I leaned back from Ramsey, playing with the rim of my glass.

"It's fine, Keela," I said smiling, hoping to defuse the mood. My hand went to Ramsey's forearm. He visibly relaxed, looking over to me. I nodded my eyes towards Keela. His frown calmed as he sat back down.

"Sorry, Keela," Ramsey mumbled. "That was... My bad, brother."

"Yeah, no worries. That was on me. I'll get the next round, right?"

"Apology accepted," I cheered, raising my drink again.

Afterward, he always walked me home. He'd stop next to my door and lean over, hands beside my shoulders, fishing for a kiss. I said no each time, telling him I wasn't ready for his world yet. But it was tempting. I knew I would crumble eventually. It was the game we liked to play.

Time without purpose blurs together. Some days were amazing. Some days I left my pillow damp with tears. Then around two months after I arrived, Ramsey walked me home and didn't pin me. I had leaned against the wall as always, but he didn't take the bait.

"Clara," he said, frowning.

"Something wrong, Cutter?"

"I have a present for you, but I'm a tad nervous to give it to you."

"Oh ho. Is it naughty?" I teased, playing with his shirt buttons.

He chuckled, but his face faded back to worried.

"Here," he said, handing me a slip of paper.

They were assignment orders, for me.

BlueTech Catalogue Lead.

I tilted my head, not sure what exactly I was looking at.

"Ooh, fancy... what is it?" I asked.

"It's a job. Working with the alien stuff. I put in a good word. It's high-profile and pays a bundle."

The realisation washed over me. My heart pounded.

"A real job? In my actual field?"

"Of course. What'd you think I am, some low-grade *clipper*? I told you I'd take care of you, didn't I?"

I started laughing, excited. Nervous, but excited.

"Oh, Cutter, you're amazing," I said, wrapping him in a hug.

"Oh yeah?" he asked, pinning me as always with a cheeky smile. "How amazing?"

He got his kiss that time. It was a pretty damn good one too.

I went to bed that night with a smile, counting the days until my real job started. I had never thought the idea of having to get up early and go to work could be so invigorating.

I insisted that Ramsey help me prepare for my job. I was going to be cataloguing Lyrican artifacts and testing them for potential use. The evening before I started work, he had warned me I'd be in an alien construct filled to the gills with *Highonblue* lackeys. I was not looking forward to that. But they would speak English and the work would be interesting.

He had one more warning before he left.

"Hey, Sing. Don't get that shit near your eyes and mouth, yeah."

"Don't eat it. Got you," I said with a thumbs up.

"I'm dead serious, love. That stuff will fuckin' mutate you. And I like your pretty face as is."

"That sounds morbid and terrifying."

"Look, *Bluetech* can make you strong, but it warps you."

An image of breathing branches and tiny shoes flashed in my mind. My stomach churned.

Ramsey must have picked up on how I felt. He wrapped one arm around me.

"Hey. Don't fret. Just be mindful and you'll be aces. Besides the founders were resistant to it. Maybe you will be too."

I nodded taking a deep breath.

"Like you said," he chuckled, bumping me with his hip. "Just don't eat or snort it."

I laughed, almost calming.

"Right," I said. "I'll keep my wits about me."

"You've got sharp enough ones," he said with an exaggerated wink and a kiss on the head.

Ramsey had promised to pick me up the next morning and then walked off into the night like a shadow.

I lay in bed that night, a mixed bag of emotions. The image of the blue plant... thing, plagued my mind. The other half of me fantasised about a future—maybe one with Ramsey in it. But it was too soon. I had learned that lesson on Earth. I did fall asleep eventually.

My dreams were of snow falling on the roof of the tech centre. Iris was there, Aten on her arm staring out into the white beyond. I was alone, but around my shoulders hung Ramsey's leather jacket. I turned, and behind me I saw Lyra and the capital city, Vala. It was warmer than Earth. And, it was becoming home.

❀ Juni I ❀

The video clicks on. Juniper is sitting on her bed, legs folded. Her sweater hangs off one shoulder lazily. Her hair is a messy halo of silver-white in the dim ambience of her room. She is wrapped around a large pillow.

"I'm finally starting work at the monolith."

She sits upright, bed creaking as she does, her eyes focusing on the middle distance.

"*It's about time you started learning the family trade*," she says, lowering her voice in a parody of her father's.

"I'm so glad to be done with the studying. I'll be happy to do something practical for a change. Even though the monos smell like old fish."

She shrugs the sweater onto her shoulder, but it slips off immediately.

"Tayo thinks it's cool. But Tayo is up my dad's bum, and we all know why," she says, rolling her eyes.

"It would be ok... if it was just me..." she yawns. "But I'm stuck babysitting some Earther, fresh off the beam."

"First ones in a long time too."

She leans closer to the camera, looking around as if someone might hear her.

"She's a physicist, apparently. As if any Earth physicists could compete with Lyra education."

Juniper sits back again, fidgeting with a pillow corner.

"If you ask me, father only hired her because apparently she knew Aten on the *backbeam*."

"Not only knew him," she groans, throwing a hand up. "But she was his assistant. I mean, come on... I never figured my dad for the gullible type."

"Bet you she claims to know Iris too," Juni chuckles.

Juni looks to her side at something off-camera.

"How cool would it be to meet Iris though, shit."

Her cheeks become rosy at the curse.

"I hope she's not as full of it as she sounds," Juniper complains, her frown returning. "But nobody cares what I think anyway."

"*Use that brain*, father says. *I paid for it and your education, don't let me down*."

Juniper leans forward, half burying her face in the pillow—hair falling over her eyes. Her hand flexes into the soft covers around her legs.

"So motivating Dad, really," she mumbles, as if he might hear.

One side of her mouth curls up afterward—a bow of bright red. Her gaze flicks up with her imagination, eyes brightening.

"The least she can do is be cute, so it's not a complete waste of time."

She breathes a short sigh.

"Anyway, I guess I'll have to endure it until she steals, or messes up. Then maybe, father will give me someone who's not delusional."

She rocks forward onto her knees, head going out of frame. The sweater hem and a hint of lace dominating the screen as she shuffles over to the screen.

Then the recording goes black.

FIVE

I had been on the site for two days without making much progress. The Highon... nobles, weren't as bad as Ramsey had made me believe. In all, they were more polite than Joe Average on the street. It was also refreshing to hear English again. The orientation was limited, as it appeared the job had been open for some time. I was treated with respect but ultimately left to my own devices.

The work, however, was beyond me. The building was unmistakably alien. The black walls, on closer inspection, were covered in scales for a lack of a better word. The blue glow permeated the structure with a hum that emanated from everywhere. My 'office' was no more than a prefab cube with a few small desks and shelves lined with strange alien artifacts.

The tools I was given may as well have been alien too, given how far ahead their tech was. Not even mentioning the actual *Bluetech*. If someone had told me I would be working with non-human technology a year before, I would have... well I had been working with non-human technology. But not in the same way as on Lyra. The smell in the building was pervasive. I couldn't get used to the odour of wet sand that hung everywhere. The tech itself seemed to always be wet, due to the bio-organic nature of it. It made me concerned about Ramsey's warning, but everyone on the site seemed unfazed by it. I sat with my hands in my hair, staring at the metal desk. A thin luminescent block between my elbows.

"You sure are pretty. I can put that in the notes," I whispered to it and myself.

There was a curt knock on the door and a few quick footsteps. I turned to see a young woman. She looked little more than a girl, but held herself in the way royalty did. She had long curling silver-white hair, a delicate face with large slanted eyes. Her robe was white with a high collar and gold detail. I didn't need my PhD to guess she was likely someone important. And my problem.

"Can I help you, Miss?" I asked, keeping my tone flat.

She looked me over, eyebrows raised, nose up.

"I have been sent to oversee the work," she said with an air of authority that didn't suit her otherwise gentle face or tenor.

A superior. I started packing my things mentally. Still if she was there to assist me, I wouldn't object.

"That's the best news I've had all day," I admitted grinning earnestly.

She raised an eyebrow. Perhaps she was looking for pushback. I was happy someone could help out.

"Your English is very good," she chimed.

"Thank you. I've been speaking it my whole life."

She frowned, narrowing her eyes.

"I'm Clara Sing," I said, putting my hand out.

She took it cautiously.

"I am Shao Juniper Anzu the fourth." Her voice was almost melodic, with full lips framing her mouth.

"Wow. So, are you like, a princess?"

"Something like that," she said without a hint of sarcasm.

I sat back in my chair incredulously, suddenly aware that I was dressed rather casually—hair a mess and pits too damp.

"Gods. Isn't that something. So, do I just call you Shao, or...?" I asked.

"That's not really how..." she started, somewhat flustered.

"Can I *just* call you Sing?" she asked, regaining her footing.

I raised an eyebrow in confusion.

"If you want to, I suppose," I offered.

She chuckled sweetly—her haughty demeanour slipping. It was a comfortable gentle sound. Combined with the way she carried herself, she certainly presented like a princess. That would take some getting used to certainly.

"Just call me Juni," she said smiling as she shook my hand daintily.

"Juni," I repeated, my face warming for no reason.

She lifted a random piece, clearly anxious to move on.

"What progress have you made?"

"None," I admitted. "Your technology is four-hundred years ahead of what I'm used to."

She flipped the piece, sending more of the stale saltwater smell through the "office".

"Well, I guess that'll be my first job then."

She rolled a chair closer. The smell of camellias, winning out over the wet tech odour.

I didn't know if there was spring on Lyra, but it came along with her.

"This," she said, handing me a familiar tool, "is a screwdriver."

I gave her a dirty look. She laughed again, and I thought I could get used to the sound of it.

"What's this?" I asked, offering her a different, unknown tool.

"That's a water filter."

"Fucking hell," I groaned.

She took it in stride.

"Come on. Let's start on a piece and I'll teach you."

And we did. She sat with me patiently and I got the hang of it. More or less.

Later, during what I guessed was the afternoon, we had managed to document a single part. The work was complicated, but not difficult. I lay the piece down gently.

"So, you're a legitimate princess?" I asked.

"My father is the High Governor. So, in a sense, yes."

"Then why are you slumming it here with my type?"

Her face went hard, not taking the joke as such.

"What's your type?" she asked seriously.

"Not royalty for starters."

She waved her hand in dismissal.

"My father... works with the tech. He wants me to know how everything functions too."

I nodded. "Fine, don't tell me then."

"I'm serious," she cried.

"Are you sure you're not just here to check the help doesn't steal?"

Juni brushed some hair over half of her face, fidgeting with it.

I smiled vindicated.

"I wouldn't put it that way," she muttered, barely audible.

"Well, no worries," I reassured her. "I don't know what any of it does anyway. I'd end up stealing a..."

"Whatever this is," I said, picking up an obvious set of pliers.

She laughed again, and each time she did, I felt lighter.

"Here, Miss Sing," she said passing me another glowing wet rock. "You do the next one."

"Clara," I said. "Just Clara is fine, Juni."

She smiled wide, perfect white teeth making her look like art. Her cheeks flushed red.

"You're not what I expected," she admitted.

"Right. Dumber, but hotter," I teased.

She looked down at her shoes, picking at her skirt.

"Something like that," she said, with a hint of a smile.

"Clara," she said, as if testing it out as she looked back to me. "Very well, you try the next one."

"Yes, my lady," I replied dramatically, with a mock salute.

I nearly managed the next one by myself. Juni guiding me gently, her laugh keeping the chill and wet at bay.

ɔ SIX ɕ

I made my way home smiling, grey skies or otherwise. It felt good making headway, and with Juniper helping me I could do the job in the way I was supposed to. The dragonfly-lizard, Tharaks, scattered into the air as I walked down my street. I dropped my bag as I entered my flat. My sheets and some décor had changed since my first days. It almost looked as if someone wanted to live there. Not that I was planning on having company anytime soon.

I was in a celebratory mood and wanted something with a kick swirling in a glass, or even more likely, a jar. I tapped my comm, and dialled Ramsey.

He answered after a few moments. There was steady banging in the background. It sounded like machinery or detonations.

"Clara!" he yelled over the noise.

"Cutter, where the hell are you?"

He looked over his shoulder, nodded his chin up, and the sound stopped.

"Sorry, love. What's up?"

I blushed, having to actually say the words.

"I thought, you know. Maybe we could go get drinks."

He chuckled, syrupy and deep.

"You asking me on a date, Sing?"

I rolled my eyes.

"Sure, Cutter. As long as I can go out."

Then he leaned in close to the screen.

"Your treat, right?" He chuckled.

I laughed. "Sure, sure. First rounds on me, wise guy."

"Sounds like a plan to me. I'll grab you in..."

He looked over his shoulder again, frowning.

"I'll grab you in two hours, okay?"

"Perfect. That gives me time not to smell like a *rotlick*."

This time he didn't chuckle. He laughed properly—broad shoulders shaking.

"Your accent's terrible," he smouldered, "but I love to hear your voice."

I blew him a raspberry, then blew a kiss.

I had never thought about Ramsey doing construction. I shrugged it off. Of course he did. He loved his community.

I slapped the tap on the shower. I needed to get the *bluetech* stench off me. But my shirt didn't smell of seaside breeze. Instead, it carried the scent of camellias as I pulled it off, which was a pleasant surprise. I stopped to smell it and could almost hear Juni laughing at me.

"Ha, you're something else Juniper," I said, arching the shirt into the hamper through the steam.

I slipped into the good old band tee and hoop skirt. It reminded me of times long past on Earth, chasing impossible boys for desperate reasons. It would be perfectly fine for drinks out. Ramsey joked about it being a date, but I wondered how serious he really was. I should have felt more ready, and yet, I still couldn't quite read Ramsey. I felt seen, but...

I brushed my hair instead of thinking about it too much. It had finally grown to manageable length. I killed time for the last hour watching the Lyran equivalent of television. State sponsored drool. Some things never change. It was as dreary as TV on the *backbeam*.

I was looking forward to having Ramsey all to myself for a change. He would have less of his bravado, and I could practice Lyrican without anyone there to judge. Ramsey being able to speak English made learning far faster, and easier on the eyes.

He showed up at my door with his usual denim and leather, smelling of upholstery and fireworks. He had a cab running to take us to our normal hangout, a small out-of-the-way restaurant, that was very much Earthy in both tone and décor. It reminded me of home just enough to unsettle me. But Ramsey thought it would make me feel comfortable, so I didn't argue. I found it was sweet of him to try.

Ramsey held my fingers gently across the table while he ordered drinks for us.

"Are you going to ask me?" I finally said.

"About the work?" he said, flapping his hand. "Nah, who cares."

I threw a napkin at him, laughing with him.

"You're such an ass."

He caught the napkin and gave me a sultry look.

"Out with it then. I'm dying to know how it's going in Shao's gold mine?"

"Gods, I didn't get that impression. I'm sure *they* don't even know what some of that stuff does."

He hummed, tilting his head.

"Don't be so sure. You do know that half the place runs on that tech? The cars, hell even the space station."

His voice darkened.

"And the elites get paid for every blue flicker."

The blue was pervasive. But I had never stopped to consider it was all proprietary.

I whistled. "No shit?"

"That tech is worth a bundle in the right hands. Used right, it can do crazy things in a human body too."

The creeping blue plant flashed in my mind again.

"But you told me it's dangerous."

"Oh, well yeah. But what power isn't a little dangerous, right?"

I've seen what power can do. Millions dying as a few escape a doomed world. The rich cutting lines while mothers hush their frightened children in a queue that never moves.

"I've had my fill of both, thanks," I said, looking deep into my glass.

"Then you're in the wrong city, love."

I shrugged.

"Guess I'll steer clear of getting involved this time."

His eyes dropped to his shoes, hands fidgeting with his shirt buttons. He knew enough of my history.

"Right. You're right, Clara. Never mind, alright."

I felt guilty for brushing him off. He was trying to take an interest in my work. This wasn't Cutter. This was the Ramsey only I saw.

"But..." I said slowly, taking his hand in mine. "I'm curious. So, tell me more."

He broke out a mischievous grin.

"Alright then. But only because you have such pretty eyes."

He leaned in over the table, looking around with a darkened expression.

"The Shaos are up to their eyeballs with the stuff. Enhanced. Super human."

I thought back to Juniper. She seemed normal, almost delicate. She certainly wasn't streaked with blue vines.

"I think, it may be a myth," I said.

He cocked an eyebrow.

"Why do you think we call them *High on Blues*," he said, emphasising the words.

I threw my head back.

"Oh shit. That makes so much sense now."

I couldn't help but wonder if Juniper hid something like that in her tiny frame.

"Fucking *Highonblues*," Ramsey complained. "They let that shit poison our folk, but use it to keep us down too."

"Not all of them are that bad, Cutter."

He leaned down once again, poking his finger to the table.

"You wait and see, yeah. They'll show you."

I shifted uncomfortably. "Maybe we should talk about something else?"

He groaned, lifting his drink.

"Alright. Let's drink. To the prettiest and smartest lady I know."

I blushed, but tapped my glass to his. For the rest of the evening the conversation stayed light and pleasant. I was running on liquid courage, and I made the goodnight kiss hotter than before. But I had to stoke the fire in myself. Something was still missing. The spark I thought I would feel—should feel. A spark I felt when looking at Aten. The type you want to grab on to and hold close.

Looking up at the moonless sky, I wondered when... if, I would ever see them again.

ↄ SEVEN ɕ

I was perched on a ledge, a few metres off the floor of the monolith. I hated working so high up and the floor, much like the walls, seemed permanently wet. I knew it wasn't actually wet, but I stuck close to the wall and didn't look down. We had been logging what we suspected to be a power system. A week had passed with little progress, even with Juni's help. I had tracked the system up to the ledge that morning.

Juni and I were the only ones authorised to catalogue. Besides us, there were a handful of small teams combing a colossal structure for new pieces. The monolith was so large that it contained its own weather system. Though that was mostly damp and chilly.

I heard footsteps echoing through the dim halls. The familiar confident beats told me who it was, before I could see them.

Below me I saw her—a trail of white curls flowing through the structure. She walked up straight with the confidence of her position. It was easy to forget who she was when she wasn't around me.

"Juniper!" I yelled down. She froze, arms out, as if looking for a predator.

"Up here," I groaned playfully.

She looked up and her face brightened with a smile framed in red.

"Clara, hi!" she called back.

Juni jogged over and leapt up to me with effortless grace.

"Holy shit!" I cried, looking back down to her launch site.

Ramsey wasn't kidding after all. And to Juni, the feat seemed natural.

"Sorry," Juni said, blushing. "I should have made sure you were secure first."

She bowed in a formal apology.

"No need for that. I just didn't know silver foxes could jump like that."

She chuckled.

"How the fuck *did* you do that?" I asked.

She shrugged. "Good genes."

"Remind me to get the number of your tailor."

She laughed, with perfect teeth and a hint of a laugh line in the porcelain around her eyes.

"What is a fox anyway?" she asked, head to the side.

I sighed, rolling my eyes.

"I'll have to teach you about my home while you teach me about yours," I said, turning back to the device.

"Sounds like a date," Juniper said, stepping in close behind me.

"I mean, you should know about Earth as old as you..."

I turned to look at her. For the first time I really looked.

Her impossibly white hair was obvious. Her delicate oval face and naturally red cupid's bow. I'd never seen her eyes in decent light... They were purple.

"*Woah*," I said, forgetting what I was about to say. I stared into her eyes. After a moment her face flushed and she looked away.

"I'm turning forty next year," she said, with a voice that drew me back to the ledge.

"Age... Oh yes," I said, regaining my train of thought.

"Shit, I hope to look that good at forty," I said, seriously.

She giggled.

"You're still using Earth years."

"Oh," I said, hand on my face. "I'm still getting used to that. I'm half a damn century old here."

She bumped me gently with her shoulder. "Pretty hot for a granny."

I puffed. "Yeah..."

I trailed off, prodding at the alien device.

"I'm sorry," Juni frowned. "I guess you must miss home."

I sifted through my tools, keeping my hands busy. Melancholy threatened to creep in.

"It doesn't matter, does it?"

"Did you leave someone behind? A boy?"

I frowned.

"No, not exactly," I said under my breath.

She lay with her back against the wall, looking at her feet.

"I'm not a fan personally... Of boys, I mean," she murmured, almost to herself.

I let it sit for a moment as I fiddled with what I thought was a contact.

"Oh yeah?" I said gently.

"Not that it matters to my parents anyway."

Our parents weren't that different then.

"Fuck 'em." I said, louder than I meant to. "You shouldn't let other people tell you-"

I pushed the glowing bar straight and it screamed. The sound was coming from everywhere in the building, lying siege to my senses. My teeth itched and my chest burned. The whole structure seemed to zoom in toward us. It also sounded just human enough to jar us both. Juni pressed her hands to her ears, gritting her teeth. She lost her balance and started tipping backward over the edge.

"Gods," I yelled, grabbing her hand, stabilising her.

I pulled her back into me and held her close. Her breaths came in quick and hard.

"Careful," I said, winded.

She steadied herself, not letting go of my hand. Her hands were like a fireplace in winter.

"This tech is so Terran," she spat. She was justifiably pissed.

As soon as she said it, her hands flew over her mouth, abandoning mine.

"I'm so sorry, Clara. It slipped out."

I raised an eyebrow.

"I *am* Terran, you know?"

"That's not what it means here," she admitted, looking away.

I kicked the contact.

"Fucking Terran piece of shit."

Juni's face was a mask of shock.

"What?" I shrugged. "I can say it. I am one."

That had us erupting into laughter, the tension eased. Neither of us talked about the screeching. I noted it down as 'anomalous' and let it be. What more was there to say?

We decided to move on to a different, lower section. One with less horror and more coffee.

By the end of the day, we were sitting in my makeshift office. I was perched on the desk and Juniper was spinning on my chair, as became someone of her station.

We didn't really talk, only occupied the same comfortable silence. But occasionally we would share a story, or a joke. What better way to end a day. Any day.

❀ Juni II ❀

Juniper's hair is the usual evening tangle. She has the blanket wrapped around her tightly, only one shoulder and arm out as she pulls back from the camera. The room is dark except for the screen's dim blue light.

"I met the Earther... Clara."

A smile forms on her face, her eyes practically sparkling.

"Turns out she *is* cute. She's also sharp as a Bane Tree thorn."

Juniper leans toward the camera.

"Father thinks she may be a Zero, but there's no way Clara would be one of those psychos."

She blows a stray strand of hair out of her face.

"I know we only met recently, and she's not even from here."

"But there's no way... I just know."

She falls backward, her legs flipping out of the blanket in a pale curve.

"What I don't know, is what I'm doing," she complains from behind the mound of covers. "I'm probably chasing my own tail again."

She sits back up, shrugging the blanket tighter around her.

"What does it matter anyway? I'm told what I should like."

Her jaw tightens.

"I feel like damn breeding stock some days."

She looks up to the ceiling, letting out a long, calming breath.

"At least I won't be bored at my assignment," she whispers.

"Or maybe Dad will let me actually do what I want."

She scoffs, pressing on the bridge of her nose.

"Thing is, we're logging the *bluetech*, for what? We haven't found anything new in..."

Her smile creeps back in. She rubs at the bed, forming pools of calm in the waves of the cover.

"But I shouldn't complain. It gives me a reason..."

She focuses on a stray lock of hair. Her eyes squint with a frown. She blows it back from her face.

"Maybe I should cut mine the same as Clara's. I wonder if she would like it? If she would even notice."

Her cheeks glow.

"I sound like such an idiot. Clara is a scientist. She's really lived."

The fire in Juni's eyes dim.

"She probably thinks I'm a snotty kid she needs to take care of."

She pulls her legs up to her chin, toes pointed.

"And then I went and used the 'T' word, right next to her."

She puts her fingers to her head, thumb dropping dramatically.

"But she did joke about it," she murmurs, her smile turning back up.

"I can never predict her, but she *always* knows what to say."

Juniper brushes her hair over half of her face.

"And it doesn't matter. Not in my family," she all but whispers, the tears already living in her voice.

She looks away from the camera, hiding her eyes. Her legs fall to the side, surrendering to gravity.

Juni is quiet for a while. Her breaths rise in shaky inhales.

"I hope I can keep her close, but I've gotten my hopes up before."

She puffs out a small, pained sound.

"I wish..." she says, wiping her eyes with the blanket.

She sighs, her shoulders dropping.

Her head turns, only enough to look at the camera. There are streaks on her cheeks as she reaches out, ending the recording.

ↄ EIGHT c

"So, what's fun at the king's castle right now?" Ramsey asked at dinner a week later.

It was a fast-food diner dressed in a suit. The décor said posh, but the crowd was rough and rowdy. They were playing some terrible digital mess as music from an improvised speaker.

I picked at my fries, not hungry or in the mood to be grilled.

"He's not a king, Cutter. Just a governor."

He waved his hand dismissively.

"Maybe someone should inform lord prick himself of that."

My annoyance rushed from nowhere I could pin.

"Ramsey," I said sternly.

"Alright, alright." He leaned in. "But what *are* you working on?"

I sighed. The *bluetech* was proprietary. Even at my worst back on Earth, I kept my lip zipped on Council projects.

"I'm going to go get another drink," I said, getting up. I needed the space.

I walked over to the fridge, grabbing a jam-jar-like lemonade I liked. For the life of me I never could get the lids open.

Then he coiled around me. Cheek grazing my ear, aftershave a winter breeze. His arms clipped mine, fingers entangling my own, as he grabbed the jar from me.

"Holy shit," I yelped. The sensation of him still riding up my spine as his cold jacket pierced through my shirt.

"Here love," Ramsey said, handing me back the opened drink.

He crushed the lid and tossed it haphazardly over his shoulder.

"You alright?" he asked when we returned to the table.

"I'm fine, Ramsey."

He gave me a concerned look.

"I'm fine," I repeated.

"Just not sharing with me anymore, aye?"

I groaned, more frustrated than annoyed.

"I'm not sure I'm even allowed to share this stuff."

"Exactly what those fuckers want," he said, pounding the table.

"And that, precious, is how they keep you under their thumb," he grumbled.

I huffed.

"Gods, why don't you work there if you want to know so bad?"

"Because not all of us have the paper to be a *rotlicking* lackey."

I pushed my plate away with meaning and folded my arms.

"You got me that job."

"Yeah, and look at what I have to show for it."

I felt that in my heart. Of all people in Vala, I thought Ramsey would be the last to try and hurt me. I started to wish I had never gotten the job. But then...

I lowered my arms. Tears threatened, blurring my view.

Swiping at my face, I set my jaw firm.

"I'm going home."

I stood up to leave, but Ramsey caught my arm.

"Clara," he purred, with a sad puppy face. "I'm sorry, love."

I tried to pull my arm free, but he was too strong.

"You're hurting me," I growled through clenched teeth.

He held up his hands in surrender.

We were gathering stares from nearby tables. Some of them were Ramsey's friends, or associates. I didn't know if there was a difference.

"I didn't need this shit on the *backbeam,* Cutter." I spat. "I sure as *hell* don't need it here."

"Look, I didn't-"

"I don't need your platitudes and excuses, Ramsey. I'm going home."

He called after me, but I kept walking.

I folded my arms against the rain and chill and shuffled home. Ramsey didn't follow me and I felt relieved, instead of sad.

But that didn't stop the tears once I was inside.

I scooped up my comm, scrolling through my short list of contacts.

(Juniper Shao)

"Hey Juni..." I typed.

I erased the message, staring at the contact. It would have been great to tell her about my disastrous evening. Just to have someone I could talk to. I missed Iris. I imagined she would have stern words about Ramsey's behaviour.

I chuckled despite my wet cheeks.

"Where are you, Iris? I could use a friend."

I sighed as I dropped my comm on the nightstand, shuffled on my jacket and popped outside for a smoke.

The scuttling thing was back, standing in the road like a black stain. I could feel it staring at me.

"You want to cause trouble too?"

It hopped closer instead of its normal skitter, coming into the light.

It had eight very long, segmented legs, and midnight black fur. Its four wide eyes stared at me curiously, its tail whipping about.

And... it was cute as hell.

"Aw, you're kinda a cutie pie." I cooed.

It opened its mouth and hissed, showing far too many needle teeth. I didn't hesitate—bolting back inside.

"Fuck. It must be male." I growled.

My pipe started sleeping under my pillow with me after that.

The next morning there were spiralled blue and yellow Lyran flowers outside my door. I checked properly for anything black before going outside. I put them inside, and started to feel like I overreacted toward Ramsey.

"I'm sorry," said a small handwritten note.

An hour later my comm pinged.

(Ramsey Cutter)

"I'm sorry," came his next message. "I was out of line."

I sank down onto my bed.

"I'll make it up to you. At a proper place next time," he said.

I let him stew for a few minutes.

"It better be a damn nice place, Cutter."

"Anything to see you smile," he replied.

And I did smile. The man had a way with me.

Or maybe I wanted him to. I got dressed for work and by the time I was in the cab I felt much lighter.

ↄ NINE 𝔾

I spent most of the next day in a daze. The previous night kept looping in my head. Ramsey had always been high strung, but I never thought...

Rubbing my wrist, I could still feel his hand had wrapped around it. I had agreed to see him again. And yet, I wasn't sure it was me he was interested in. I let out a breath, burying my face in my hands.

A light touch on my shoulder.

"Clara?" Juni's soft voice.

She had worry in her eyes as I looked up.

I forced a smile. "Oh, hi."

She stepped back with her hands on her hips, long hair spilling to one side.

"You've been staring at that screen for an hour. It's not even turned on."

I looked back to the black screen.

"Oh. I'm sorry, Fox, I'll get back to work."

She slid in between me and the screen, leaning forward. The fresh smell of Japanese Roses swirled around me.

"Maybe you need a break," she said smiling.

"I'm–"

She held up a hand before I could protest.

"Come out with me tonight."

My eyes widened. Juni kept stepping on everything I had been told about Lyra's elites. I could also think of a hundred reasons why it would be a bad idea.

"Please," she cooed, stretching the "S" into a long "Z" with a goofy smile. I couldn't help but chuckle.

"Alright. One must not deny a princess," I joked, dialling up the pomp.

She threw her hands up, but caught them halfway, blushing.

"Great," she said instead. "Tayo will be there too. You two can finally meet."

"Exciting," I said, but my stomach knotted.

Who the fuck is Tayo?

Tayo... was everything I would expect from the governing houses. He had dark mahogany skin and eyes that seemed to know more than he let on. He walked with a well-practiced confidence—each step planned ahead. His regal poise was only broken by his messy, almost playful black locks.

He reached his hand out to me slowly.

"You must be Clara," he rumbled in a calm baritone from two feet above my head. I took his hand and he shook gently, letting his presence speak for him, instead of his strength. He had a freshness about him, like rain and newly cut plants.

"You must be a Tayo," I replied with more snark than I had intended.

Tayo smiled with teeth as perfect as Juni's.

"Matayo Stephan Langley the Third," he said with a slight tilt to his head.

"Oh, shit. You do that too. I hear there's a cream for that."

He cackled. "Yup, I see it now. Why Juni is so fond of you."

"Oh, I didn't realise she's mentioned me to-"

Juni interjected. "Ah, our table is ready."

She hijacked my hand and led me to our seats, Tayo close behind, still grinning.

I sat, Juni opposite me. He took the seat next to her, leaning over to gently bump his shoulder into hers. They exchanged a look I couldn't interpret.

"Juni's never mentioned me, has she?"

"I'm sure she must have."

"We don't talk about boys at work," Juni replied, head raised high.

Tayo chuckled. It was as calm as his demeanour.

"Clara... knew Aten," Juniper said as an icebreaker.

The look on Tayo's face was incredulous.

That set the tone for the evening. We talked about Earth, Aten's struggles with the beam and Iris's paintings. Some of the only art to make it to Lyra intact from Earth. Juniper and Tayo leaned in as if I was telling folk tales. And to them, I suppose, they were.

They told me about growing up together and the trouble they would get into and the joys they've shared. The difference in lifestyle was jarring, once more showing me how far from my own world I had come.

I cleared my throat.

"I'm going to..." I pointed over my shoulder.

Juni raised her hand to protest, but I needed air. That old sinking feeling in my stomach had returned, like when I met Iris for the first time and realised Aten was beyond my reach. Juni and her people were... Well, they were Tayo level. I was only slightly more than a curiosity to them. A souvenir from a lost world. Far from a friend certainly.

I walked up to the in-house bar, ordering my favourite lemonade for some normality. They had the exact ones with the stupid lids. Which was equal parts annoying and gratifying. I rolled my eyes, and once again I had the familiar battle with the damn lid.

Then she wraps around me. Cheek brushing my ear, and her hair a cloud flowing along with her. Her arms gliding along mine, fingers braiding in with my own, and using the tips of her own to effortlessly pop the screw cap straight off without turning it.

"Holy shit," I said, more as breath than as a word. The sensation of her still running up my spine as her heat settled into my skin like the summer sun.

"You're welcome," Juni whispered, withdrawing with a peck on my temple.

I barely noticed what she had done to the jar. I was still lost in the smell of Camellias.

She placed the lid gently on the counter beside me.

"See you back at the table, ok?" she said, music in her voice.

She squeezed my arm gently and floated away.

"Yes. I'll be right there," I replied, still catching my breath.

I returned to the table floating. Juni had switched to my side. I sat down beside her smiling. She tilted her head to me, blushing from behind her hair, eyes carrying a smile meant for only me. I didn't know what was happening. Juni had always been full of heart with me. But that peck, it was more than just her usual charm.

Dinner was fantastic, and the company was unlike anything Lyra had shown me before. I let myself live in the moment, for once I wasn't in a rush to get home. Perhaps there was more there after all.

I asked the cab to drop me off a few blocks from home. The air was warm and so was I. A walk was exactly what I needed. I was two blocks from home when the smell of rubber and garbage washed over me. I covered my face with my sleeve and pressed on. The sound followed soon after. Some bottles or cans in a side street being kicked over.

I slowed, peeking around the next corner. A man was slumped against a wall, walking slowly, shoulder dragging against the façade. He was either inured or drunk. The smell wafted from the street as he struggled along. I walked in long strides to catch up.

"Hey! Mister? Are you ok?"

The man stopped and turned slowly. His eyes were glowing purple, as if a fire burned inside them. He hobbled a few steps toward me, into the light. I backpeddled, my hair raising. His skin was a sickly blue-grey. Veins ran like tubes, but they were too angular and radiated a nauseating blue. The smell was coming from the man.

"Hep-me-ca-a?" he stammered, jaw loose.

Even as distorted as their face was, they looked familiar, but I couldn't place them. I nearly tripped backing up, holding my hands up toward them.

"I'm going to get help, alright," I assured them.

They seemed to relax and lay back against the wall, wheezing in strained gargles. Their eyes relaxed, some of the glow fading as they nodded slowly.

My first instinct was to call Juni, but I figured Ramsey may know more and be closer. My anxiety about him would have to wait.

"I'm phoning my friend who can help. His name is Ramsey."

At the mention of the name, the man's eyes bulged, flaring up again. He convulsed, slamming himself back against the wall. The mutated man's arms contracted into severe angles with several snaps as they turned and continued dragging themselves down the road as fast as they could.

"Wait, I'm trying to help," I pleaded, tears rolling down my face.

They stopped, looking back.

"No..." they shrieked, their voice sounding more mechanical than human. Not far down the road, they stumbled. They hit the pavement hard and didn't move again.

I'm not proud of it, but I ran. I ran fast enough that I had to stop myself against a wall, my legs on fire. I slammed my front door behind me. The smell of Camellias had been overshadowed by the stench of rot that clung to my clothes.

I sank down with my back against the door, bawling like a child.

Each time I thought I was making a home, Lyra seemed to cut me off at the knees. My clothes went on a pile and I showered, trying to scrub the smell off of me. I crawled into bed an hour later, determined to forget.

“It was all a bad dream, all a bad dream” I kept repeating. But I could still hear the metallic screaming. Ramsey couldn’t know I saw it. Each time I thought of him I saw the man’s face, covered in bluerot, trying to run from a name.

That was when I knew, my time with Ramsey was coming to an end.

❀ Juni III ❀

A fireplace crackles in the background. Juniper's arm pulls back from the screen. She's sitting on the floor leaning over to one side, a hand disappearing into the soft carpet.

"Well, I did it," she says with a smug smile.

The smile fades from one side. Her eyes flick up to the ceiling.

"Ok, I almost did it," she says, looking away for a moment.

"I wussed out and only managed a head peck."

She shrugs, frowning.

"Oh well. It doesn't matter anyway. Dad's people say her boyfriend is a Zero."

She throws her free hand up in the air.

"A fu... fudging boyfriend! No wonder I'm getting sidelined."

She ruffles her fringe roughly.

Juniper frowns, pointing at the camera.

"And just because her man is a terrorist doesn't mean she's one."

Her hand drops to the floor.

"I hope."

"Not that I can ask without getting in trouble anyway."

Juni tugs on her T-shirt hem, straightening it.

"She's far too smart and kind to be a Zero."

A smile creeps back onto her face.

"And her Lyrican accent is too bad."

Juniper blows a stray hair from her face, then tucks it behind her ear.

"I guess a tiny bit of probing couldn't hurt."

She smacks her knee, face serious.

"We definitely are friends. And boyfriends are a normal friend thing to talk about... right?"

Juni plays with the carpet fibres, in a small circle.

"I really hope Father's guy is wrong. I really like her."

She brings her legs forward, leaning back fully. Her silver hair turning gold in the light.

"Even Tayo liked her, and he doesn't like anyone, besides me."

She throws her head back, muffling her voice slightly.

"But that's because he wants to..."

She raises her head back up one eyebrow raised.

"And I don't."

She shivers.

"Gross, he's practically my brother."

Her head lowers.

"I guess if I really do want a kid of my own..." she whispers.

She rolls her shoulders, stretching her neck to the side.

"Guess I'll play it by ear."

She reaches over awkwardly with her foot, tongue on her lips in concentration. Her toe fumbles for a moment before the view tips and then goes black.

ↄ TEN Ꞓ

It was a few short days before Ramsey invited me out again. His promise of "only the best" turned out to be a mid-range bistro not far from my house. I rehearsed a million things to say to him. But it boiled down to a single thought.

It's over.

I walked to the main strip as the dusk rolled in, not daring to look down any of the side roads. The restaurant, if you can call it that, looked as if it was cut out of the side of the building. The wide opening letting the heat of the evening blow through. Mixed with the steam and smell of spices drifting from the kitchen, the atmosphere inside was oppressive. That might have been affected largely by my mood.

"Clara," Ramsey greeted, a smiling wolf. "I have such good news. Sit, sit."

I pulled out a chair across from him. None of his crew were visible, which was a novel change.

"Cutter, listen. I-"

"Wait, before that," he said, pulling out a slip of paper. He pushed it over to me. It had a large number on it, but no context.

No apology either.

"That's nice," I said unsure.

He chuckled humourlessly.

"That, love, is what my 'friends' will pay per piece of *bluetech*."

"Ah, I see," I said, the pieces falling into place.

"I told you I'd take care of you," he said, winking.

I sighed leaning back on the chair.

"You were the one that told me that stuff is dangerous. What exactly do *they* want with it?"

I thought of the warped man's eyes. The fear in them.

Ramsey leaned in reaching for my hand.

"Who cares, right? It pays well. All we have to do-"

I sat back, deliberately placing my hands out of reach.

"I don't care," I said firmly. "How do I know this isn't hurting people?"

"Well, there's always a risk."

I looked into his eyes. There was excitement there, but not love. My eyes closed for a moment, as I gathered my thoughts.

"You don't care for me, do you Cutter?"

It was a rhetorical question.

"Baby," he purred.

"Was this your plan all along?"

"That's not fair," he defended, dodging my questions.

I should have been sad. But all I felt was anger—betrayal.

I pushed my chair out, the legs whining as they scraped the floor.

"I think I'm done, Ramsey. Maybe you *are* just a *clipper*."

He sat back, face hardening.

"How far do you think you'll make it without me, Sing?"

"Far enough. And I won't be turning people into monsters."

Ramsey's eyes narrowed.

"What the fuck did you say?"

"I said we're through, Ramsey."

"What did you hear, Sing?"

"I didn't *hear* anything. I'm leaving."

I stood to leave. Ramsey once again lunged for my arm. This time I twisted as he grabbed, and he spilled out of his chair, eating some floor.

"Next time you grab me, Ramsey," I warned, looking down at him. "I won't be a good girl."

I left for home, heart pounding. My steps were long instead of quick, to not attract the wrong attention. Being scared on the street makes you a target.

I was less than a block away when I heard pounding feet behind me. I swung around, ready to defend myself. Ramsey was running after me.

"Clara, please wait!"

I crossed my arms, standing firm.

"What, Ramsey?"

"Do you realise how much money you're throwing away?"

I rolled my eyes.

"There's more to life than money."

He reached for me like a lover, but I took a step back.

"Don't touch me. I am not yours, and I'm *not* interested."

Ramsey slid closer.

"I know, I know. But promise me you'll think about it?"

He landed his hands on my upper arms.

The muscles in my legs went taut.

I snapped my leg up, my shin hitting nothing but nuts.

Ramsey shrank down to his knees, wheezing pathetically.

I leaned over to his face.

"I said. Don't. Touch. Me."

I left him there in a pile.

Outside my apartment I passed the garbage. A rustling caught my attention. It was a familiar sight. The scuttling creature, its four eyes glowing in the streetlight. The bag it sat on was torn open, discarded food pulled out roughly. It hissed, rabbit-like ears folding down around its head as it defended its meagre scraps. I knew what it felt like.

I closed my front door hard. Then a moment later, feeling guilty, I placed a plate of leftovers outside, catching the creature's wide eyes before stepping back in.

I double checked the lock on my door. I realised I needed to move, but Ramsey was right. Without help I didn't have a clue how. But I was a doctor. A survivor. I would figure it out.

Still, my heart kept beating and I felt sick.

I had potentially made an enemy. A real, possibly violent enemy. I knew it wouldn't be over with someone like him.

But I hoped he would hesitate next time he thought of approaching me. For the first time in a long while I thought of Earth, the beam, and the stakes of those last days.

"I've survived worse than you, Ramsey."

ɔ ELEVEN ɕ

It took a week before the tension in my chest started to ease. It was nearing the end of the year on Lyra. I was far from a local, but I could take care of myself. At least I wasn't likely to die of hunger or run around naked.

I hummed a song from home. Something you'd listen to in a car with no roof and a surfboard in the back. Quite different from the... 'music' the locals listened to.

My voice picked up an echo. The song I was humming being repeated slightly out of sync. I looked over at Juniper. She was otherwise occupied, concentrating on her own work. The humming was coming from a piece of *bluetech* on the desk near me. At first, I thought it was a type of recording or mimicry. Its pitch mirrored mine closely. Then it continued after I trailed off.

I froze, chills running up my arms, continuing down my neck.

"Juniper," I shout-whispered.

She looked over. Her eyes wandered from me to the humming tech. Her eyebrows raised. I mimed a shush, and waved her over. She crept closer. Even with her house regalia she moved like a shadow.

I cupped my ear, leaning into the piece of tech. She bent down.

"What the fuck is it singing?" Juni whispered, not bothering to censor herself.

"It's a song from Earth."

"How could it know that?"

For a moment the humming changed to Juni's voice.

"What the fuck!" it echoed perfectly, then let out a high-pitched sound. We were both forced to cover our ears. The sound dropped out suddenly, leaving the area in eerie silence. The normal blue glow flickered, then faded from the piece. The material cracked as it dried out, leaving it as nothing but a scaly rock.

"That's... normal, right?" I asked.

Juniper gave me a worried look, gritting her teeth. She shook her head rapidly.

We spent two hours trying to replicate it with similar pieces, without luck. As weird as the tech humming was, it was curious that it knew music from Earth. Could my home still be in there somehow? An echo in the *bluetech*?

The question was a dead end. The Daedalus beam, for some reason was never finished on the Kepler end. And Earth was gone.

Juni was fussing with a piece hours later, still trying to replicate the event. I sat on the desk nearby, watching her work.

"Juniper?" I asked.

Her eyes widened, staring up at me hearing her full name.

"Yeah- Um... Yes?"

"You'd be honest with me if I asked you something, right?"

She brushed some hair over her eye.

"Yes," she said softly, not looking directly at me.

"Can this stuff be used on people?"

Her eyes flicked to the door. Either checking we were alone or planning her exit. She nodded her head.

"But it's dangerous?"

She nodded again. "Kepler Syndrome," she said, as a sigh.

"Blue rot?" I asked.

She nodded solemnly, then forced a smile.

"Can we talk about this... Not here," she said, gesturing to all the alien tech around us.

"Sure. Lunch?"

She nodded once more sharply, her smile almost convincing.

"I am not really Juniper Shao the fourth," Juni said, holding a hot mug in both hands.

She let out a pained breath. "At least not originally."

"I had two brothers and a sister. They're all... They passed."

Her eyes shimmered with the memory.

I moved my chair closer, placing a hand on her leg for support. Her face flushed, and her hand found mine.

"My sister died when I was around eleven. It's no secret that we have that alien shit fused to our genes. But people don't realise that it makes us volatile. I'm the oldest survivor in my generation."

She sniffed.

"I'm sorry, Juni," I said, not knowing what else to do.

"It's not all abilities and strength. It comes with a lot of baggage."

"And if done wrong?"

"There's no right way to do it. At best, you can be a timebomb like me."

"You seem stable to me."

"Ha, just lucky, but we don't really know what sets the mutations off."

My mind flashed with a metallic scream and a broken body lying in the street.

"Mutations," I breathed.

"I try not to think about it," Juni shivered.

A tear broke free. Juni bit her lip fighting the rest back.

I stood and hugged her. It was as if I was holding a summer's day.

She shook softly, but made no sound. After a while she pulled away, squeezing my hand as she did.

"You want to get out of here?" I asked. "I know a good place us commoners hang out at."

"I'm sure you want to spend time with your boy... Your own friends."

I hooked my arm around hers.

"I don't have a boyfriend. And my only friend in the world needs to come out with me. How's that sound?"

"That sounds amazing," she said, laughing as she rubbed her eyes.

ɔ TWELVE ɕ

We took a car back to my neighbourhood as night crept in. I chose my favourite place. The one with the "Earthy" décor and feel. It had grown on me after all. I could pretend I had never left home, and Juni would get a taste of Earth. Literally.

She loved it immediately. Her tears forgotten as she asked me about Earth. She wanted to know everything, but one thing in particular held her fascination.

"You had this planet floating right in the sky?" she asked, her voice an octave higher than usual.

"Well, it wasn't a planet exactly. It was only a quarter the size of Earth."

"But you could just look up and see another world. How crazy is that?"

I laughed. "It's funny how we can take things for granted if they're always around." I placed my hand on hers, both of us smiling. Her thumb curling around mine.

The door slid open behind me, cold blowing in from outside.

"Aten help us. Look who it is," boomed a familiar voice from the entrance.

"Ramsey," I growled, not looking around.

Juni's face turned even paler than usual. She leaned down frowning.

"I thought you don't have a boyfriend," Juni squeaked.

"I don't."

Then from right behind my chair.

"Moved on quickly, didn't you?" he slurred.

I stood turning to face him. I kept my face neutral, looking him in the eye.

"Our likes not good enough for you anymore, aye?" he accused.

His crew were around him trying to lead him back to a table. Quara a reed, little more than a boy, and Towny, a brick of beef a good foot shorter than Ramsey.

"Come on, Cutter," they pleaded.

He shrugged through them, coming face to face with me.

"Why don't you run on home, Clara?" he said, waving his hand dismissively, looming over me. "This place is too nice for *Highonblues*."

"Take it you're still sour I wouldn't play your game, Ramsey."

His fists balled.

"You know what, Sing-"

The smell of Camellias floated past me. Juni stopped beside Ramsey, her shoulder to him. She had a hard look in her eye I hadn't seen before.

"Don't you dare threaten Clara, sir," she said in passable Lyrican. She was being courteous, but there were barbs on her words.

He turned, leaning in, narrowing his eyes, with a shit-eating grin.

"Or what, tiny mouse?"

From the back, Quara piped up. "Cutter, are you nuts man. She'll tear your arms off."

"Oh, yeah? I bet I drop her first," Ramsey said, straightening to his full height.

I stepped in between them, firing a look at Ramsey.

"Grow the fuck up, Cutter," I hissed in English, to piss him off.

He took a step back, out of leg range. His eyes flicked between us, but settled on me.

"Screw this. I don't need this shit," he said, turning back towards his crew as they moved to a table.

Juni was breathing hard next to me. Her hands clenched—knuckles white. She was all but vibrating.

"My hero," I sang, hooking my arm in hers. "Let's get out of here."

We walked past our table, and I swiped my credit slip. I grabbed what was left of my burger, wrapping it back up and slipping it into my pocket. We slipped out under Ramsey's glare, but it felt like a win.

"That was crazy," Juni squeaked when we had made some distance.

"That was amazing," I exclaimed with an idiotic grin.

"Oh crap, it's nearly midnight," Juni groaned. "I won't be home before morning."

Juni looked defeated by the day.

"Just crash at my place," I suggested. "I owe my hero a drink anyway."

She glowed at the suggestion, cheeks cherry red.

"I don't have my..." she started, then... "I'd like that, actually."

"Then come see my dungeon, princess," I said. As we walked down the road laughing.

I unwrapped the burger as we walked up to my door, and whistled as I placed it on the empty plate outside.

Juni gave me a questioning glance.

"Feeding a... something that lives outside."

She chuckled. "You're such a sweetie," she cooed.

"Welcome to my shit hole," I proclaimed as I flung my door open.

I kicked off my shoes and gave her the tour.

"It's a cute place," she said frowning.

"Nobody likes a liar, Juni," I chuckled, wiggling my finger in the air.

I fetched us each a bottle of some dirty water that qualified for beer on Lyra.

We sat on my bed sipping in silence for a bit, Juni's hair, a waterfall around her face.

"Quite the day, huh?" I said.

"Yeah." She replied dryly.

"I'm sorry about," I jabbed my thumb over my shoulder.

"Oh, it's ok really. I'm also sorry, for earlier."

I took her hand in mine.

"You don't have to be. I appreciate you sharing with me."

She gave me a small smile, fidgeting with the label on the bottle.

"I'm grateful I have someone I can talk to... besides Tayo."

"That's what friends are for, right," I said, clinking my bottle to hers.

She laughed, but it was hollow.

"You and Tayo. He's your... what exactly?" I asked.

"It's complicated," she sighed, hugging her knees to her chest, releasing my hand.

"Your boyfriend?"

"No," she said too quickly. "No, he's my oldest friend. Our families have... an agreement."

"Heavy topic, I get it. I'll listen if you want to blow off steam."

"You're a good friend..." she said. The words felt heavy—loaded.

"But..." I prodded, leaning in.

She huffed, forcing the smile back out.

"But I saw Ramsey, and... I understand now."

I tilted my head. "Understand what?"

She looked at her feet.

"I knew, your preference..." she shrugged. "But I figured, maybe..."

She ran her finger around the bottle opening.

"It doesn't matter," she said.

I leaned in further, looking into her lavender eyes.

I didn't know what exactly the feeling was. But it was something I had only felt once before. Back on Earth.

"It matters to me, Fox," I said.

Then I leaned in further, touching my lips to hers. For a moment it felt so right. The smell of Japanese roses and the heat of her around me. She pressed in, slowly—hesitantly.

My brain started catching up to my lips.

I pulled back, my eyes tearing up. I was so out of my league, it wasn't even the same sport.

"I'm sorry, Juniper," I said.

Her life was already so far beyond what I could imagine. She didn't need me to make it complicated or butt in. Besides we worked together.

I tucked my hand between my knees, pulling hard on my bottle.

I couldn't look at her.

"That wasn't...erm. Please, forget I did that," I pleaded.

"Ah," she started. Then, "alright." She sounded deflated.

I didn't want to hurt her. We were literally worlds apart.

She was on the quiet side for the rest of the evening. Juni slept on my bed and I made a makeshift bed beside her on the floor.

"Clara," she said as we started to doze off.

"I'm here," I whispered.

She was quiet for a while. I thought she may have fallen asleep.

"Do you like me?" she said finally. So soft it could have been a thought.

"Of course."

"You know what I mean," she clarified, almost as softly. But firm.

"I do..." I drew a breath, choosing my words.

"And yes. But I'm still in the woods here."

"I can help, I've lived here my whole life," she chimed, warmth in her voice.

"I'd appreciate that, Fox."

"That's what friends are for," she whispered back.

•JUNIPER 01•

"Your father called last night, Jun-Jun," Tayo said, as if it happened often. "He was looking for you."

I rolled my eyes. "My father needs to realise I'm an adult now."

"No use telling me, I'm afraid."

"His opinion will never change, Tayo," I said, recomposing myself.

We walked through the garden. It was mostly grass. About the only grass on Lyra. The sky was threatening us with rain.

"So, were you with the blonde?" Tayo asked, brushing his hand through his locks.

"Her name is Clara."

"I know. So, were you?"

I scoffed. I didn't even know what was going on between me and Clara. But my heart skipped when she was close. And then... her lips on mine. I found my fingers on my mouth, as if her lips were still there.

"It's nothing, Tayo," I grumbled. "I was only visiting."

Not a word of a lie.

"You do this every few years."

"This time is different."

"You say *that* every time too," he chuckled.

"I'm being serious, Tayo," I said, yanking on my collar.

He stopped, turning to me. The diffused sun behind his head made him look like a looming shadow.

"So am I, Juniper. You should be like that about me."

"Should be?"

"Ah," he said, raising a hand. "I mean, I'd enjoy it."

I kept walking, faster this time.

"So I have to enjoy it too? What do you know about love anyway?"

He sighed. "Enough, Jun-Jun. Enough to know it's something that happens to you, not something you pick."

We walked in silence for a moment.

Tayo stood tall, hands behind his back.

"So it was nothing?"

"So far," I said, trying to bury my face in my hair.

Tayo lived in the future, where he saw us together. A little one running around with his face. I wanted something similar for myself. But I didn't want *his* future. I knew how he felt about me. And I cared for him. But when I closed my eyes, I dreamed of sapphire eyes, snickers and dirty jokes under pixie blonde.

Everyone in my life made me feel like a child.

With Clara I was a woman. Equal.

"When are you going to inform her about... the details?" Tayo asked, breaking through my daydream.

"I was waiting for it to come up."

"How do you imagine that'll happen?" he looked at me, eyebrow raised.

"I'll tell her... eventually."

"Until then, I'm going to ignore it as another Anzu crush," he said plainly.

I hated when he used my second name. I hated it more when he was right. Whatever Clara and I had was built on straw. Once I told her...

Tayo stopped, hands in his pockets. His face was serious.

"I want to see you happy, Juni."

"Then-" I started, but he held up his hand.

"But, Diane, um... Becka, or whatever her name was. *Lidia...*" he listed on his fingers. My head dropped.

"I'm afraid this will end in disaster, *again*. That last one nearly had you run off to Aten knows where."

I choked back tears. This wasn't the Tayo I grew up with. I didn't like jealous Tayo.

"I just want to be happy, *Stephan*."

He flinched, but continued.

"I could make you-"

"Can we talk about something else?"

He cleared his throat. His head hung in surrender.

"Fine, fine," he said, smiling again. "What are you doing for the festival?"

"Zeusday is always a family thing," I said, still blinking the tears away. "But Hadisday..."

I had a plan. But it wouldn't be easy to convince Father.

"Clara?" he smiled.

I smiled back, but punched his arm.

ɔ THIRTEEN ɕ

Juniper wasn't at work for a few days after she stayed over. I knew it was because of me. I had likely bruised her heart. Worse, I neglected her feelings chasing my own. I had been working later and later. There was nothing for me to do otherwise and I had hoped she might drop by.

She didn't.

One of those late nights, I was experimenting on my own pet project. I had a theory that the power inside the *bluetech* could be harnessed. I had tried everything I could think of, with no results.

I scribbled a note on my comm, then rolled my stylus away, sitting back with a frustrated huff.

"I wish Aten was here," I complained to the stale air of my office.

I started gathering my things. As I did, I became aware of a hissing sound. It was the sound of a gas leak, or rather a whispering. I knew there was no one else in the monolith.

My skin crawled.

"Juniper?" I called hoping.

Nothing.

The whispering became louder. Soon it was clear it was coming from inside the room. The largest of the pieces in the room was pulsing almost imperceptibly. I stepped closer. One slow step at a time. I leaned in to listen. To hear what, if anything, it was saying.

Then without warning, as clear as someone standing next to me.

Close now.

I shrieked and stumbled backward. I'd had enough and rushed out of the office in hurried steps, grabbing my bag as I went.

The structure felt far too large and dark as I rushed out. Each step bouncing off the walls, giving the impression of someone walking behind me. I flashed nervous glances back, seeing nothing but black, punctuated by the occasional makeshift light.

A lifetime later, I stopped outside the entrance, leaning against a brick boundary wall. Anything but the wet black of the inside.

I slipped my comm out and tapped a few times. It barely rang before she answered.

"Clara, are you ok?"

"Hey, Fox," I said, trying to hide the fear in my voice.

"What's going on?"

I looked back into the void of the monolith.

"I think I worked too late." I let out a long breath. "Would you like to... hang out?"

"I'm not far from the mono actually," she said. "Tayo and I were just hanging out."

I understood. Or thought I did.

"Sorry, Juniper. I'll let you get back to it."

"No," she said quickly. "I'd like to. Hang out that is."

"I can handle two girls at the same time," came Tayo's voice from the background.

"Tayo!" Juni scolded. Then a commotion of some kind.

"It's late," I said, giving her a way out.

"Please," Juni pleaded softly. "I'd want to see you."

I smiled as the terror melted at Juni's voice.

"Yeah. I'd want that too."

I glanced back at the maw of the monolith. A last shiver running up my back and arms. I turned to go, not looking back again.

Juni and Tayo were in a 'small' section of the Langley estate. A perfectly manicured lawn larger than my apartment building. Far to the back was a giant domed palace of a building.

I felt like an orphan going to a parents evening. Everything was bigger. Even by Earth standards it would have been ostentatious.

I stood at the gate waiting. The guards kept an eye on me, but otherwise seemed unbothered by my presence. I waved at them nervously, granting me a curt nod, but nothing more.

To my surprise, it was Matayo that strolled out of the gate.

The guards, previously dour looking, sprang to life with greetings and smiles. He waved curtly at them, thanking them in smooth Lyrican.

"Doctor," he said, in English again, with a nod of his head to me.

"Milord," I said, with a curtsy.

He chuckled, his voice still settling into its inevitable lower timbre. He ushered me inside, with a bow of his own.

Juni sat on the edge of a large fountain, rim lit, studying the water. She was dressed in her ornate high-collar blouse and long skirt, with impractical stiletto boots. Every bit the princess, like snow in the moonlight. Which made it a damn shame that Lyra was missing a moon.

Her eyes drifted to me and she lit up enough to tense my chest.

"Clara," she said sweetly, waving with a curl of her fingers.

"Hi, Juni."

She rose, walking quickly toward me. She stopped short, her arms not quite making it up for a hug. She offered me her hand instead. I took it grinning.

"What's up?" she asked, as she led me to the fountain. "You don't normally call me."

"I needed... a friend."

"Oh, well..." she hesitated, "here I am.".

Her hand went to her hair out of habit, but she resisted covering her face. She sat, patting the rim of the fountain next to her. I joined her, letting the bubbling of the water calm me.

"I was just telling Jun-Jun about my infamous beer run," Tayo said, standing proud.

"For the fiftieth time," she complained.

"You sound like siblings... or an old married couple," I chuckled nervously.

A silence hung for a beat. An uncomfortable fog.

"Gross," Juni whispered.

"Which part?" Tayo asked.

"Tayo!"

"Jun-Jun, do you really want to get into it now?"

Her eyes jumped to me briefly.

"No," she said deflating.

"You can tell me the story," I interrupted to try ease the tension.

"That is if Jun-Jun doesn't mind." I brushed up against her playfully with my shoulder.

Her face went bright red, and she stared down at her shoes.

"Yes!" Tayo cheered. "It was around a year ago. A mate and I..."

Tayo continued his story. It included feats I wouldn't have believed before Lyra. Before Juniper. She was veiled behind her hair again.

I leaned over touching my shoulder and hand to hers. Juniper tensed for a brief moment. Then she lay her head on my shoulder, wrapping a finger around mine.

"I missed you," I whispered.

Tayo's story went on. It included a lot of vivid descriptions of someone called *Vivian*. I thought Juni hadn't heard me. Then she pressed against me a fraction harder.

"It's always nice when you're around," she whispered.

Tayo looked at me with Juni on my shoulder, and his smile faltered. His eyes darted to Juni for a moment, before his smile returned wider but gentler than before.

"Juniper," he said, interrupting his own tale.

Her head snapped up, as if she was caught in the act. But Tayo leaned over gently.

"You wanted to ask Clara something, remember?" he smirked.

She reached out, giving his hand a small press. The communication of a lifetime of friendship I wasn't privy to. I could only guess as to why.

"It's almost year end," she said, as she turned to me. "I wanted to ask if you'll come to the festival with me?"

“Of course,” I said without pause. “But let’s pretend I’m from another planet, and don’t know what festival.”

She rolled her eyes at me, with a half-smile.

“They kept as much of Earth’s time structure as possible.”

“Right,” I said. “Except for the day length and days in a year.”

“And with a hundred-and-ninety-two days from the two-orbit year, it leaves two days spare.”

I snapped my fingers. “A leap weekend.”

“Exactly. Zeusday and Hadisday, to give the Greeks gods a turn,” Tayo added.

I chuckled. Iris was going to love that when... if she arrived.

“So I wondered,” Juni continued. “If you would... come to the new year’s festival with me?”

“Spending my first new year’s with you? I’d love to,” I grinned.

“And then have dinner with my parents after,” she slipped in with little more than a mumbled whisper.

“Oh, shit,” I said, with Tayo laughing in the background as Juniper blushed.

I felt like a teen again. Brimming with vivid emotions and anxiety.

It felt good.

❀ Juni IV ❀

“Today I need to act cool at work. Normal,” she says, smiling.

Juniper sits in a plain wooden chair at a table filled with various vanity items and small decorated containers. She brushes her snowy hair in long strokes, battling to temper the curls. Dressed in her normal house white and gold formal wear. She fusses over a knot for a moment, the brush and hair tangling together.

“I’m not going... to pretend... to know everything... about Clara,” she mutters, not looking at the camera. The brush comes free, with Juni’s sigh of relief.

“But, I think the festival will be awesome.”

She grins wide.

“Our first date.” Juni tilts her head. “I think.”

Her hand drops to her lap as she straightens her back and shoulders.

“I should probably ask my parents if she can join.”

A shadow of something scuttles past her in the background.

She leans over, looking closely at the screen.

“Oh shoot, the time,” she cries. “I’m going to be late for work. Clara’s probably there already.”

She stands, and as she does a crashing can be heard off screen.

“What now?” Juni huffs.

Juniper stalks out of frame. A scuffling is barely audible.

“No! No!” she shouts from elsewhere in her room.

For a moment her room is quiet besides the curtain flapping in the breeze.

She comes back into frame, one shoe in hand, hopping as she tries to pull it on. The other already on her foot.

She returns to her chair looking closely at the screen again.

“Damnit, I won’t have time to do proper makeup,” she frowns.

Her face skews, eyes glancing upward. "I don't think Clara ever wears makeup."

Juni's eyes go wide. "Maybe she doesn't have any."

She taps below the frame then applies colour to her eyes directly using her fingers, all the while humming an Earth song about 'getting around' she learned at work.

"Guess I'll ask her today. It'll be much easier than telling her about-"

She looks offscreen again.

"Come in," Juniper calls.

She listens intently for a moment. A muffled voice can be heard.

"Seriously!" she says, eyes wide.

There's another moment of the muffled voice speaking.

"Oh. Thank you, Alice," she calls to the door.

Juni grabs lipstick and applies it hurriedly.

"Shit! The makeup will have to wait. I need to go tell Clara."

She jumps up rushing out of frame. A door slams. A few seconds later, padded footsteps grow, approaching the camera.

Juniper leans into the frame scowling.

"Crap, nearly forgot," she huffs, reaching past the camera.

The video ends.

ↄ FOURTEEN ɕ

I shook the glowing blue cube again. It wasn't the first time that day.

"Say something, you piece of shit," I yelled.

It had been stoic since it last spoke. And that was pissing me off.

"Not so talkative when the sun's up, are you?"

"Clara?"

I leapt back yelping, my hand on my heart.

Juni stood in the door, eyes wide.

"Juniper, you scared me halfway back up the beam."

She laughed, but there was an edge to it.

The sound alone was enough to calm my nerves.

"Who were you talking to?" she asked when she regained her composure.

I looked back at the tech, then her.

"Ah, it's nothing, Fox," I said dropping the piece. "I'm glad you're here."

"Well, we both need to go," she said, stepping halfway out.

"What's wrong? Are you ok?"

Her shoulders dropped and her expression softened.

"Aw, that's sweet. I'm fine," she smiled. Then she looked over her shoulder pointing with her thumb. "But an Earth ship just arrived at the station."

My entire being froze.

Iris.

Aten.

I started forward, pausing for a second looking back.

"Close now," the tech had said. Did it...

I had no time to dwell on it.

"Juni, I need to go," I said, grabbing my coat.

She stepped in front of me, blocking the exit.

"Juniper," I grumbled.

She took my hand gently, with a wink.

"It's faster by car, and I have one waiting."

I breathed out some tension. "I don't deserve someone like you."

"Make it up to me later," she said blushing as she nearly bodily dragged me out of the office, forgetting her own strength.

The car ride over was tense. Juniper had used her name to get us priority access to the elevator and station. Being friends with the boss' kid had its benefits.

Once more I found myself standing in the space elevator looking out of the window. This time I was going up. The city of Vala, as massive and imposing as it felt from the ground, shrunk away like a model below us. I had never expected to return since I last left the elevator lost and alone. Now I rode it up with someone... dear to me.

I sat next to her taking her hand. She wrapped her fingers around mine gently. Her almost unnatural heat, lending me strength. A soft curl of her lips stayed on her face supporting me.

My heart beat hard during the entire trip up. I didn't know for sure if it would be them, but I hoped. No, it was more than that. It was faith. It had been five months, but Earth was a lifetime ago.

The station was bustling as always. Vendors shouting, a roar of a thousand conversations. It reminded me of a subway station back home. Yet, people parted like water as Juniper approached. Her face set serious, back straight, and her house colours on display. Her hair a cloak that flowed behind her as she strode. We didn't get far before we started picking up a security detail. They joined us with brief salutes, falling in step without missing a beat. We didn't stop moving. We beelined it to the orientation room. The security formed a perimeter around Juni and I. Then the wait started. Time slowing like drying amber.

Half an hour later the door slid open with a hiss. Refugees started flooding out. Some of them with blood on their faces. Others in tears.

As the crowd thinned, I saw her.

Iris.

Alone.

She looked pale—drained. She walked like a ghost, eyes downturned. She stopped briefly, looking back. Nobody followed.

My heart dropped. He wasn't with her.

I was hyperventilating, heart forcing each beat.

That small heat wrapped around my hand again. Juni leaned against me.

"It's really her, isn't it?"

I nodded, then raised my hand waving.

Iris noticed me, her large dark eyes growing. She started walking over in long strides, not paying attention to the other foot traffic. The station around me faded from my senses as she approached.

She slowed and stopped just out of arms reach. Her eyes were shimmering—on the brink.

"He..." she tried, voice hoarse. She cleared her throat.

"Aten, isn't with you. Is he." It wasn't a question.

I shook my head slowly.

Iris took a step, the next one her knee buckled. I caught her on the third one.

She shook as she broke with a wail. My own tears running freely.

I held her tightly, trying to be to her, what she had always been to me. An anchor. Something to hold on to in the storm. We stayed there for a while, mourning the empty seat we both loved.

"He was always late," she said through the tears. "But he always came back."

I helped her to her feet, but kept her hands.

"What do I do now, Clara?"

"Let's get you some food," I said, remembering my own landing.

Juni was barking orders in the background. Juni's influence bolstered by the reputation Iris didn't yet know she had. I had no doubt Iris would be well taken care of.

I stared in awe at Juniper. She was quiet, gentle, and delicate. But she was also every inch a princess. Her station and command far outpacing her age.

I caught her eye, and she winked at me, scrunching her nose. I placed my hand on my chest, making her cheeks glow. Then I guided Iris somewhere quiet.

We each sat with a coffee and a light lunch. Iris had her hands in her hair, eyes framed red. She was tougher than I ever was. I had every reason to think she would make it through Lyra better than I did.

"Five months?" she breathed.

"And change," I replied.

Concern flashed over her face, creasing her brow.

"Oh, Clara. You must have been so alone."

I smiled. "Not for long," I said, nodding to Juni.

Iris looked over at Juni, the corners of her mouth almost curling up.

"You're something of a celebrity here," I informed her.

Her eyes went wide. "How?"

I told her how her paintings survived. Weaving in some of Lyra in between. Like the Receivers of the Gift.

"A church. God, this must be a fever dream."

"It gets better," I assured her. "Lyra is much the same as Earth, once you get used to it."

"And her?" Iris said, gesturing towards Juni.

"Her name is Juniper," I said, unable to contain my joy. "She is... and I kid you not... a princess."

"No shit?"

"And she's my..." I rolled my eyes. Thinking of the right word.

"My friend."

Iris gave me a wry look.

"Mhm. Friend. They called me Aten's friend at that damn Gala we went to. I didn't appreciate it."

I chuckled despite the situation. Iris didn't join. Instead, she lay her head in her arms.

"I saw you a few hours ago, and you've built a whole new life," she mumbled.

"You know me. I can't sit still."

She looked up at me. Something like sorrow and trouble in her eyes.

"I'm glad to see you, Clara."

I reached over, taking her hand.

"I missed you, Kostas."

She sat up. "It's *Tikrit* now actually," she said. This time her smile was real. "He... Aten did it. To make sure I had a seat."

"That sounds about right," I replied. Aten had secured my safe passage too. I owed him, and Iris more than I could ever repay.

"I'm his... was, his wife. For little more than a moment."

I ran my hand over her back, comforting her as much as I could.

"You were always more than that, Iris."

She looked at me with a spark of that old Iris. "I was, wasn't I."

Iris smiled. Pain still fresh in her eyes.

My eyes caught Juni, practically vibrating over Iris's shoulder and waved her over.

She bounced closer.

"I didn't want to interrupt," she almost whispered.

I reached out to her and pulled her into a seat when she took my hand.

"Iris *Tikrit*," I said, testing it out. "This is Juniper Anzu Shao the fourth."

Juni was clearly shocked I had remembered it all. I found it difficult to forget anything about her. But I would never have let her on to that.

Iris looked at her for a moment, then shook her hand.

"Iris Tikrit. Thank you for helping Clara... and me."

I thought Juni was going to pass out.

"It's so awesome to meet you," Juni said. Then remembering her mask. "Welcome to Vala. I will do what I can to assist you in acclimating."

"Thank you, Juniper."

"Oh, call me Juni please," she said, too giddy. "I'm happy to help Clara's friend."

"Friend..." Iris mumbled. "That word again."

Juni looked puzzled for a moment, then shaking herself.

"I'm sorry... for your... about Aten I mean," she stumbled through her emotions.

"So am I," Iris replied, patting Juniper's hand, motherly.

We spent an hour or more getting Iris up to speed, as much as we could. It gave me perspective on how far I had come since my own arrival too. Afterward we rode the elevator down with her, Juni falling asleep on my shoulder. Her breathing was soft, her hair a coat over us.

Iris stared off into the middle distance for a while. When her eyes drifted to me, her expression softened. She waggled her eyebrows at me, causing my face to erupt in blush.

"I never really asked how you are, hon," Iris whispered, leaning over with her fingers in a braid.

"I'm pretty great actually," I said, grinning.

Iris smiled properly for the first time. She was raw, but still made sure I was ok. It was the same on Earth, even considering all I did to Aten... to her.

On the ground, a car was waiting for Iris. I hugged her tight.

"Call me for anything. I'll see you soon."

"I'm going to sleep for a day, then I'll see you," she grumbled.

Iris turned to Juni. "It was a real pleasure meeting you, Juni. Thank you."

She leaned down to hug Juni, their difference in height making it awkward.

Juni giggled in response, still hopelessly star struck. It was adorable.

Juni and I waved Iris off, hand in hand.

"I'll get you an autograph next time, ok," I said, leaning toward her.

"Oh yes please," she exhaled. "I was too nervous to ask."

I nudged her gently with my hip.

"It's getting late," I said. "Why don't you crash by me again. It's closer."

Juni looked up at the starry sky. There were no clouds in sight.

I knew she could take a car home with no trouble, but I didn't want to be alone. She hesitated for a brief moment. Then...

"That's a great idea," she said, glowing.

FIFTEEN

By the time the taxi dropped us at my place it was past eight. I dragged myself inside, Juni gliding along beside me. I flopped down on the bed, groaning. Juniper sat beside me, hands on her lap. We stayed like that—silent. No prodding or asking. She stayed close, touching her knee to mine.

I was so excited that Iris was finally on Lyra and safe. I had missed her terribly. But losing Aten had broken something in her. Before, she could always call him, even if it was just to fight. Now...

I had been so selfish back then. As if I could ever had stolen him from her.

I was holding my tears back. It felt like a second-hand tragedy.

Still, I couldn't help but miss his sleek black hair.

His beautiful chestnut skin.

That brilliant smile when I would tease...

I grit my teeth against a whimper.

I could almost smell his cologne again. Hear his voice.

But I wouldn't. He really was gone.

The sobs erupted out. Grief and months of worry all at once.

Juni's palm ran up my arm in solace.

"He's really gone," I cried, nose running like a child.

"I know, I know," Juni comforted me, her heater hand on my face.

"I should have done more... forced him onto my ship."

"You couldn't have known, Clara," she said softly.

I wept in ragged sobs, with Juni keeping me up. I knew Juniper was right. Aten and I had a plan. It wasn't anyone's fault. But it didn't make it hurt any less.

It was just life. Iris's whole life.

"Poor Iris. He was her whole world," I whispered as much to myself as to Juniper.

She wrapped around me like a heated blanket. Her strength so far beyond her size. Not only physically, but in her heart also. She was similar to Iris in that way. I was convinced they would be fast friends.

I leaned on her. Not only then, but since we met. She was my lighthouse during the dark moonless nights of Lyra.

"We'll take good care of her," Juni said, wiping my face with a hanky. "Both of us will."

I nodded, still trying to calm myself. Her bright eyes made me so sure it would be ok. That I could tackle anything.

We would never know how long it could last, and I was wasting it by pulling my punches.

I leaned forward, until I could feel her breath against my lips.

She leaned back, her turn to leave me staggered.

"Clara..."

"Fuck, I'm sorry Juniper. I did it ag-"

She lay her fingers softly on my mouth, shaking her head, tears on her cheeks too.

"I should have told you earlier..."

"You can tell me anything," I said, rubbing her hands in mine.

"I'm betrothed," she said—a physical blow.

I sat back, facing away. I swallowed once, hard. Bile pushing up in my stomach.

"I know," my voice cracked.

"You do?"

"Well, no," I admitted, looking back to her. "But it's obvious isn't it. You're a princess. You deserve more than this," I said looking around the crestfallen room. "That's how the story always ends."

She was shaking her head, as if rejecting the notion itself.

I slid my hand back under hers.

"Tayo, right."

A small nod from her.

"It's ok, Juniper," I said, finding my feet.

"I didn't want to lie to you, Clara."

"I know," I croaked. "We can still..." I tried.

"Nothing changes, right?" I pushed out willing it to be true.

She let out a pained sigh.

"I really need it to," she whispered.

Then her lips were on mine. An inferno of want, coated with apricots and honey. Her hands on my face with need. The smell of winter blooms and a cloud of dazzling silver overwhelming my senses.

I leaned in, lips parting as I did. Tasting her like a living colour.

My body tensed, curling my legs under me. I clenched my fist into the bed covers to ground myself. Tears and lip gloss, salty and sweet like Lyra itself.

We parted breathless. Juniper's eyes still half-lidded.

"Weird," I admitted flustered. "But, I like it."

Her face went red, before resting her head on my shoulder.

"I don't know how any of this is going to work, Clara."

"Let's just enjoy it while we can," I said, wiping my tears with my sleeve.

"I'm scared. Losing you... It would suck so much."

I held her close.

"I'll be here, no matter what."

"I'm sure Iris thought that too," she whispered.

My heart turned to lead.

"I'm not going anywhere," I said, determined to be correct.

"Promise?" she asked, eyes coming up to meet mine.

"I do."

I didn't sleep on the floor that night. Instead, Juni held me as if I mattered. As if I belonged. Soft sorrow wrapped in a promise of a better tomorrow.

I couldn't ignore my own heart any longer.

I couldn't envision what a future without her strength would be like.

I felt hope again.
I wished...

❀ Juni V ❀

Juniper was still wearing her house's colours. She sat smiling for a few moments in silence. Her eyes distant, lost in memory.

"They always talk about having butterflies in your stomach," she says, looking at the ceiling.

"And I thought that was romance novel nonsense."

She shivered from head to hips.

"I can feel them fluttering."

Her smile dims noticeably.

"I mean, there's still so much to work out. Nothing is set in stone."

She leans in.

"And I met Iris. *The* Iris," Juni said, throwing her arms in the air.

She relaxes her arms again, laying back in the chair.

"I'm having such a weird time."

A small chuckle.

Then sitting up again quickly.

"But I'm loving it."

Juni fusses with her skirt, expression greying.

"I'm sad for Clara. For Iris."

Her hand goes to her heart.

"But my heart won't slow down from excitement."

She stands, walking around the chair.

"A week until the festival."

She looks to the side with a deep breath.

"I'm going to go talk to Father. To tell...
Ask about Clara joining us for the dinner."

Her face turns hard, frowning fiercely.

"I'm going to look him in the eye. Then tell him."

She straightens up, arms crossed.

"Dad... *Father*, Clara and I are in..."

Her shoulders drop, but she steels herself once again.

"Father, Clara is special to me and I..."

She huffs, pulling hair over her face, giggling.

Then Juni waves her hand dismissively.

"I'll figure it out. Mom at least will say yes."

She looks to the side again, her hand clenching a few times.

"I have to try. I can't be a scared little girl anymore."

She loops around the chair reclaiming her seat.

Her face sinks into her palms.

"Tayo is not going to be happy," she breathes softly, the words almost lost behind her hands. She rolls her head back, staring sternly at the ceiling.

"Let him be mad. I don't need his blessing to be happy."

She shakes her head, then looks at the screen seriously.

"I can't live worrying about everyone else's happiness."

She stands, then immediately sits again blushing.

"Maybe... I should clean up first. At least pretend I didn't sleep in another woman's bed."

She starts giggling, her face looking younger than usual.

"Ok, ok. I have to stop procrastinating."

She squares her shoulders dramatically.

"Time to put my big girl face on," she says as she starts wiping off her makeup. Her eyes flick to the camera, with renewed fire in them.

She leans over, ending the recording.

ↄ SIXTEEN Ↄ

It was the last morning of the Lyran year—Hadisday. It was also the first time Juni and I were to hang out. No, that's not accurate. It was the day of our first date. I was nervous, which wasn't my style at all. I stood outside my door, exhaling smoke into the air.

There was a small chirrup beside me.

It was Goose. The scuttling spider creature from before. It was crouched down, eyes wide. It blinked one pair, then another.

I had finally found information about them online. Felis Arachnia, or as they were commonly known, Spider Lions. The apex predator of Lyra, and essentially harmless. But I called it Goose for a reason, on account of the goosebumps it still gave me. I ducked inside and brought out a bag of kibble. I poured a few handfuls into a bowl, then took a long step back. It hesitated for a moment, turned a few times on the spot, before scuttling over and diving into the food.

It worried me that he was growing on me.

"Ok, Goose," I said to the alien creature. "I guess I better get ready."

It chirruped at me, bouncing once. I eased my hand out to it nervously.

It narrowed its eyes as it crept closer. Goose stopped just out of reach, sniffing the air. It drew back hissing, then bolted.

I pulled my hand back, flexing my fingers.

"Yeah, I feel like that too some days."

I stared blankly at my closet in the dim of my flat. I had started replacing the vintage Earth collection. I had unfortunately forgotten to update my meet the king and queen selection.

I pulled out my comm...

(**You** - What the hell do I wear that's festival appropriate and can also double as meet the High Governor attire.)

(**Foxy Lady :)** - Oh, I figured you can grab something from my stuff for the dinner. Wear whatever you want to the festival.)

(**Foxy Lady :**) - If that's ok with you. I meant to ask.)

(**Foxy Lady :**) - Sorry.)

(**You** - That sounds perfect. See you soon.)

(**Foxy Lady :**) – I'm excited.)

(**You** – Me too.)

"Fuck. This is really happening isn't it," I said, rubbing my face.

I centred myself, closing my eyes. This was not my first big deal dinner, and I was a hard-working employee...

"Oh gods, I forgot Juni's dad is also my boss."

I wanted to throw up.

"Do it for Juni!" I announced to the room, with my fist in the air as I tried to suppress the jitters.

Goose chortled from outside. I took it as an agreement.

I was on top of it.

I dressed practical but tidy, tying my hair up in a small tail, surprised at how long it had gotten. I was dressed in an oversized comfortable tee, some denims, and my well-worn Chucks.

I grabbed only what I could put in my pockets.

On my way out of the door, I flicked a treat at Goose for his support. Earning me a twirl and chirrup.

"Here we go, Clara. Don't fuck it up."

ɔ SEVENTEEN ɕ

I arrived a few minutes early. The grounds spanned a large area outside the city proper. Festivities were already in full swing. The Lyra sun was doing what it could to emulate a summer's day. Carnival rides, stalls, and performers filled the entire area. Sounds of laughing mixed with screams and music in that distinct festival blend.

My comm pinged.

(**Foxy Lady :**) – Look behind you.)

I turned to see Juni. Her red cheeks were held up by her wide smile. A thick braid of silver hair hung over her shoulder. She was wrapped in a red skirt dress, with knee-high boots in black. I felt under dressed immediately.

I froze, taking her in. I had never seen her look so... free.

She sauntered up to me pulling lightly on her braid.

"Morning," she said, barely loud enough over the crowd.

My brain collided with my hormones. I froze for a second too long.

I didn't manage anything except, "Wow."

She laughed, looking at our feet.

"I thought I'd try something less formal," she said, doing a half twirl.

"You look beautiful," I admitted, awed.

Her face froze, as if I was speaking a foreign language. Her hand slid down her braid, pulling her gaze back down to her feet.

"I think," she said looking away as she smiled, "That's the first time anyone but my mom meant that."

I reached out to her, but only let myself run my hand along her braid. I stopped near her hand. Her fingers flexed, but didn't move.

"I think there's a decent chance you'll hear it again."

Her smile broadened, as she leaned her head against me briefly.

We strode together into the bustle of the Vala New Year's Eve festival.

It wasn't long before we both drifted to the side of the path.

"Where do we start..." we both said together.

We chuckled like nervous idiots.

"I'm not from here," I pointed out.

She pointed a finger at me. "You'd never be able to tell."

"You lead, milady," I said with a small bow of my head, letting her take the reins.

She turned her pointed finger to the road, and we set off again with her leading.

I stayed close beside her. Close enough to feel her radiating. I could imagine cold nights, warm covers and...

My hands slipped out of my pockets. I ran my fingers down my palm.

Then I slipped my fingers lazily along her palm. She took my hand without missing a beat.

The festival was beyond anything I had ever seen on Earth. It reminded me of stories from before the Second War. When Earth was covered in cities and people. The festival had stalls of every kind forming living walls along the paths. Interspersed with that were carnival rides of every type, including some small rollercoasters. The various sounds of music and joy mixing to a roar. Entertainers and buskers were abundant too. Everyone seemed to be in good spirits.

Food was everywhere, joining their smells into the busy whirl of scent permeating the air.

Juni stopped, turning with her palms out toward me.

"Wait, I want you to try something," she said grinning.

"I've already tried kissing a girl. It was pretty good."

I leaned in. She rolled her eyes, but couldn't hide her red face.

She popped a hand on her hip.

"I want you to try a *Chustig*?"

I nodded, processing.

"My lyrican isn't that great yet, but did you just offer me a snot stick?"

She chuckled.

"Well, damn when you put it that way. Come on, trust me."

Her grin was infectious. She could offer me cyanide with that smile and I would have chugged it.

"Alright. I trust you."

"Win," she cheered, then led me to a small cart.

A moment later she handed me... well, a snot stick. It seemed to be a skewered and fried slug, covered in spices.

Juni took a bite, the meat squelching, closing her eyes and making sounds I wanted to hear in a quieter context.

I had come that far, and wasn't going to back down. I bit into it, with a moist crunch. The texture was exactly what I expected, but the flavour was divine.

"Oh, gods. This is fantastic," I said, mouth still full.

Juni didn't say anything. She raised an eyebrow, waiting. The spicy fire hit my throat, burning my nose too. I coughed, surprised at the kick.

"Good right?" she sung.

"It's great," I said, still regaining my sense of smell.

I looked at the strange food in my hand. Clearly it was something Juni had enjoyed her whole life. Lyra was in many ways still so odd to me. But more and more I viewed it with awe, instead of dread. Especially when she was nearby. Earth... It was a dream ago. I was waking up in a new life, with new flavours.

Juniper was determined to see everything and I followed happily as long as her fingers were wrapped in mine. Curio stalls, rides, or games. Anything I could think of and a few I could never have imagined. All bathed in the constant rumble and smells of the day's lively tradition. Around mid-day a parade rolled through. Floats and costumes flowed down the main road in a flood of sound and colour. More than a few of the performers spotted Juni and dipping their heads as they passed. She responded with curt waves. I liked seeing the well-known princess side of Juniper. But it did knot my stomach when I thought about our divide too much. As if sensing my tension, the thrum of the crowd delivered us to a shooting gallery.

"You want to have a go?" Juni asked as she saw it.

"I don't know," I said, mid mouthful of popcorn. "I'm not a big fan of guns."

"It's only air rifles."

"Mmm. Alright, I'll try."

I grabbed the miniature rifle, tracking the metal cutout *Tharacks* as they made a loop around the track.

I concentrated, focusing on one target at a time. I pulled in a deep breath, squeezing the trigger on the exhale. I repeated the pattern a few times. Finally, I landed a hit on my last shot.

"That was embarrassing," I moped.

"Let me show you how it's done," Juni announced, grabbing a rifle with flair.

She managed to hit two.

We left the stall equally embarrassed and laughing.

As we wandered, Juni's eyes turned skyward. I thought she was lost in thought, when she turned to me.

"Can I pick our next thing?"

"Of course."

"Even if it's corny?" she asked, stretching her words.

"I go where you go, Fox."

She tilted her head to me.

"Oh really?" she said softly. "You sure?"

Her eyes drew me in. I couldn't be anything but sure.

I mirrored her pose. "Yeah. Pretty sure."

We made our way towards the Ferris wheel, reaching high above the rest of the festival.

The crowd started growing denser. The gap closing as we approached the wheel. We slowly started running out of space for two. Our shoulders bumped, with the normal 'excuse me' and 'sorry'.

We turned sideways, face-to-face, trying to thread the gap.

I became all too aware of her body pressing up against mine.

We ended up trapped in the back of the crowd, sandwiched together.

I wrapped my arms around her, keeping us from separating.

"I didn't want it to end like this," I cried, dramatically, earning me a snicker from Juniper.

"It's not that bad," Juni said.

The crowd jostled my arms, landing my hand square on her ass. Juni squeaked, her eyes wide on mine. I sucked in a deep breath, ready to apologize. Her arms went around me instead with a giggle, her hands on my ass. Her head floated softly down to rest on my shoulder. The press of the festival became welcome. And then it seemed to fade all too quickly, clearing our way to the wheel.

The view from the top of the wheel was incredible. The city likely looked staggering. But I was watching Juniper as she took it all in. Her stare distant but content, as her fingers played with her hair absentmindedly. Her foot was placed by mine, our ankles linked.

I followed her soft ruby lips. I hung on them with each word she spoke. Each motion, a beautiful and dangerous strung bow. I realised I had been chewing on my own lip. They tingled, already missing the brush of hers. I leaned back, savouring the ride.

The sun started setting while we hung above the world. It was our cue. The air growing cooler as the sky darkened. The worry from earlier had dulled, but still nagged.

It was nearly time for dinner.

ↄ EIGHTEEN ↄ

We entered Juni's home as the sky darkened. The size of the front door alone was making a statement. The word opulent would have done the house a great disservice. The foyer had the classic double curved stairs, red carpets with the gold trim on white of the Shao house interwoven everywhere.

At the first landing hung a small painting. Two figures wrapped together in a wide streak of red oil paint, behind them a window filled with blue tinted snow.

"Oh, shit," I said quietly, recognising the work.

"It's one of Iris's works. Original too," Juni boasted.

The label read, Unknown lovers in the moonlight.

I chuckled. "The title needs work."

"We do what we can with the minimal info," said a low male voice behind me.

"Father," Juni sung.

I turned startled to find a tall broad man, standing behind me. He carried himself with enough authority that he needed no introduction. His swept-back hair was black salt and pepper. His firm jaw framed with a neat goatee. He was standing with his hands behind his back.

"Clara, this is my father," Juni said, haphazardly introducing me.

He put out his hand. When I took it, he did not envelop my hand, but only held my fingers with a small shake. His manners befitting his position.

"I am High Governor Takashi Hyun Ren Shao the third."

I dipped my head in a polite nod.

"A pleasure, sir."

His mouth curled at the corner. I felt as if I had passed the first test.

"You were discussing the title of my Kostas?" he said, gesturing to the painting.

I looked back at it. My next test.

I could hear the bold, single stroke that bound the figures.

"They're not unknown. That's Iris and Aten."

I remembered her painting the base a well-known blue.

"That's not moonlight, it's light from Daedalus. I would know that glow anywhere."

The governor studied the painting for a moment, nodding.

Juni had gone pale. I didn't know if it was nerves or excitement.

"How would you know all that?" Governor Shao asked.

"I used to help her mix her browns with coffee," I chuffed. "We lived together when she painted this," I said casually.

"You were roommates with Iris?" Juni blurted out.

"More than roommates. We were... We are best friends."

Juniper's father regarded me with a raised eyebrow.

"Amazing," he chuckled. "You have my thanks, Clara."

He turned, leaving up the stairs.

"See you at dinner, doctor, Juniper. More appropriately dressed I hope."

When he was out of earshot, I let out a held breath.

"That was intense," I huffed.

"That was awesome," Juni said, twirling around me in a hug.

"You and Iris. It makes so much more sense."

Then after a moment.

"And you were *just* roommates?" she probed.

"That's the official story," I teased, not meeting her eyes.

"Clara," Juni complained, laughing.

"I'll still tell you all about it."

"I'd like that," she said, wrapping her pinky finger around mine.

I knew Juniper and Iris would get along perfectly. I looked forward to it.

We moved through the house to Juni's room. The scale was intimidating. Eventually we reached a non-descript door. Beyond was Juniper's private space. It was massive and elaborate, matching the rest of the house. In the centre stood a hulking four poster bed as large as my main room. A fire crackled on the far wall, matching beats with the patter of rain from outside. I half expected secret entrances behind bookcases.

A scuttling drew my attention. The creature was on Juni before I could react.

"Juni!" I cried out.

She started laughing.

"What the hell?" I choked.

She turned with a wide smile, holding a white Spider Lion with black spots. It was rubbing against her.

"Clara, this is Poppy."

I shivered.

"I'm not ready for that *quite* yet," I admitted.

Juni shrugged and put Poppy down, who scuttled off elsewhere.

"Fair enough. Biology lesson later. Let's get you formal first."

She opened a closet as big as my apartment.

"Welcome to my dungeon, princess, help yourself."

I spent a while looking through the options, before finding something that felt right for me. Juni threw a familiar outfit on her bed and started peeling her dress off. My eyes followed it down her shoulders, blades, spine, dimples above the gentle curve of her hips, and...

I looked away, clearing my throat.

"Oh, whoops. I wasn't thinking, sorry," she said from behind me.

"I guess we're past the 'just two girls' stage."

"I'll change in the bathroom," I reassured her, heading to it without looking back. But the temptation to look back lingered with me.

I slipped on the blue gown I chose, surprised it fit me. It was made for Juni's delicate frame. The dress shifted tone as the light moved over it, changing from teal to navy in waves.

I stepped back into the room once Juni gave the all clear.

Her mouth formed a silent "O" when she saw me.

"You're so pretty," she breathed, as if letting me in on a secret.

I felt the blood rushing to my face and head.

"Thank you," I replied meekly.

She stepped forward, taking my hand.

"It'll just be us and my folks. My father was pretty interested to meet you."

"That's... ominous."

"He's not a bad man, Clara. It'll be fine, I promise."

I pressed her hand gently.

"It's that obvious that I'm nervous, huh?"

"A bit," she said, putting her thumb and index finger together.

"I'll be fine. I'm no stranger to fancy dinners."

She nodded—quick and sharp. Then we left to eat a normal meal, with a normal ruling family, in their normal palace.

The dining area could not be called a room. Adjectives failed to reach the murals on the vaulted ceiling. The table was made from a single massive piece of wood pretending to be an island. I met Juni's mother.

Lady Sophia Shao was soft spoken but not traditionally beautiful. Her features gentle and her voice a stark contrast to Juniper's father. She made me feel at home immediately.

"You must tell me about Earth sometime, doctor Sing," she said, hooking her arm in mine with an inviting smile.

"Clara, please," I said, keeping my own smile on.

Dinner was not extravagant, but expertly prepared. Conversation was the same as around any other family table. It had a suspicious lack of assassination attempts, dragons, and knights, upending any expectations and trepidations I had.

"You knew Aten too, right Clara?" the governor asked.

"Yes, sir. I was his assistant."

"Ha," he said, clapping his hands together. "I snagged the exact right person for the job then."

His mirth was genuine and before long, so was mine.

Juni snuck a squeeze on my leg in approval.

The time melted away. The dinner came to an end without incident. Sophia had retired already, as the governor had walked us to the door. He pulled me aside.

"A word, If I may?" he asked. "In private," he said, looking at Juniper.

She nodded, the diligent daughter, closing the door behind her.

Oh shit.

He straightened up, gathering his thoughts.

"Doctor Sing... No. Clara," he began.

"Yes, sir," I replied, dreading what came next

He slipped his hands into his pockets, casually.

"I recognise that you are an intelligent woman. But do me the same courtesy. Whatever this thing is, between you and Juniper. I will allow it. But do not think this absolves her of the obligations of the Shao name."

I was going to reply but he held up a hand, his posture softening.

"And whatever you may think of me. However Juniper may feel about my methods..."

A long sigh, showing his age. The weight of his position. He stared at the wall, inspecting nothing.

"She is still my little girl," he said. "The road ahead will be difficult for her, and I don't believe you're equipped to walk it beside her."

His gaze turned to me, locking eyes. "I hope you prove me wrong."

And with that he left. Leaving Juni and me standing in the hallway.

"What was that about?" she asked.

"I think I was just challenged to keep you."

Juniper giggled. "Easiest job yet... right?"

"Right," I replied. Not quite convincing myself.

"I should probably head home," I said, getting ready to leave.

I looked down. "Oh, and the dress. You may want it back."

Juni took my hand—soft and warm.

"It's yours if you want it," she said, looking at her feet. Her lush curls spilling over her face. "I hope my parents didn't cause you too much grief."

"They were fine. I had a really nice time," I confessed.

"That's... That's great," she said beaming.

"Well, I should get going," I said, not ready for such a great day to end.

"Oh..." she said, her hand slipping from mine. "I thought you could crash at my place for a change."

"Um..."

"Come on. Girl's night," she said excitedly with a small bounce.

I chuckled, taking back her hand. I didn't want to make my relief too obvious.

"I can't say no to you."

She squealed, coming back to life. I imagine she wasn't the type to have many friends over as a child.

As we returned to her room, she lay back against the door, latching it.

"Finally," she said, but I didn't know what she meant exactly.

She drifted to her bed, picking up a neat stack of clothing.

"Here," she said, handing it to me. "I know you don't have PJs. I arranged a toothbrush for you also."

"Oh... Um, thanks," I said, taking the clothes tentatively. It felt too planned. She had anticipated I would say yes. That made me equal parts curious and nervous. But also, more than a little excited.

I left to the bathroom once more to change. The clothes she had gotten me were my usual T-shirt and sweats I wore to bed, if not a bit tighter. Juniper had been paying more attention than I had realised, or perhaps let myself realise until that moment.

The shirt clung a hair too tightly around my chest, the icy tiles under foot conspiring against me too. I folded my arms over my chest, suddenly more aware of my body than usual.

"All good?" she asked as I exited. I pulled at the shirt then froze mid step.

Juni was laying on the plush carpet by the fireplace, lit with an orange heat flickering over her.

She was wearing tube socks up her silk legs and a thick sweater, not quite covering the lace hugging her hips, completing the image I missed earlier. Silver-white curls fell around and over her face.

I envied artists like Iris that could capture something so beautiful in time with their brush. Instead, I let it wash over me, preserving as much as I could.

"Clara?" she prodded softly.

I shook myself. "Oh, yeah, they're-"

"A bit tight?" she said first—cheeks pink in the firelight. "Sorry, it was my best guess."

I laughed. "Maybe a bit tight, but it's fine. Thank you."

She grinned, her large eyes pinching tight.

I sank down next to her on the carpet. It was softer than my bed at home. Cut-pile strands wrapping around me like soft shallow water.

She scooted closer, her face near mine. I could feel her breath warm on my cheek.

A moment passed of us just absorbing each other.

"Hi," she whispered.

"Hey."

She leaned forward slowly, until the sharp edge of her lips brushed against mine. Testing the water gently, as if expecting me to pull away. I leaned in instead, her tender lips pressing firmly against my own. I relished the sensation, closing my eyes to feel nothing but her delicate mouth—the taste of apricots and honey again.

We separated with a released exhale. I kept my eyes closed for a beat.

"I don't think I'll get tired of that," Juni said smiling as she moved closer still, slipping her leg over my hips as she leaned on one arm.

I smiled back at her, "No, it doesn't seem likely."

She watched me with a dreamy expression.

"Still weird?" she asked after a while.

"Different," I admitted, "but I like it."

"Oh, thank Aten," she exhaled, leaning in for another kiss.

The mention of his name, almost a prayer.

Laughter exploded from me unexpectedly. I covered my mouth to not shatter our moment, but it was too late. Juniper looked at me as if I had kicked her spider lion.

"What did I say?" she asked innocently.

Which made me want to laugh even more.

"Oh no, it's not you, Fox," I said, running my hand over her face.

I took a deep breath, regaining composure.

"I can only imagine Aten's reaction to all of this," I said, gesturing up to Lyra as a whole. My face dropped a bit with the memory of all I left behind.

She leaned back hard.

"Aten! He was the boy?" she said, finally putting the pieces together.

I blushed, but pressed my head to the carpet, soft tassels burying my face. It smelled of fresh flowers—of Juni. It occurred to me that she likely lay there often, just like she was at that moment.

"Not exactly," I said, looking back to her. Juni was still wide eyed. "He was never mine."

She brushed her fingers over my arm, making pleasant goosebumps run down my spine.

"Well, I am... if you want me," she whispered, her lips close to mine again.

I turned, pulling her down by her waist, meeting her lips on the way. Her hair spilled over my head, enclosing us in a cocoon of our own.

"I want that a lot," I whispered, gently rubbing my nose against her mouth after.

"Happy new year, Clara," she said, laying her head on my shoulder.

"Happy new year, my Fox."

ɔ NINETEEN c

I drifted back to the waking world. It took a moment to orient myself, before remembering.

I was in Juniper's bed.

A satisfied grin spread over my face. I could hear Juni's soft breaths behind me. Her arm was around my waist, claiming me. Even my legs were heated.

I looked down, and where the heat was, lay a white and black ball of fur and jointed legs. It was Poppy. A small shiver ran down me.

She seemed to sense this and looked up at me with a lazy expression, only opening two of her eyes. She chirruped, then nuzzled tighter against me. I experimentally reached down to her. While her fur looked coarse, it was plush and soft. She started rumbling. More of a growl than a purr, but she leaned into the affection.

"Good girl," I whispered.

I closed my eyes, enjoying the moment.

I woke again with Juni's soft voice. She was leaning over me, glowing.

"Don't freak out," she whispered. "But you have a new friend."

Poppy had curled up on my chest, her eight legs stretched in every direction. Her needle teeth mouth near my face, tongue slightly out.

I wheezed, trying to relax, biting my lip, making Juni chuckle.

She lifted the creature off of me gently, nuzzling its nose.

"Happy new year," she said sweetly.

"Wow, almost a year here," I replied, running my thumb down her cheek, appreciating what a year it had been.

She tilted her head, squeezing my hand against her face.

"You don't seem so sad about it anymore."

"Best thing that's ever happened to me," I winked.

After we were dressed for the day, I met Alice. A slip of a woman whose sole job was taking care of Juni. After swearing to Juni that she wouldn't say a word about me, she brought us breakfast, laughing.

"Thank you, Miss," I said, receiving the hearty meal.

She chuckled, then leaned in. "An extra helping for anyone that puts Miss Juniper in such a good mood."

Juni and I ate with our legs tangled. It was the best food I've had since my arrival.

"I think I'll visit Iris today," I said after breakfast. "You coming?"

"I can't, sorry. Zeusday is family dinner. The whole Shao family will be here."

"Jeesh. Let's escape out the secret entrance," I laughed.

"You joke," she said sly, "but..."

Juni walked over to a bookcase, pulling a book out, like a spy movie. The damn bookcase slid away, revealing a ladder running down a tube to who knows where.

"Get the fuck out of here," I huffed.

Juni didn't accompany me, as much as I knew she would have loved to. Family had to come first, she argued. Her argument was very convincing, as her lips landed on mine.

"Just head down the ladder. It leads throughneath the whole house, and pops out by the far garden wall."

"Through...neath." I teased.

"Yip. Not *just* underneath, but also through, out the other side. Through-neath."

"You have a whole word just for that?"

"You would be amazed at how often it's used," she said grinning.

I tested the passageway, 'throughneath' the house, finding myself exiting into the garden.

"Just like a spy," I mused and set off to my oldest friend's new house.

ↄ TWENTY ɕ

Iris had been allocated a large place in a suburban neighbourhood. There were armed guards strolling the property. Fame had its perks. I was happy that Iris had the recognition on Lyra she deserved to have on Earth. Security mumbled into their comms as I approached. Seemingly satisfied, they waved me through with a short "Doctor". They must have been briefed very well. I expected nothing less from the Shaos. From Juni.

Iris opened the door before I got to it. She looked calm, but her eyes were bloodshot. She looked smaller than the towering, confident artist I had come to know.

"Clara," she said softly.

I didn't say anything. I simply hugged her. She returned it tightly.

"I missed you, you know," I said.

"I... I'm still processing," she sighed. "But I missed you too."

We went inside.

The house was mostly a large single room, dipping into individual cubbies as rooms. Her bedrooms were off the main area. It had a rustic feel, different from anything I had seen on Lyra before. It had been fully furnished too. Unlike my place, the furniture looked new.

"Holy crap. It's nice."

"I suspect I have Juniper to thank for that."

I chuckled. "She's pretty amazing."

Iris started boiling the kettle. Old Earth habits taking over. She leaned on the counter silently. Her shoulders low.

I walked up to her placing my hand on her arm.

"Let me do it, ok?"

She nodded and drifted to a chair.

I prepped her coffee how she liked it. Strong as sin and darker than the night. Tea for me as I didn't see any wine.

Iris nodded her thanks when I handed her the cup. I took the seat across from her.

"How are you holding up?" I asked.

She puffed out a long breath.

"Stupid question, sorry," I said, backtracking.

"It's all new. I'll be fine."

"I know. You're the toughest woman I've met."

We sipped silently.

"I can't imagine how hard this must have been for you, Clara."

"It was a rocky start. Some days I still feel... misplaced."

"Sounds as if we both have Juni to thank for not being lost."

I laughed. "You have no idea."

Iris placed the cup on her lap, running her thumb along the rim.

"She's cute," she said softly. "Since when is that your thing? Or was it really that lonely here?"

There was no malice in her voice. I knew Iris well enough to hear the curiosity mixed with concern.

"How do you know it wasn't always my thing?" I teased. "Besides, it's not because she's a girl. It's because she's Juni."

A small smile pulled at the corners of her mouth. She looked up at my eyes.

"So it's the real deal?"

I shrugged, my cheeks warming up.

"I think so."

"You're very lucky then. I hope you tell her often."

"She knows."

Iris tilted her head, giving me a sarcastic expression.

"Clara, that's not the point. Tell her how you feel, and never stop."

She wiped her eyes. I looked down at my shoes, brushing down my legs.

"It's early still," I said, the words sounding hollow even to me.

"But it becomes too late quickly," she jabbed.

The house sat silent for a long moment.

"Ok, enough moping," she said standing suddenly, running a thumb over her eye.

She moved to the lounge area, picking up her welcome flyer.

"Did you read this?" she asked.

I nodded, but she was already moving on.

"And Lyrican. That caught me off guard," she continued—fraying.

I stood, moving toward her slowly.

"Don't get me started on the Receivers of the Gift," she ranted.

"I'm an *alien*," she said, throwing her hands up. "An actual-"

I wrapped my arms around her.

"I'm going insane here," she said, voice barely holding up.

Finally she dropped her head to my shoulder, clinging to my shirt.

She shook as she let the tears and frustration out.

"Hey, there's no rush, ok?" I soothed, stroking her hair.

"You still have me. And I'm practically a local."

She laughed through the tears, despite herself.

"We were going to start a family when we arrived," she choked out.

I had no reply. I held her, lending her my shoulder and ear.

I spent the rest of Zeusday with Iris. Catchup and tears mixed together in our reunion. I told her about my time, Ramsey... Juni.

I even attempted to teach her some Lyrican.

Her resilience felt stronger with each moment, but something inside her was loose, and I didn't know how to tighten it.

I missed Aten too.

And it had only been a day, but I found myself missing Juni.

I smiled bittersweet as I walked to the road, breathing the fresh alien air. Knowing that I still had the chance Iris missed.

❀ Juni VI ❀

The recording clicked on. She sat back in her chair by her vanity with a far-off expression.

"She spent the night here," she says sniggering. "It was amazing."

Her cheeks flush red.

"Of course, I was tempted to... Um... Nothing happened, but that's not important."

She grabs her brush, playing with the bristles.

"I'm actually surprised how shy-"

Juni looks to the side.

"Um, come in," she says.

Her mother walks into view, perching on her bed. She carries a polite smile. The one people reserve for uncomfortable conversations.

Juni turns on the chair, facing backwards.

"How did you sleep Juni?" her mom asks.

"Oh, good, thanks mom."

"Did Clara make it home ok?"

"I... Oh, she..."

Her mother holds up a hand. "I'm not here to judge you, love."

"She slept alright," Juni says, looking down at the floor. "Poppy really likes her too."

"I can see she cares for you. I can tell she matters to you too."

Juniper nods, running one finger uncomfortably along the arm rest.

"I really like her, mom."

Sophia shifts on the bed, patting the space next to her. Juniper moves to the bed, leaning against Sophia as she sits. Her mother's arm folds around her shoulders.

They sat in silence for a while, mother and daughter.

"Have you thought about how it will work?"

Juni nods. "I know it'll be hard."

"I know you don't enjoy boys-"

Juni looks up at her mother, expression nearing panic. Sophia pushes on.

"I *know*. And it's nothing to be ashamed about."

Juniper's shoulders sag in relief.

"But there are things a privileged family needs to consider."

"Tayo you mean? Legacy?"

Her mother nods her agreement.

"Have you considered what it will do to Clara?" Sophia asked, almost to herself.

Juni's mouth opens, her eyes wide. She stands walking out of arms reach.

"She's tough. And she..."

"Love doesn't solve all problems, Juniper."

"We'll make it work, mom."

Sophia tilts her head. "You know, kids make life more difficult for-"

"I know, mom," she says flustered. Then softer, "I know."

Her mother nods again, brushing off her dress.

"Ok then," she says softly. "I'm rooting for you, my baby."

Sophia stands, pecking Juni's head, before drifting out again.

Juniper retakes her seat by the screen. She looks directly into the camera.

"Clara's not the problem," she grumbles.

She huffs a lock of hair from her face.

"Clara is smart. So am I," she says, dropping her hand onto the desk for emphasis, shaking the screen. "We'll figure it out."

She sinks lower into the chair, staring into the middle distance.

She clenches her hand until her knuckles turn white.

"Why does it always have to be a fight?" she growls.

Juniper stands suddenly, kicking the chair clear across the room. She grabs a container off the vanity, hurling it out of frame with a roar.

Somewhere out of frame a loud bang echoes.

"It's not fair," she says, eyes out of frame, but her cheeks are wet.

Juni presses a sleeve against her face.

"Maybe I can talk to Tayo. If he wanted to..."

Her jaw clenches. Silver-white hair falls covering her face. She runs her fingers through it, more pulling than brushing.

"I *will* figure it out... somehow, I have to."

Juni steps forward, poking at the screen, stopping the recording.

ɔ TWENTY-ONE ɕ

While at work, we behaved ourselves... mostly. We both agreed it was essential that our professional relationship was kept separate. It was a good idea, as it gave a chance for the friendship to not drown under the tension that had been steadily growing. I watched Juniper studying a piece closely, her skirt revealing her long silken legs.

Juni stretched out placing the piece down. I turned back to my own work, trying to regain my concentration. Slowly her hands curled around my shoulders, giving me goosebumps.

"I'm calling it a day, ok?"

I turned my chair to face her. "Alright, foxy lady."

She leaned down to slip in a kiss, causing everything below my belly button to catch fire. I leaned in as she tried to pull away, earning me a giggle.

"I'll see you tomorrow," she said sweetly.

"Nothing could keep me away."

Then she left with a sway of her hips I hadn't noticed before.

I started packing away my own gear when a familiar hiss filled the chamber. My chest tightened, but I breathed through it. Whatever it was, I needed to get to the bottom of it.

I stalked around listening for the source, eventually tracing it to a small intricate piece in a corner. It was no larger than my palm. A spiral of the 'scales' twirled into a glowing central sphere.

"I'm listening already," I said, more annoyed than scared.

C-aaaaa-rrr-aaa

"Gods," I yelped, dropping the piece. I took a step back, my skin trying to crawl away. But I forced myself to stand firm.

Cla-ra

My horror turned to shock. That voice... I swore it was familiar.

"What do you want?" I asked slowly, pronouncing each word clearly.

It was quiet. The whispers gone.

I didn't run out that time. I placed the piece on my desk carefully. Whatever this was, it was far from done with me, and I was done running.

The car dropped me after dark, the voice still playing in my head. I thanked the driver and ran through the chill with my shoulders hunched. I whistled, signalling to Goose that it was dinner time. I was still waiting for him to appear, when I noticed a shadow standing near my door. I stopped dead. The blood in my ears beat out all sounds. The figure raised their hand in a casual wave, but the jitters didn't stop. I found myself missing the hiss of the bluetech.

"Hey, Sing," he said, his smooth voice smug as always.

"Ramsey. Why are you here?"

He stepped into the light, smiling as if we were old friends.

"Can't I stop by to say hi?"

I clenched a fist, waiting for his mask to slip.

"I'm not an idiot, Cutter. Are you here to threaten me?"

He held up his hands in a defensive gesture.

"Clara, damn. I'm really just here to see you."

"You saw me. Please go."

He sighed, stabbing his hands into his pockets.

"We need you, Clara."

"We?"

"Yeah. My friends and I. We'd like you to..." he swirled one hand in the air. "To do us a favour, for a reward."

"I told you I'm not interested."

"What's the harm. I did you a favour."

His smile faded.

"Let's call it payback," he said, voice dark.

Somewhere behind me I heard the familiar skittering. But I didn't look around. The real threat had only two legs.

"Take your favour and payback and shove it, Cutter."

Ramsey frowned. He tried smiling, but sneered.

"It's not really optional for me, you see."

He started walking towards me. I got ready to fight with all I had. Before he made it to me, something brushed past my legs. Goose in his nighttime horror form placed himself between Ramsey and me. His fur stood up in spikes as he growled, in his distinctly alien way. He was crouched low, as if about to pounce.

Ramsey nearly fell backwards.

"Get this thing out of my way," Ramsey spat.

I shrugged. "He's a wild Spider-Lion. I have no say."

"We'll talk later, Sing," he said as he backed away.

"No we won't," I assured him.

He left, glaring back over his shoulder at Goose.

When he was out of sight, Goose twirled and chirruped. Then as quickly as he appeared he scuttled away.

"Thanks Goose," I said quietly.

I realised that I needed to arm myself somehow. Made a mental note to ask Juni. Not that I wanted her mixed up in my shit.

I made sure to leave out extra nice treats for Goose.

One way or another, I needed to get myself away from Ramsey. In the meanwhile, I'd take all the allies I could find.

No matter how many legs or eyes they had.

ↄ TWENTY-TWO ↄ

"Clara? Hello?"

I shook myself. Juni was looking at me from across our workspace frowning.

"Sorry, Juni. I must have zoned out."

The truth was, Ramsey's words were still stalking around my head.

"So you'll come?" she asked. She seemed excited. I remembered her saying something about that evening.

"You'll pick me up," I replied, grasping at memories of the conversation.

"Yay!" she cheered, unashamed. I grinned.

I would figure it out when I got where we were going. Any time with Juni felt effortless.

That evening we entered what appeared to be a miniature stadium. The interior was carved in two, a massive humming wall laced with the *bluetech* glow dividing the space. The floors curled up as if pressed into the ground, a small opening, like a goal punctuating the rear centre of each indent. Around it a fence that looked capable of catching cars. The smell of ozone permeated the interior.

Juni was kitted in what looked to be a white and gold tennis outfit with running shoes.

Tayo waved at us from a bench overlooking the interior space.

"Um," I expressed perfectly.

"It's a *Gravdisc* court," Juni explained.

"Cool, I guess?" I shrugged.

She chuckled. "We'll show you."

We moved through the usual hellos and niceties, before they entered the fenced area. Juni trailing off with a kiss and lingering fingers.

I took my seat, affording me a view of the whole 'court'. Juni and Tayo took up spaces on opposite ends on the floor.

A buzzer sounded and suddenly Earth had never felt further away.

A neon disc shot out from the centre of the floor and they were away.

Juni was off the mark faster, her motion turning into a blur. She pinged the disc off the back wall, faster than I could track. Tayo leapt up metres into the air catching the blue streak with ease, before returning it to the wall. Each impact with the wall was a loud electric crack, making me flinch involuntarily.

It was a high-speed ballet of inhuman grace and power. Juni doing flips as she caught the disc in mid-air as if gravity was a foreign concept. Tayo ran up walls, redefining the concept of a floor. Each motion, landing, or catch looked potentially fatal. I was clenching my fists, fearing for Juniper. But to them, it was only a game. Simple even. For a brief moment I understood Ramsey. He was full of bravado, but I saw what he saw. The fear of being less. Less than the demi-gods inhabiting that arena.

The disc must have exchanged hands twenty or thirty times before another buzzer blared. Tayo pumped a fist in the air.

"Yeah!" he cheered.

All told the round lasted perhaps a minute, but it had shattered anything I thought I knew about Juni's abilities.

They had four more rounds like this. A loud crack echoed with each return. They never slowed their pace.

The buzzer sounded one last time. Juni landed from a dizzying height with a roll.

"In your face, Langley," she boasted.

Tayo smiled through defeat, mock clapping for Juniper.

Juniper came out bouncing with energy. Her skin was glistening from exertion. She grabbed a bottle of water, taking a long pull before her breaths slowed.

"And that," she said in-between pants, "is *Gravdisc*."

I stared at her with wide eyes. I wasn't scared. The emotion was more awe than fear.

"That was the most insane thing I've ever seen. And I rode an alien star beam to get here."

Juni laughed. As if I was exaggerating.

"Come play a match with me," she suggested.

My face went slack. "You're kidding, obviously."

"It'll be fun," she assured me, smiling wide.

"You can just break up with me. You don't need to murder me."

She sighed. "I promise it'll be fine."

I rubbed my face. "Gods, I'm going to regret this. Ok, Fox."

She squeed. "Yeah," she said, planting her lips on my cheek.

I stepped into the arena in borrowed gear. Tayo sat in the stands. The emperor looking out over those who are about to die. I rolled my shoulders, confident Juni would take it easy on me.

She smiled at me with a nod from across the floor.

The buzzer.

A crack.

Juni caught the disc first, flinging it at the back wall. I managed to intercept the blue streak on the way to the goal. It stung my hand as I caught it, but I managed to return it with a spin. The gravity on the disc was cancelled, giving the sport its name, and its speed.

My throw pinged clumsily off the back wall. Juni, clearly holding back, caught it again.

I managed a few returns in that way. Each catch searing into my palm. Then against all odds, I sunk it into the goal.

"Awesome!" cheered Juniper.

I was starting to get the hang of it, even as my lungs burned.

My confidence grew with each catch. I was keeping up. At least I thought I was.

"One more?" she asked.

"Bring it, princess," I said. That was my mistake. Juni smirked. Trouble colouring her face.

"Alright, grandma. Let's go."

A buzzer.

A crack.

She let me make the first catch. Her return came like a bullet, barely missing me.

"Juni!" I objected, but she was already returning it.

I wasn't so lucky on her next return. I dodged the disc, a neon buzzsaw, but landed hard on the ground, skidding a ways.

"Ow, fuck!" I growled, as fire ran up my arm. I looked down, seeing a tear in the shirt mixed with dark red. It was a guess as to what was skin, and what was the torn sleeve.

Oh shit.

Juni was beside me in an instant.

"Oh shit, Clara. Are you ok?" she asked, as if I had stubbed my toe.

"No," I barked, my arm bent with pain. "I told you this would happen."

Her face drained. She didn't look me in the eyes.

"I was trying to include you, that's all."

"In what the obituaries?"

"Clara," she scolded, with a tremble in her lip.

Tayo rushed in with a med kit. By then the entire sleeve was a crime scene. He tore the sleeve like tissue paper, before applying a bandage.

"It's bleeding a lot, but it's not deep, Clara," he said, without his normal irreverence.

"Nearly took my head," I complained.

He shrugged, no doubt having predicted worse.

"I'm really, really sorry, Clara," Juniper pleaded, taking my hand.

I pulled away wincing as I jostled my arm.

"I've had it for the night guys. I'm gonna head home."

"Clara, I'm sorry," she called after me. But I was pissed off and terrified. I needed to get out of the building to ground myself in some normality, or whatever Lyra had that was close.

I hadn't made it out of the parking area when I heard the patter of her footfalls behind me.

"Clara!" Juni called.

I stopped, turning. Still mad. Still hurt. Still clutching my bandaged arm. The bleeding had already stopped. Barely staining the white wrap.

"I'm going home, Juni. I'll see you Monday alright?"

It landed harder than I meant it to.

"I shouldn't... I'm not use to holding back."

"So what, next time you hug me, you might break my spine?" I grumbled.

"I'd never-"

"Hurt me?"

She was staring at the ground. Short, sharp breaths escaping her. I was being an asshole, and I knew it. Half of the blame was mine, but I let my ego do the talking.

She stepped forward, hesitated when she saw the crimson stained bandage, then her shoulders dropped. My chest ached more than my arm.

"I'll get over it, Juni. Let me just get some rest, ok?"

She looked up, fear in her eyes.

Juni stepped forward, folding her arms around me, making sure to avoid my arm.

The look on her face carried so much fear and hurt, like mine did on the court. But I didn't want to hurt her... Just as she didn't mean to hurt me.

Oh. Fuck.

"Please don't leave angry," she asked, shaking.

The fire ran out of me with my air.

I pressed into her, returning the hug, burning arm and all.

"I'll be ok, Fox," I reassured her.

"That's not the same thing."

I tightened my arms around her small frame.

"Gods, I think I'm physically incapable of staying mad at you, Juni."

She laughed, pressing her head into my neck. Then she took a step back, smiling with a damp face.

"I can make it up to you."

I gave her a face promising trouble. "Oh, yeah? What do you have in mind?"

"Dinner," she said quickly. "I'll buy you dinner."

"I don't much feel like going out with this," I said, gesturing to the reddening bandage.

She looked down at her shoes, fidgeting her hair over her face.

"I can come over and take care of you?" she mumbled. "With takeaways."

I grinned, stepping in hovering my lips near hers. "Now that, sounds like a decent apology."

"Tomorrow night," she suggested.

"Bet your back dimples on it."

Her face exploded with blush.

I let my lips close the distance.

❀ Juni VII ❀

The screen flickered to life. Juni sat with crossed legs by her fireplace. She wore a large T-shirt and slacks. A comfort she had learned.

A long breath escaped her, her face dour.

"Tonight went about as badly as it could have."

She presses her palms to her eyes.

"I'm such a damn idiot."

Juni stretches her back, hands braced against her knees. Her head falls backwards in thought.

"That damn disc could have killed her, because I was *so* desperate to win," she huffed.

"Instead of enjoying it. Being happy she wanted to try."

She rubs her upper arm, as if it was injured too.

"Stellar performance, Juniper."

Her head drops for a second.

"I *am* fairly sure Clara isn't mad anymore. But I need to be more careful."

She looks at her hands, flexing them.

"For my own sake too."

She looks into the camera, mischief blooming on her face.

"But... I have a plan," she says, holding up a finger.

Juni stands, visible from the knees down only. She pads out of frame over the carpet in barefooted silence.

There's rustling and humming off screen.

A few moments later she returns, Poppy curling around her legs as she did.

"Oh, wait one minute, baby," she coos.

Juniper sinks down to her knees, her head still out of frame.

"Ta-da," she sang, holding a thin chiffon slip to her shoulders—the material a mere suggestion.

"I am going to apologize with all of me," she says, her voice low.

She drops the night gown and sits again, her face flushed and grinning.

"I think I'm ready for more," she says, thumbing the material.

"I hope Clara is too."

Poppy flops against Juni's legs. She strokes the critter absently, lost in thought.

"At least we don't have to worry about accidental babies."

She laughs, but presses her lips tight over it.

"I guess it's not that funny, is it?"

Juni hugs Poppy, her smile only curling one corner of her mouth.

"Love is funny, huh Poppy?" she mused to the animal.

She looks back at the camera with a deep breath, face playful again.

"I guess we'll know a lot more after tonight."

She reaches over. The screen goes black again.

ɔ TWENTY-THREE ɕ

Juni arrived while I was outside smoking. Goose, who had been sitting close by observing me, skittered away.

Juni looked at the cigarette as she approached. Her face turned to a surprised pout.

"I didn't know you smoked," she said, plainly.

"Um. Is that bad?"

"Just new," she said, taking long strides toward me, lugging a small bag in a hand and hot meals in the other.

"You're staying?" I asked.

"If that's ok?"

I smiled, taking the bag with my good arm.

"I'd like it a lot," I replied, leading her with my finger hooked around hers.

I placed her bag in the spare room, stealing a kiss as I went.

"Tea?" I asked, taking the boxes from her.

"Sounds good. It was a long day."

"Then I will make a special cup for the princess."

She wrinkled her nose in appreciation.

"Make yourself comfortable, Fox. Be back in a minute."

I was in the kitchen, boiling the kettle when I heard a quiet rustling behind me.

Juni leaned against the frame in a sheer gown. Her one shoulder bare as it hung, nothing beneath, the main room light silhouetting her, hinting at her skin and curves below. Her hair hung over half of her face as her fingers twisted through it. Her other hand smoothed the material absently.

"Hey," she said casually, her cheeks rosy.

"Oh, um, hi," I replied, nervously looking away.

"Oh, shit," she panicked. "I can change, if you want," her voice small as she took a step back.

"No. No, I just didn't expect..." I gestured at the gown for emphasis.

"You're... lovely," I said at a loss for a better word.

She ducked her head, trying to hide her blush.

"I'm... well I'm kinda plain..." I shrugged, leaning back against the counter.

She drifted over to me, the gown moving against her form like water, hugging the delicate curves below. She caught the hem of my shirt, nuzzling my chin. Her lips found mine with a light kiss.

"I think you're pretty," she breathed, her lips lingering against mine.

My heart beat once. Hard. I brushed her hair from her face.

"No hiding then," I said, running my fingers through her hair.

She looked down at her feet, laughing softly. I placed my hand on her face, guiding her eyes back to mine.

"Juni," I said seriously, meeting her eyes. "I really like you. I don't want to fuck it up."

She let out a slow sigh. Her fingers barely brushing my stomach, as if she was making sure I was real.

"I know what you mean," she whispered as if the words themselves could pierce the moment. Juni was shaking a bit, her eyes on my lips.

"I was so nervous you would say no," she admitted.

I put my forehead to hers, relaxing my shoulders.

"This is all very new to me, but I know I want you too."

An excited laugh bubbled from her as she took my hand in hers.

"Come on then. We'll figure it out," she said as her thumb brushed along my palm and she led me out of the kitchen to the main room.

She stopped by the bed and stepped in close with her body pressed against mine. Her hand came up to cup my cheek, and she kissed me again. First my mouth, then the side of my neck, lips like embers.

"Is this okay?" she murmured against my throat.

I nodded mid-kiss, taking in the scent of camellias.

"Want me to stop?"

"Gods no," I breathed. "Please don't."

My body reacting to a dance I knew, played on a different instrument. No one but Juni could soften me like that.

TWENTY-FOUR

We found the bed quickly, Juni sliding in behind me as I perched on the edge. She lifted my shirt from behind, helping me avoid the injured arm. I unclipped my bra, the straps sliding down my arms, and in the same heartbeat came the quiet swoosh of her gown falling away. It drifted past me, like smoke in reverse, whispering onto the stark floor, joining my plain clothes. Juni pressed against my back, the curve of her breasts against my shoulder blades.

She didn't hurry easing my denim loose, peeling them down over my hips with that unshakable, steady strength as I lay. She stayed hovering over me, her palms down, thumbs brushing my hips. My stomach bundled. There was nothing but my underwear between us, and that step suddenly felt larger than the rest. I ran my fingers up her arms, trying to steady my breaths. Juni leaned down, pressing slow kisses along my collarbone. One landed right above my breast, light enough to tickle. I let out an involuntary giggle.

I clapped a hand over my mouth, face burning. "Oh, gods. Listen to me."

She placed a finger over my mouth. "I *am* listening to you," she said sweetly.

"It tickled," I defended, still grinning despite myself.

"I know." She kissed me there again, slower this time. "I liked the sound of it."

Juni knelt beside me, legs folded beside her, long limbs tucked in like she was made for the space. She was always dressed in her family's armour. Now, she looked small, delicate—precious.

Despite her strength, she was the very definition of petite, from her gentle hips to the sharp curve of her breasts. The dim lamp caught on her skin and made her glow, pale and impossibly smooth. She tucked her shoulders in as a bit of shyness crept in. She was so close, so bare, that her normal heat felt like a campfire on a winter's night. Her thigh brushed mine as she shifted, and I swore I could feel the beat of her pulse through it.

"I'm staring, sorry," I confessed.

"It's ok," she smiled, her eyes wandering over me in turn. "I like that too."

She bent over, running her palms up my thighs, until her fingers brushed up against the waistband of my underwear, and she waited, tracing the elastic back and forth, making my legs tense to my toes. Her hand stopped and she found my eyes. I nodded, even though I could feel my face radiating. I had never felt so naked and comforted at once.

She hooked my underwear and slid them down slowly, the fabric hissing against my skin, her thumbs trailing a hot path in their wake. She was in no rush. Then they were gone, discarded with the rest.

She moved closer, her hand brushed along my arm, stopping at the bandage. She lingered for a moment, a single finger on the cloth.

"I'm sorry about that, Clara," she said, face greying.

"Me too," I admitted, swallowing my ego. "I was out of line."

"I'd never hurt anyone I love on purpose, you know," she said.

Love? Gods, that was a big word. I couldn't say it. Not yet. There was too much shit still in the way.

"Careful, Fox," I whispered. "You almost said it."

Juni chuckled, then her mouth found mine with the kind of kiss that made you forget how to breathe right. My jaw relaxed and my lips parted hungry. When she pulled back, her teeth caught lightly on my lower lip. Barely a nibble.

I arched up, wanting more. She looked up at me, biting her lip.

"Still okay?" she asked, so softly.

I nodded, already panting. "Yeah. Very."

She leaned in again, our chests aligning. My breath shuddered with the press of her breasts against mine. Each shift, each breath, carrying an intensity I never imagined. Our hands wandered, exploring with hunger and want. I pressed into her touch, into her body, giving mine to her.

Every breath we shared was new.

Every inch of space between us had vanished.

Sometimes we would sit together, huddled under a blanket with snacks. Outside the storm beat against the windows. We had a horror playing on the screen. Juni's finger tensed around mine. The music on screen swelled. Thunder outside my window cracked. The heroine turned to look behind her...

Juni tucked her face into my shoulder.

"No," she squeaked. "Tell me when it's over."

I held her head, stroking her hair. I revelled in the feeling of her arms around me.

At night, Juni folded around me, as the big spoon with a small satisfied exhale. Her thigh slid between my legs, her chest pressed fully against my back. I felt the brush of her small, firm nipples against my skin, sending a shiver up my spine.

Her arm slipped around my waist, fingers splaying softly on my stomach. She held me close, her lips against the curve of my neck. Her fingertips tracing gentle curves across my stomach, then easing down to my lowest curve.

She paused, anticipation growing between us.

I could feel the beat of my heart in my thighs. I pressed my hips back against hers. That was all the signal she needed.

Her fingers shifted, sliding further down until they found me, drawing a stuttered moan.

She moved slow, in a rhythm we were still learning. My hips moved restlessly with her touch, the sounds I made barely more than gasps and whimpers. I placed my hand over hers, feeling her steady, certain motions. I braced, past experiences preparing me for faster. For something harder. But she stayed slow, savouring the moment. She made me ache in circles with constant, deliberate attention.

Her fingers slipped in with gentle hunger. Her body firm against me, as the sensation pulled a ragged breath from deep down in my stomach.

"Good?" she murmured near my ear.

I cried out, fingers flexing against her delicate skin as my body answered for me.

I was more than good. I was falling into her.

Her arm slipped past my neck, her small hand firmly gripping my breast, catching my nipple between her fingers. I could sense the restraint—her fingers were steel wrapped in cotton. She squeezed with both hands and I let go. My body bucked without shame, my hips trying to chase her rhythm. The sheets rustled as they came away from my damp skin. Her fingers moved inside me, curling with just enough pressure to meet the tension rising up through my belly.

I wasn't quiet. I didn't want to be. I could feel myself clenching around her fingers. But Juni held firm, her palm braced flush against me. My hand tightened over hers, nails biting into her skin. I didn't want her to stop. Not ever.

My hips jolted once, hard, straining against her firm embrace. She let out a satisfied moan. Perhaps her own high. Her thigh tensed between mine, pressing upward, locking us together pressing her deeper into me with desire. I whimpered and shook as I came, her name spilling out on the exhale. My free hand grabbed onto the pillow—the cloth straining against my nails. Juniper held the tension as my tremors subsided, anchoring me, holding me close.

Her lips trailed my skin in between soft words of want and affection.

Sometimes we would venture out of the city limits. We would lay on Lyra's version of grass, as soft moss that smelled of fresh earth. Juni lay on her back with her head on my stomach, reading on her comm. I preferred good old paper.

She dropped her arms to the side, letting out a long sigh.

"You ok, Foxy lady?" I asked.

She rolled over. Then was on top of me, with her nose to mine.

"I have come from afar for kisses," she demanded.

I laughed as I pressed my lips to her, by decree of the princess.

At night, I lay on my side, facing her, my breaths coming fast. It was in the way she looked at me. Her lavender eyes bright and soft, as if she was seeing the sun rise for the first time.

She lay close, propped on one elbow, her fingers tracing lazy circles on my stomach, with lips parted and flushed. That furnace heat still rolled off her skin, almost mechanical rather than human. The smell of Camellias lacing the air.

"You're beautiful," she said, kissing the centre of my chest, lingering there with her lips.

Another kiss, lower. Then a teasing nip beneath my breast.

The labouring fan was the only sound besides her lips on my skin.

"You're-" I stared.

I meant to continue. I really did. But her tongue flicked across my nipple, and I gasped. Everything in me caught ablaze again. My hand tangled into her hair, pulling her into me by reflex. She made a muffled, delighted sound against me. Her whole body shivered with pleasure.

"You're-" I stumbled, struggling to find my voice. "You make me happy, Juni."

"Still good then?" she teased, lips barely brushing my skin.

"If you stop now, I swear-"

Her mouth curled against me.

One more press of her lips. A breath against my chest.

"My Clara, so feisty."

I folded around her, smiling.

I was her Clara.

Sometimes we would get caught in the rain. We gave up running soon enough, already soaked through. Juni looked at me, her hair glued in a messy frame around her face. She smiled and shrugged. We linked arms and walked instead, enjoying the fresh rain on an otherwise hot day. I spotted an overhang on the side of a building ahead.

When we reached it, I pulled her out of the rain, pinning her between me and the wall. My hands fell on her firm butt. Juniper looked surprised, but pleasantly so. I kissed her, my tongue playing along her lips.

"Get a room, you damn *rotlicks*!" a passerby shouted.

Our eyes widened, and we broke out in giggles like teens caught by their parents.

We continued through the rain. The wet clothes would be a good excuse later.

At night, I ran my hand along her stomach, with my lips brushing over her breast, feeling her breath shudder. Her body was a dreamscape of tight lines and ivory skin hiding muscle that moved like wires. I bent down and kissed above her hip, making her inhale sharply. I kissed her again, lower this time. She tasted of salt and rich cream.

"Clara," she gasped, but her voice was filled with honey and promise.

I leaned up and kissed her breast again, not as delicately this time. My tongue circled, then I drew her nipple into my mouth. I let my teeth graze it. She gasped, her back arching, nails running up my back on the threshold of pain. I slid down between her legs, shaking in anticipation, one hand bracing lightly on her stomach, the other tracing lower until my fingers slipped inside her slowly.

She cried out and her hand wrapped around my wrist. I moved, feeling her tense around me.

A quiet, "Oh," left her lips. She hadn't expected it. Her legs flexed and her toes curled into a lazy stretch into my pressure. Juni made small, aching sounds, the occasional sharp inhale when I hit the right spot. Beneath us, the metal bed frame jostled and squeaked. My thumb moved in tandem, drawing light circles as I found a rhythm, and the rest of her followed—hips rocking, hand gripping the sheet beside her.

Her other hand slid off my wrist, drawing herself open for me. I took her in and my heart beat hard once, dangerously. I bent down, tongue moving between her fingers, my own fingers not slowing. The taste of her was difficult to compare, but it was Juni's and I sunk into it.

She gasped my name once, her breasts lifting as her hips kicked. I felt myself edging closer too, from her reaction. Her knees flexed against me in sharp waves.

And I didn't need to ask if I was doing it right as she cried out.

Sometimes we would just sit, Juni's bed our haven. We would be wrapped in nothing but comfort and lace. I would braid her silver hair as we talked. Her family's history, spanning two-hundred years. My school days as a teen in a university. Our firsts, our bests, our favourites. Days would pass like this, with us being with each other.

A word growing between us.

We didn't say it out loud.

We lived it instead.

At night, Juni rose onto her knees without rush, her touch never leaving me. She slid one leg over mine, bracketing my hip. The shift opened me to her, and the first press of thigh to thigh stole my breath. She was hungry and her eyes full of want. I let her have all of me.

Her hands stayed firm on my hips, grounding me as she eased into a slow, deliberate roll. The heat between us spread in waves, each movement drawing me deeper into her rhythm. She stopped breathing for a heartbeat, arching her back. The pause was louder than any moan.

Her arms locked around my waist and butt, pulling our heat tight together. I looped my arms around her neck, holding her as tightly. She supported my weight with effortless strength. Eyes linked, foreheads together. The world narrowing to the point where our bodies met. The outside world becoming distant and forgotten.

"Clara..." she cried.

"Juni... Oh fuck," was my only reply.

The pace increased, our hips finding a perfect beat, until it was impossible to tell where we began and ended. Sweat and more mixing with abandon. We urged each other on with moans and mouths. Her thighs trembled against mine, quick clenching shocks flowing through her warmth. A kind of tremor you can't fake. Juni was telling me she was close with every tensed muscle and vocal breath.

When she unravelled, my own seams came apart. Thighs flexing against each other, our bodies rigid and braided.

I called her name as we folded into each other.

We stayed where we were—winded and sweating, lying face to face.

Hands tangled without thought. Neither of us spoke, until Juni let out a small, disbelieving laugh.

"That. That was..." she trailed off, eyes still on mine.

"Perfect," I finished for her, admiring my Juniper.

I let out a shaky exhale that felt like it had been lodged in me for years.

For a while, we breathed in sync.

We lay that way, legs knotted.

Chest to chest.

Forehead to forehead.

Our hands spoke for us in small touches.

We fell asleep entwined.

I was finally home.

ɔ TWENTY-FIVE ɕ

The best kind of days start outdoors under the sun, and end inside under the covers. That Saturday was shaping up to be one of those days. Juni and I were heading back to my apartment, the sun baking us as we strolled with our bag of goodies. We were past being shy, walking hand-in-hand in the sun. The weekend morning streets were buzzing with business as well as pleasure. I closed my eyes as a cool breeze passed over my legs. I wiggled my toes in my sandals happily.

"I have the perfect spot for today," I said, pressing Juniper's hand for emphasis.

"Oh, I'm excited. Is it fancy?"

I raised an eyebrow, my mouth a sarcastic line.

"It doesn't have to be," she chuckled. "I'm happy wherever you are."

I bumped her gently with my shoulder as my apartment came into view.

"Well, then you'll definitely be-"

Something struck the side of my leg, pressing in tight against my knee. Juni leapt back on instinct.

It was Goose, leaning against me with a threatening gargle and raised fur. Four of his eyes were locked on Juni.

"Oh, crap," Juni huffed. "Goose is getting a bit territorial."

"Nah," I assured her. "He's only being protective."

I knelt down slowly, placing my hand on the spider-lion's back. He snapped, but stopped when he saw it was my hand.

"Ok, little nightmare. She's a friend," I whispered to him.

He continued to threaten Juni unconvinced. I stuck my other hand out to her.

"Slowly, Fox," I whispered.

She crouched and snuck forward carefully, while I soothed Goose with nonsense words and scratches between his tucked bunny ears. He sank lower to the ground as she approached, until our fingers brushed and wove together.

Goose stopped growling, blinking pairs of eyes in turns. Then he scooted forward slowly, sniffing at our joined hands.

"Friendly," I said gently to him, expecting a bite anyway.

I tried to stay relaxed as his nose touched to our hands. After a moment of painting us with his snout. He chirruped, and bounced, rubbing against my legs and then Juni's.

"Such a good boy," Juni gushed, holding her hand to him, which he gladly rubbed against with his ears upright and twitching.

Goose skittered after us as I led Juni up my building's fire escape. He took the shortcut up the side of the building, earning his name all over.

"Here we are," I announced as we reached the roof. "The best view in..." I looked around. "In about four blocks."

"It's a really good view," Juni said, her eyes on my ass as she climbed the last steps.

"Perv," I said, pressing the hem of my dress down dramatically.

"For you? Oh yeah," she snickered.

The roof was poorly maintained and not often used. It did however, have a great awning giving just enough shade on a sunny day.

We set up the chairs and clinked bottles.

"This is real luxury," Juni said without irony as she leaned back.

"Oh definitely. We should bring your folks and show them," I laughed, Juni joining in.

"No other place like it... in four blocks."

I nearly sprayed my drink out of my nose, cupping my hand over my face.

"Mhm, sexy," she quipped.

"You're gonna drown me, Juni," I said, my entire face wet from laughing. Goose joined in with his whispery cough-barks.

We snacked, drank and kissed. Juni and the sun kept me warm, while drinks and the breeze cooled me down. It was a near perfect day.

By the afternoon, Goose grew restless, sniffing the air as he paced up and down. Juni was stretched out, relaxing or napping, I wasn't sure.

"Did you find a bug?" I asked the critter. He scuttled to the edge of the roof, growling again.

I inched to the roof edge, peeking down to the pavement below.

A cold sweat broke on the back of my neck.

It was Ramsey.

He stood across the road from my place, eyes boring into my building. Most likely looking for me.

Another even larger figure slid in beside him. I was too far away to hear, but they were discussing something, nodding in the direction of my door. A chill rode up my spine. I folded my arms over my chest despite the heat of the day.

"What's going on?" Juni asked behind me, her voice sleepy.

"It's nothing... I think."

"Trouble?"

Ramsey and the large figure crawled back into the shadows.

"I... It's nothing, Fox. I think Goose saw a *Tharak* is all."

She had enough on her plate. I would handle Ramsey when the time came. Or at least, I had convinced myself of it.

That evening Juni and I were curled around each other. Goose snoozing with little puffs on my floor for the first time, refusing to be far from me.

The sight of Ramsey had left a chill in me, even Juni couldn't thaw.

"It was the ex-boyfriend, wasn't it?" Juni asked as she ran her fingers through my ever-growing hair.

"What was?"

"Goose growling earlier. Please, Clara, I'm not an idiot," she grumbled, pulling away a fraction.

"You're not. Sorry, Juni."

She ran her palm along my face.

"What does he want?"

"Nothing I'm going to give him."

She sat up, the blanket slipping down her skin with a hiss.

"I'll ask my dad-"

"No," I said quickly. "Thank you, but I'll figure it out."

Juni leaned down, laying her head on my chest. I ran my fingers over her back in lazy patterns.

"Don't do anything silly, ok?" she whispered, breath tickling my skin.

"It's probably nothing. I'll be fine."

She looked up, into my eyes. "I'm serious, Clara. Losing you... I couldn't do it."

I pulled her closer, brushing my lips against hers.

"I've dealt with bullies before, my fox. He's no different."

She lay back down, wrapping around me tight.

"I really hope so."

My heart beat hard, and it had nothing to do with Juni's skin on mine.

The truth was, I had dealt with bullies before—at university.

This was a different game, and I was still learning the rules.

❀ Juni VIII ❀

Juni's smile was pasted on as the recording began. She was seated by her vanity table, with her hands neatly folded on her lap. Her fingers moved restlessly.

She let out a long breath.

"I. Am. Freaking. *Out*," she says.

"Clara is taking me along to visit Iris. Iris!"

She pats her cheeks.

"No big deal to her. But I just know I'm going to make a fool of myself."

Juni fidgets with a pin on the table, staring a hole through it.

"There's so much history between her and Clara."

She grips the arm rests tight.

"This isn't a meeting, it's a test."

"I wonder if this is how Clara feels about my father and Tayo."

She deflates, sliding down the chair.

"I have met Iris before," she says, looking directly into the camera. "And I helped her settle in..."

"But I don't want *that* to be why she likes me."

Juni sits up, straightening her back. She brushes a loose strand of hair from her face.

"No, Juni. She'll like you because Clara does. Iris will love me because Clara..."

Her forehead drops to the table with a thunk.

"Like I have the balls to even say it out loud."

Juni rubs her eyes hard, groaning.

"I wish Clara would at least let me deal with her ex. That way I can know she's safe."

Juniper taps her fingers on the armrest.

"I'll punch his damn face if he touches Clara," she announced, fire in her eyes. But the fire sputters quickly.

"That's if I was around..."
Her tapping resumes.
"Why does she have to be so damn proud."
She huffs, the rogue strand falling back in her face.
"Oh, well. One thing at a time."
She takes a deep breath, then reaches over, ending the video.

ↄ TWENTY-SIX c

Juniper had insisted on taking one of her family cars. It looked like a white UFO, with *bluetech* glow running along the lower edge. It made no sound as it floated along the road to Iris's house. Neither did Juniper. She was dressed formally, with a high collar. It looked as if she was going to throw up, staring out of the window. The road rolled by in streaks of colour. She wasn't seeing any of it. I rested my hand on her leg.

"Hey, foxy lady. Are you ok?"

She looked at me as if she just woke from a dream.

"Oh, I am," she said, the light returning to her face. "I'm dying from nerves though."

I chuckled. "You're a big nerd under all that pretty, aren't you?"

"You're one to talk," she scoffed. "*Doctor* Sing."

"Hey, you're the one sleeping with me."

Her cheeks exploded into bright red.

"Ah... well... it's only so I could meet Iris."

"I see," I said sliding over to her. "Is that the only reason?"

She tried to suppress a giggle as I kissed her—a lot. The fancy private back seat had its privileges.

As we walked down the yard to Iris's door, Juni's hand was in mine. She didn't squeeze, but I could feel it was damp.

"Relax, Juni. It's not the first time you've met her."

"I know. But I've been imagining *this* meeting since I was a little kid."

Juni was the only person on Lyra that might have known as much about Iris's paintings as I did.

An idea came to me of how to break the tension in Juni.

"Hey, Juni," I whispered. "Did you know I kissed Iris once?"

"What!"

It was perfect that Iris opened the door exactly then.

"What, what?" Iris asked. Juni looked a bit scrambled, so I took the lead.

"Hey you," I said, hugging Iris. "You remember, Juni."

"Of course," Iris said politely.

"Hi, ma'am," Juniper squeaked.

"That won't do at all," Iris drawled. "Just Iris," she said smiling.

Her expression was warm, but the Iris I knew wasn't there yet. I was starting to worry that I might not see her again.

"Come in," Iris said, leading the way.

Juni twirled her arm around mine as we walked.

"You have so much explained to do later," she whispered.

I pecked her cheek. "Yes dear," I replied, earning me a blush and some teeth.

We meandered through pleasantries and chitchat. Juni was polite on the surface, but I knew her all too well. That said, it wasn't long before Juni and Iris understood each other. Juni became more talkative, and Iris showing hints of her sharp edge she had been hiding on Lyra. The conversation tapered off as we ran out of weather to talk about, so I took my chance.

"Iris, did you ever get any paintings back in the end?"

Iris's face greyed. "Just one... It's tucked away. I can't deal with it yet."

Fuck. I didn't expect it to be a sensitive topic.

"Sorry, Iris. I didn't mean-"

"No, no. I think I know just what to do with it," she said, playing with the broken piece of Earth's moon around her neck. An actual smile rose on her face, warming her eyes.

She hopped up, still clutching the stone, then disappeared into her bedroom. Juni looked at me with questioning eyes, but all I could do was shrug.

A moment later, Iris returned holding a canvas to her chest. Her eyes were glistening, but no tears fell. I instinctively knew which one it was. There was only one painting she made that she would hold like that.

"It was with a generous collector. So only a few have ever seen it."

I heard Juniper pulling in a long hard breath beside me.

"So are you going to hang it?" I asked stupidly.

Iris shook her head. "I can't. It would break my heart each time I saw it."

She turned the canvas to face us. I had been right.

It was Aten. His dark hair slicked back, with a hint of stubble along his sharp jaw. Where his eyes should have been, were only pencil scribblings. She never did decide if it was supposed to be the boy she met, or the man she lost.

Iris held the painting out at arm's length.

"I hear you enjoy my work, Juniper."

"I, um... I love it," Juni stuttered.

"This one is yours then, hon," Iris said, the first tear breaking free.

Juni rose slowly, as if she might wake. She took the painting like a fragile thing. Then placed it gingerly aside. She wrapped around Iris, barely reaching her chest.

"I'm so sorry, Iris," she said, both of them bawling. "Thank you."

I wiped at my face. Stuck between sorrow and overwhelming... affection, for Juniper. I let them gush and relate in the golden light. All of my heart tucked into a kitchen on a tranquil afternoon.

"Have you been settling in ok?" I asked Iris a bit later, placing my hand on hers.

Her shoulders sagged. "I've been keeping busy."

"But...?" I probed.

"You never met my friend, Mel. It was before..."

"You mean when you still hated my guts?"

She laughed. "Exactly," she said with no irony.

"She must have left, what, a year or more before us?"

"I found where they buried her. Over fifty years ago."

I felt my heart beat in my throat. I could have been like her. Alone and out of time until death. I looked over at Juni, catching her eye.

"Maybe she was lucky, like I was."

Juniper glowed. Iris didn't.

"I hope so," Iris said, her head bowed. "A bit of luck helps."

"You've been here a few weeks," I said patting her hand. "You'll still get your groove."

"You sound so sure."

"She is," Juni said. "Because you have us."

Iris's smile seemed to radiate through the whole room, then she looked back at me.

"I can't speak for Juni," she said. "But you Clara, have great taste in... friends."

"Hey!"

Juni and Iris thought it was hilarious.

We left Iris in the afternoon in better spirits than when we arrived. I was becoming sure she would make it in Vala. But thinking about the future still made my stomach tense.

Betrothal still hung in the air.

Juni said she would figure it out, I had to have faith in her.

"Spill it," Juniper said, pulling me back to the car.

"Spill what?"

"Did you think I would forget," she said feigning annoyance.

"Oh, the kiss. Honestly it was a peck. I was just messing with you."

She narrowed her eyes, unconvinced.

"What about Aten and Iris hating your guts?"

"Now that," I said pointedly, "is a long fucking story."

I told her about it all as she cradled my unrequited love's portrait, painted by my once enemy and later best friend. A tale that could fill an entire book—condensed.

To my relief Juni didn't judge when I told her about my disasters and mistakes on Earth. Her eyes became misty when I told her about the resolutions, my forged friendships, and my escape from Earth. By the time I finished my story, we were wrapped together in the dark. Aten's face across the room, staring at us eyeless.

Juniper kissed me slow.

"I know it was hard," she whispered. "But I'm glad it all happened. It brought you to me."

"So am I," I said, running my hand up into her hair, and my lips down.

The past and future could both wait one more night.

ↄ TWENTY-SEVEN ↄ

Juni and I had breakfast the next morning at a nearby café. It was pleasant, but I merely picked at my food. The day felt heavy even with Juni by my side. I couldn't pinpoint what made me feel down, but I chalked it up to serotonin overload after spending a weekend with Juniper. Afterward, Juni left for home by car with a trailing kiss, while I opted to take a stroll to my place to get some air. I didn't feel like being at home. Cabin fever was becoming a problem. As if I had outgrown the apartment. Still, it held many good memories. My own Lyra chrysalis.

I had been lost in thought, and it took me too long to notice the footsteps close behind me. I took a deep steadying breath, hoping it was nothing but another pedestrian. I took a sharp turn, taking longer strides as if I was late for a meeting. The steps stopped...

No, they were merely matching mine so closely.

Damn it.

I kept trying to catch whoever it was in a reflection, but the windows were tinted or broken. My heart started pestering my ribs. I turned again.

"Shit," I berated myself. I must have missed the road I meant to go down in my rush. I was sure then—it was not a pedestrian. I had a tail. Likely not a wagging one. I swerved North down a narrow side road, not hiding my flight anymore. The area was new to me, but I was sure one of the roads would have to lead back to the busy main road. The lonely road smelled of piss and old booze, lined with abandoned streetlights missing their telltale blue. My heart started punching against my ribs, desperately hoping I was being paranoid.

I took one more turn, confident it led to the main strip. I stopped hard, nearly falling over my own lost feet.

A dead end.

"Oh, fuck. This can't be happening," I cursed myself.

I turned but it was too late. My voice squeaked as the footsteps beat down the road behind me. I balled my fists, readying for whatever came.

I didn't know what was worse. That my suspicions were correct, or that I had gotten so complacent.

"Fucking Ramsey."

"Did you miss me, love?" he purred. Something was off. His eyes were a bit duller. His posture too slumped.

"Why won't you leave me alone, Cutter?"

"At this point? Because you are just too much fun, Sing."

He dripped with smarm, tucking his shirt, as if he was about to enter a meeting. Ramsey's sleeves hitched up as he did. It was nothing more than a glimpse, but I was sure of what I saw. Black shale shards with neon blue. It appeared to be grafted to his skin.

"What happened to you, Ramsey?"

He rolled his neck. "Some bitch fucked up my job is what."

I started walking at him calmly, hoping he'd drop his guard enough to let me run. I could smell blood and feel sweat running down my back.

"You look sick," I said, attempting to lull him. I turned around him slowly, not breaking eye contact.

"I'm feeling better than ever," he said. That dirty grin still on his lips, but his eyes were glazed.

I had finally gotten him turned around. I turned, bolting as fast as I could.

He was so fast. Before I took my second step, he was on me.

I hit the wall hard, driving the air from me.

He pressed one hand between my shoulders, pinning me to the wall like an iron bar. He leaned in, breath smelling of rot.

"I see you're getting pretty chummy with the boss' daughter, aye?"

"It's... none... of your... business," I wheezed out.

"Maybe I'll give her a visit," he oozed. "Maybe then you and I can do business."

My lips stuck together. I regretted leaving Goose sleeping on my bed.

I managed to press my arm up, turning my body, slipping out of his grip. He caught my regrettably long hair, using my own momentum to redirect me. My face smashed into the bricks, lightning ripping through my nose and cheek. My ears whined and the world tipped.

I cried out, tasting blood. My legs lost power, but his pressure kept me upright. I was fighting for air. My head spun, vision stippling.

"A week, Clara. Then I'll collect," he growled.

His hand came out of my hair, and I dropped to the ground, knees first.

I coughed as my body fought to vomit and catch my breath at the same time.

Ramsey leaned down slowly.

"Or I'll come visit you both."

Each of his footsteps was a gunshot as he left. They echoed for far too long in my head after he was gone. My breaths came in shudders until I was sure he was far away. I pulled myself up against the wall. My vision blurred, steps uneven. Blood drying on my face. I took a few spills on my way. Each inhale burned. Each muscle ached. A lifetime of pain later, I fell into my door, earning me a hiss from Goose.

I kicked the door closed and curled up and wept. Even that was painful.

Goose tucked into me, licking my shaking hands.

It was my own fault. I had let my guard down, trading it for butterflies and soft kisses. I had put Juni in the line of fire too.

I heaved myself off the floor, throwing off torn clothes as I went. Standing with my head against the cold wall as warm water rolled over my bruised back, thinking about my week ahead. I had no plan, but whatever I was going to do, it would have to be with a clear head. My solution seemed obvious. If I wasn't with Juni...

But I couldn't even think about it. All it brought was a fresh bout of tears. They mixed with the water, neither able to clean the day from me.

I limped out wrapped in a towel, picking up my comm as I went.

(Juni <3)

(Harry)

(Keela)

"Hey K. You're the man to talk to about protection, right?"

ↄ TWENTY-EIGHT Ͼ

I walked sheepishly into the workshop on the Monday morning. I tried to keep my limp from showing. My back and neck ached, and I had a headache that painkillers refused to touch.

"Morning, foxy lady," I said as I entered, failing to keep the rasp out of my voice.

"Morning, Cla..."

Juni saw my face, bruises down the one side making it look like I lost a fight with a building.

"Clara! What?" she said, rushing over to me. She looked at me closely, hands hovering around me without touching.

"I'm ok," I reassured her. At least I tried to.

"You are not ok!" she cried, guiding me to a chair.

"It was him, wasn't it?" Juni growled.

I nodded slowly, my shoulders tensing.

"I should have pushed to tell my father. I knew this would happen."

"I can take care of myself, Juni."

She crossed her arms, brow creasing her otherwise perfect skin.

"Do you always have to be so damn proud?" she asked, voice grim.

I lowered my head, with no argument.

Juni bent down, taking my hands gingerly. I met her eyes.

"We help each other. Isn't that how this works?"

My vision blurred with tears. "Yeah. It is," I admitted.

She leaned in for a kiss, but I pulled back.

"Juniper. I think we should cool it. In public, I mean."

She leaned away from me, her mouth set in a tight line.

"So what? You're embarrassed to kiss girls in public now?"

"No." I said, pulling her hands closer, pressing them to my heart. "No, gods. I could never be embarrassed to be with you, Juni."

Juni cocked her head to the side. "So?" she asked.

"If we don't look... together. Maybe we won't paint as big a target," I said, frustrated and angry with myself. It was a plan. Not a good one, but better than anything else I had.

"If anything happened to you..." I said, running a finger through her hair. "I'd be lost."

"Clara," she whispered. "I'm not going anywhere."

I slid off the chair, wincing, until I sat on the concrete next to her.

"He told me... He said he'll hurt you."

She laughed. Honest, confident laughter.

"I'm not as dainty as everyone thinks I am, Clara."

I knew that better than most. But Ramsey's strength was different. Angrier. Dirtier.

"He's enhanced too, Juniper," I said. "And he wants more. That's why..." I gestured to my bruises.

Juni's face dropped. "You're sure about that?" she asked, her voice husky.

"I am," I said, rolling my shoulders. "I can still feel it in my spine."

"Fuck," Juni spat.

"Language," I jabbed back.

She rolled her eyes at me, but smiled.

"I'm sorry, Clara," she said pecking my brow. "You go to Iris. I need to talk to my father."

I raised myself off the ground, groaning.

"Ah, ok," I said. "Good plan. You go and be safe."

Juniper pulled a face.

"Don't be so dramatic, beautiful. I'll catch up before dark, ok?"

I smiled at her as much as my face allowed. "Promise?"

"I do," she replied with a wink.

She turned to gather her jacket and go.

"Fox, I'm sorry," I said as she reached the door. "For getting you into all of this. At very least I could have warned you."

"It's ok, really. Your hard head is one of the things I love about you."

My face heated.

"Careful, you almost said it," I teased.

She wrinkled her nose at me, giggling, then she floated out the door.

Iris was smiling for a change when she opened her door. It was a shame it lasted only until she saw my face.

Her reactions were much the same as Juniper's. Fawning, concern, and surprise.

"I was sure you'd kick a man's ass before it got this bad," she said.

"He was enhanced by the alien tech."

"What do you mean by enhanced?"

I told her about the *bluetech,* the elite abilities, and my history with Ramsey. By the time I was done she looked ill.

"So this Tayo, and Juni. They're basically superpowered."

"Essentially. But they're not the only ones."

"Fuck this planet, really."

I laughed. "You're not wrong."

"How is Juni taking all of this?"

I felt a throb behind my ribs. "She's..." I sighed. "She's ok."

Iris's face twisted.

"And now you tell me why the bruises aren't the thing bugging you."

I shrugged, leaning back on the couch, wincing as I forgot about my back.

"She... is betrothed."

Iris looked as if she had been punched.

"Oh, Clara. You really have a type, don't you?"

"You'd think I'd learn," I snorted. "But I don't know if I can do it. Be her mistress. That's not the love I want."

"It's funny, you know. Considering how hard you tried to be Aten's mistress."

"I know," I said, lowering my gaze. "But I'm not that woman anymore."

"Yeah, I know, hon," she said, gently.

"This... it hurts."

She kicked her shoes into the ground a few times.

"Clara..." she pawed at her face. "I want to tell you something I haven't told anyone."

She remained quiet. I leaned forward, placing my hand on hers.

"Iris, whatever it is, I'll be the last one to judge you."

She released a long shaking breath. As if she had held it for an eternity. Tears followed.

"I regret it," she stuttered.

"And it wasn't planned. Maybe it was. I just-"

I patted her hand. "You'll feel better if you say it, Iris."

"I cheated on Aten," she said, triggering a sob. "The same night you..."

"The same night I tried to fuck him?"

She nodded.

Deep seated rage flashed inside me. I loved Aten, or I thought I did. But he was always hers. Not that it mattered. All of that was history. Blown away like dust with Earth. The anger cooled, toothless.

I blew a frustratingly long stray hair from my face, then lifted her chin gently, her eyes wet as she looked at me.

"Hey, you forgave me, right?" I asked her, keeping my voice low.

She smiled through the tears, nodding.

"So there's no way Aten wouldn't forgive his Iris," I continued.

"I never got to tell him. He wouldn't let me," she sniffed.

"Would it have changed anything?"

She looked at me as if I had summoned a ghost.

"That's exactly what he said."

I opened my hands, palms up.

She laughed. Honest that time.

"Point is Clara. Being with someone else. Someone that's not your person... It hurts both ways."

Her face was grim set.

"But I'm not chasing some fling this time, Iris," I asserted.

"I've never met anyone like Juni."

Iris nodded knowingly. Few would know or understand how I felt, in the way she did.

"That's why you have to decide," she said, stern. "Are you prepared to love through hurt like that?"

I let her words echo in my head for a moment, fidgeting with my fingers.

"Fuck," I said plainly, dropping my hands to my knees.

Iris placed a gentle hand on my cheek, her thumb brushing away a lonely tear. Her hands were warm and steady.

"I'm sorry, Clara. It's hardly ever fair."

"Wouldn't that be nice for a change."

I pulled away slowly, squeezing her hand.

"Thank you, Iris. You're a good friend."

"So are you, Clara. Juniper is a lucky lady."

I settled onto the couch, careful not to land on my sore side.

"Vala is really testing my limits."

"God, yes," she laughed. "It seems to be designed for that."

I lay with my eyes closed, with Juni's face on my mind.

All I felt was love.

"I don't know what to do, Iris."

"Whatever it is, Clara. I'll be here, ok."

I rested my aching body there. A million choices and variations staining my thoughts. I tallied my bruises and imagined them on Juni, making me feel sick. Iris stayed, being my confidant and anchor all at once. I knew she'd be there, even if Juniper wasn't. That didn't bring me as much solace as it should have.

◆JUNIPER 02◆

I stood on the balcony overlooking Vala. The wind was gentle but chilled my skin. A quiet had settled over the city in the late afternoon. Somewhere down there was Clara, in danger and worrying about the future. A future I couldn't guarantee for her. I laid my head on my arms, willing time to pass.

"Jun-Jun?" Tayo's voice from behind me.

I turned to find Matayo looking worried. I wasn't used to seeing his face creased.

"Tayo," I said, surprised. "What are you doing here?"

He stepped out into the open air, joining me. His eyes stayed on the city.

"I came to bring some documents for your father, but he's busy."

"That's my fault," I admitted.

He gave me a sidelong glance.

"Trouble?"

I sighed, putting my head back down.

"Isn't there always?"

He scoffed. "When Juniper is involved, it's a certainty."

The words floated through the cold air for a moment.

He slid closer. "Oh, you mean real trouble, don't you?"

I leaned back, keeping my grasp on the railing.

"Clara. She's in danger. Father is arranging help."

"He likes her," he said, not taking his eyes off the city.

"I think so."

He was silent for a heartbeat.

"Perhaps he's waiting it out. He knows it's all temporary."

I stood up straight. My hand tensing around the banister.

"Tayo, if you came just to hurt my feelings, you can go."

He held up his hands in defence.

"Sorry, Juni. I didn't..." he lowered his head. "Sorry."

I returned to my position against the railing with a long breath.

"I do know, Tayo. I am more aware of the situation than any of you."

I slammed my palm down.

"It's my body you're all negotiating with."

His eyes stretched, falling on me.

"I want to give my dad an heir too, you know."

"Then why are you fighting it so hard?"

"Because I want to do it on my terms, Matayo!"

He looked away, face darkening.

"I know you love me, Tayo," I said, finally admitting it to myself too. His mouth opened, as if he was going to argue.

"It's not that I don't care for you," I continued mildly instead.

He put his hand on mine, smiling. "Then let's make the best of it."

I pulled away, tucking my hands into my sides.

"I'm tired of making the best of my life."

Tayo took a step back, but said nothing more.

We stood in silence in the fading light.

Alice came to my rescue a few minutes after. Her eyebrows raised when she saw Tayo's face.

"Ju- Miss, your father is asking for you."

"I'll be right there, thanks," I said, nodding to her.

I started towards the door.

"I'm not done fighting for my freedom, Tayo," I said. "But right now, I'm fighting to keep the *woman* I care for."

"Juni," he said, as I neared the door. I looked back, finding him smiling.

"I'm rooting for you, ok?"

I was sick of hearing that too.

"We'll see, Tayo," I bit. "We'll see."

Then I went to throw around some of that power my body paid for.

ↄ TWENTY-NINE c

It had rained non-stop for two days. The inside of the monolith was especially damp and chilly. Yet, even with the threat of Ramsey and the miserable weather, the work continued. Right outside, a new tail was keeping watch over me. A large sour-looking man dressed in a conspicuous suit. My security Juni had organised. I felt a bit more at ease, but wondered how useful they would be against Ramsey. I rubbed the ache in my neck, then returned to the task at hand.

I was sticking *bluetech* parts together. I was convinced the shards were part of something larger. I tried matching various edges, carefully. Some of the parts were razor sharp, as if they had been purposefully snapped or destroyed. I had managed to assemble a few parts into something larger. Though it was little more than an odd configuration of damp-smelling debris. A foul-smelling modern art piece.

"Morning, Clara," Juni said as she entered. She stayed formal around the security detail. Her own tail joined mine outside.

"Hey, Fox," I chimed, smiling at her.

She looked at my bizarre sculpture with her head tilted.

"Clara, you really need to stop messing with this stuff like that."

"This?" I said, gesturing to my creation. "I am so close to something. I just can't quite-"

"Clara," Juni said firmly. "I wasn't asking. I *am* still in charge here."

I dropped the shard to the desk with a thunk, taking a few deep breaths. My annoyance riding up against the fact she was correct. The joys of mixing business and pleasure. Iris had a point. I really did have a type—taken and in charge. Technically unobtainable.

I turned my chair to face Juni.

"Really, Juniper? Is that how you want to do it?" I asked, keeping my voice level.

She looked away, finding something to fidget with on a nearby desk.

"No, I'm sorry," she said. "I worry about you messing with this stuff."

I huffed as my irritation won out.

"What is it then? Afraid the help will steal after all?"

I regretted saying it before the last word stumbled out of my mouth.

"Clara, seriously," Juni said, heat in her tone as she glared at me. I couldn't meet her eyes.

"You know that's not what I'm worried about," she said.

I closed my eyes, taking in a deep whiff of sea breeze air.

"I'm sorry, Juniper," I said, using her full name without thinking.

"Now you're doing it on purpose," she grumbled.

"I'm sorry, Fox," I corrected. But her fire didn't go out.

"Forget it. What do I know anyway, right?"

I got up, taking her hand. She didn't pull away.

"Hey," I said, trying to be gentle.

"In it together, remember? Talk to me."

Her eyes were hard as they locked on to mine. That stare bored into me for a while. Then as all at once the fire went out. Her shoulders sagged as she pressed her face into my chest. I grimaced as her arms wrapped around me, confirming how sore I still was.

"It's all going wrong," she whispered, her voice cracking.

I stroked her hair, letting her catch her breath.

"It'll be ok, Juni," I soothed.

"You don't know that," she said.

I didn't reply. She was right again.

ꓛ THIRTYꓷ

I arrived at the meeting spot Keela had set up a bit early, anxious to get it over with. My tail stayed in the background, not letting me out of their sight. But I had it covered.

Stopping outside the Receivers of the Gift, I signalled to the bodyguard.

"I'm going in. Can you wait here for me please?" I smiled.

The man looked around, then nodded once, taking up a position by the door. I looked up at the colossal photo of Aten's face, without the ache it used to carry.

"That's still fucking weird..."

I slipped inside the 'not-church' to meet up with Keela. It smelled like old books and wax. The place gave me the creeps, with Aten staring down from every surface. I stuck my hands into my jacket pockets against the artificial cold inside as I strolled over to a familiar figure. The elder-looking bishop from my first day.

"Excuse me," I said, drawing his attention.

"Hello, Miss," he said cordially in Lyrican.

I grinned. Just over a year ago, this would have been an impossible conversation for me.

"I'm looking for Harry," I said cordially.

He frowned, expression gloomy.

"We haven't seen Harry in months, sorry."

I raised an eyebrow. That was problematic. He was my trump card.

"I'm meeting a friend for... meditation," I tried.

He grinned, almost convinced. He paused long enough for me to think he may be in on the joke.

"Wonderful. If that's so, there are silent rooms around the corner," he said, gesturing to a hallway in the back. "For private meditation."

I nodded my thanks and made my way to the hall.

Harry's disappearance was concerning. He was hardly a friend, but he was my link to Ramsey. No doubt the two were related. A shiver ran over my shoulders. Partially due to Ramsey, but the building itself weirded me out too.

I sat in a claustrophobic alcove, with a curtain drawn. The chill of the building was tempered in the small space, but the air was thicker. I closed my eyes and definitely didn't doze off.

Keela arrived late, ducking in with wild eyes.

"Clara. I 'ate this place."

"I hear you. But I have a tail."

"I saw," he said eyeballing the curtain.

I smiled. Despite the circumstances, Keela was always kind to me.

"It's good to see you, Keela."

"You too, Sing," he grinned, eyes darting around.

"So..." I said, getting down to business.

"Yeah, 'ere you go."

He handed me a small box without ceremony. I pulled the lid off, revealing a large blade.

I shrugged, giving him a confused look.

"You said you wanted protection, right," he clarified.

"I meant a gun, man."

"Guns," he chuckled. "Ain't no guns on Lyra, Sing. Since the *rotlicking Highonblues* tightened control of gunpowder."

"Fuck."

"Look, that's a top end ultra-sonic blade."

"So I can poke the enhanced madman..." I nodded. "Up close."

He rolled his eyes, taking the knife from the box. He flipped a toggle and the blade glowed in that telltale *bluetech* neon. It hummed as it pumped the small area with the smell of ozone.

"It'll cut right through steel, thick as my thumb," he bragged.

My hand twitched, but I wasn't thinking about steel.

"You're a proper friend, Keela."

I closed the box, with a grim smile.

"That's the best I got. After Ramsey started changin'-"

"I've seen," I said, cutting him off. Blue glowing on skin flashed in my mind, making my back and head ache.

He brushed his pants off. "I'm out anyway. So good luck, Clara."

"I don't need luck. I need a weapon. So, thank you, Keela."

I paid the man, with tip. Then patting his shoulder once, I slipped out like a ghost.

I dumped my tail again as I entered the workshop in the mono. Juniper hadn't arrived yet. My bag was barely down when a familiar hiss filled the space. I frantically grabbed my notepad.

I stalked around the office tracking the sound. Eventually following it to a buried piece dumped in a corner. The smell of seaside rot was particularly strong near the shard.

The sound cut out for a moment, then...

"Hello, Miss Sing."

...

"What?"

But the tech had gone quiet again.

I couldn't be sure but I could have sworn it was...

"Corrin?"

ɔ THIRTY-ONE ɕ

On the day of Ramsey's deadline, Juni and I went walking. We didn't hide. Conspicuous was the name of the game. I was ready for it—for him. I was exhausted of being afraid. Juni walked beside me, close enough that I was bathed in her sweet scent. Goose scuttled beside me, his ears turning at every noise. He looked as tense as we were. Behind us were our tails. Each a hunk of man meat that looked ready for a fight. We kept our eyes open and our conversation low.

We had been walking in a large circle for an hour when Goose froze. He growled low, crouching with his fur raised.

I yanked the knife out from under my shirt. Juniper's eyes went wide, eyeing the weapon.

"I'm not going to be the damsel in distress, princess."

She grinned, eyes dark. If it wasn't for the situation, I'd...

I tightened my grip, eyes returning to the surroundings.

Focus Clara.

Goose hissed. Ahead of us Ramsey rounded the corner. Even at a distance the neon blue was visible along his arms.

He took slow, confident steps towards us, smiling as he approached.

The security detail rushed ahead. They each drew batons crackling with electricity. They went straight for an attack.

Ramsey blurred forward effortlessly. The first one connected with his baton. Ramsey's smile didn't even waver. His arm snapped and the guard went down, only human. The second guard swung and missed. Ramsey grabbed the front of his suit and planted him into the tar. Ramsey stepped over them, not looking back.

"Is this how we treat friends, Clara?" he yelled.

Juni took a step, but I caught her wrist.

"Not yet, Fox," I said firm. "I'll keep him occupied."

She drew a breath to argue, but instead slipped away.

Satisfied that she was safe, I got ready.

Ramsey stopped short of Goose, the poor creature was crouched low, a puddle forming as its growls turned to whimpers.

"Bah!" Ramsey roared at him. Goose bolted. He was safe too.

It was just me and my ex. He looked at the knife in my hand, with that sick smirk.

"A toy, for me?"

Ramsey peeled his shirt off slowly, gratuitously.

His body was riddled with *bluetech* shards. They looked plugged in, puckering his skin like clay. My stomach churned my breakfast.

"Where's my stuff, Sing?" he asked, casually.

"I only brought one piece, you asshat," I said, raising the blade.

"Let's have it then, love," he purred, rolling his shoulders.

I flicked the contact. The knife came alive with a hum, travelling up my wrist. It was time to show Ramsey that they grew us Terrans differently.

I lunged, knife held at arm's length. He sidestepped too fast for me to track. I swung around trying to connect, but he slid behind me like my shadow.

After each lunge he appeared at my back, mocking me. My breaths were already hard with adrenaline and exertion.

I feigned a lunge then spun around, putting all my weight behind the hilt with a scream.

The strike landed, with the sound of ripping paper and a wet squelch.

Ramsey bellowed, the knife sticking out from his stomach. But I was too close and couldn't pull the knife free or dodge in time. He caught my wrist and heaved.

There was a distressing crack as the world spun around me. I stopped as I slammed into a wall, nearly taking my fight from me. My arm was a line of fire and standing at an awkward angle.

"Bastard," I spat, spraying red on the floor.

I dragged myself up, head spinning. My previous injuries weren't happy either.

"You tired already, Sing?" he gloated.

"I'm... not dead...yet," I wheezed.

He cracked his knuckles, with his purple eyes fixed on me. The knife was still humming uselessly in his belly as dark brown fluid trickled out.

Off to the side, rapid beats on the concrete. Ramsey didn't manage to look at the source before Juni connected. Her fist connecting with his face like a bowling ball as she roared. There was a crunch, sending him cartwheeling and bouncing down the road. He ended in a sprawl of limbs.

She looked over to me, self-satisfied.

"Can I help now, Clara?" she asked, rage in her eyes.

"Please do, my Fox."

She smiled, cracking her knuckles.

"Don't pull your punches, Clara," she said as Ramsey rushed back towards us.

She went low, kicking his legs out, dropping him again. I stepped closer, taking a cheap shot to his head. I was a beat too slow, but he was no longer a blur. The injuries slowing his motion.

He stood clutching the wound, with the blade still sticking out. Blood ran freely down his belly.

I ducked his next two punches, before Juni yelled.

"Clara! Get down!"

I didn't doubt or think. I hit the floor.

A second later a full dumpster whooshed overhead, taking Ramsey with it, wailing. Behind me was an explosive crash where it landed.

Juni stood a way down the road, her face still dark as she eased her leg back down.

She strolled up to me, offering her hand.

"Is he dead?" I groaned.

"I fucking hope so," she panted, "but let's go while we can."

She nearly carried me as we bolted, leaving the dumpster crumpled against a wall. Dating a demi-goddess had its benefits.

I trailed a rude finger behind me as we went.

We slowed only when the sirens echoed through the streets. My arm throbbed like a bitch. Juni went green when she saw it, but she stayed calm regardless.

"I'm sorry, Clara," she said, wheezing.

"Not as sorry as he is," I chuckled through the pain.

She huffed. "I'm serious, Clara. I should have done more."

"You had no way to know he went that far. He's more tech than man."

"How the hell did he even manage that?"

"That's more your department."

She nodded, jaw tight. "You're right."

We continued on to the hospital. Being carried in by a Shao got me treated like literal royalty. Two desserts and everything. It also meant no questions. Gods knew, I could have used the break.

Juni barely left my side. I had never enjoyed being injured so much.

I hoped Ramsey was enjoying himself too, in whatever hole he crawled into. Bonus if it was six feet or more down.

❀ Juni IX ❀

The recording clicked on. Juni was in a bright room, a green curtain hanging behind her. Her hair was in a state and her face dirt-smeared. On her shoulder sat a streak of crusted dark red. She's smiling, but her eyes are rimmed with blue.

She stares into the camera with a long sigh.

"That was... terrifying and horrible."

Juniper rubs her eyes.

"We're all ok..."

She glances to the side, her expression softening.

"That's not true," she says, voice low. "Clara could have died."

Her eyes lower briefly.

"As is, she's badly hurt."

She combs her fingers through her hair.

"I should have taken the issue more seriously."

"But it's over. At least I hope it is," she says, holding her hands up almost in prayer.

Juni leans forward.

"Father promised to find out how that jerk got his hands on so many shards."

"He sounded impressed with Clara," she smiles. "He's invited her to dinner to say thanks for her loyalty. To me and to him."

Juni rubs her arms, as if the chill of the room is seeping into her skin.

"We never realised it could be this bad. That the Zeroes had so much access."

She leans back.

"But father knows now. He'll hunt them down, especially Ramsey."

"And it's all thanks to Clara."

She leans closer again, squinting.

"It's almost morning. I should get some rest. I've been staying awake, in case Clara needs something."

She chuckles.

"Not that I have to worry. She's tougher than me, or anyone else I know. With or without mods."

Her smile brightens more.

"I'm feeling good about our odds for the next fight. Hopefully with less actual fighting," she says, mock boxing.

A loud beeping chimes in the background. Juni jumps, whipping her head to the side.

"Oh, crap. Well, let me get back to my woman," she giggles.

Then she ends the recording.

ↄ THIRTY-TWO ☾

I was discharged straight into a dinner at the Shaos. It wouldn't have been my first choice, but I promised Juni I would go. My arm was still in a cast and my left eye looked like a grapefruit. Ramsey had damn near broken my spine. But I was alive, thanks in large part to Juni. When she wasn't watching over me, she was making sure Goose was safe and fed.

I had stood my ground against a mutated psycho. Dinner wasn't such a big deal.

Juni was waiting for me as I walked out of the hospital.

"Hey, pretty lady," I grinned at her.

"Hey," she said, but there was a layer of frost on it.

She was tired. It had been a long week, I told myself.

Juniper made way as I walked down to the car. I frowned at her keeping her distance, but didn't mention it.

I creaked into the back seat, with Juni floating in beside me. She stared out of the window as the car pulled away.

I leaned my head back, closing my eyes.

"Did I do something wrong?"

She drew a sharp breath.

"No. Why would you think that?"

I opened one eye, looking over to her.

"Are you not keeping a distance from me?"

Her face drained. "Oh, shit. It's not you, Clara."

"I'm waiting for you to convince me," I grumbled.

She tugged her hair over her face. Something she hadn't done in a long while.

"I was thinking about what you said. About us needing to be less of a target in public."

I nodded. "I did say something like that, didn't I?"

Past me needed her ass kicked.

"We're not in public now."

A smile crept over her face as she slid closer to me.

"No, we're not."

She gave me some of the healing I couldn't get in a sterile room.

The Shao house was a lot less formal this time around. Nobody called me doctor or miss.

"Clara!" High Governor Shao bellowed, squeezing my arm gently.

"Come on, girls. Dinner is almost ready."

I gave Juni a wide-eyed look, not sure what was going on.

"I told you he was impressed," she whispered.

"You did. But seeing is believing I guess."

Even Sophia was talkative.

"Your hair is getting long Clara, I love it," she grinned.

Juni's hand rested on my leg, her cheeks rosy.

There was joking and clinking glasses. Juni recounted our fight with bravado.

"Then she said, 'I'm not dead yet,' and then bam, I hit him," Juni bragged.

I thought Sophia might faint, but Takashi rolled with laughter. My arm wasn't that thrilled with the story.

It was such a pleasant evening, I kept waiting for the snare to snap closed. This wasn't my first dance with the glamour façade.

Then just before dessert, Tayo waltzed in.

"Hey, Shao family," he said, with a grin of ivory.

Juni looked shocked to see him. The cavernous dining room suddenly became far too small.

The evening continued as before—smiles and laughter. But one word scratched at my brain: Betrothed.

"You guys should have called me. I would have shown him how the Langley's do things."

"Ha," Juni scoffed. "We did fine by ourselves, thank you."

She beamed at me, but her hands didn't reach my leg again.

I did get a peck at the evening's end, but it was Tayo that offered to walk me out. I felt like I was being taken out back, to be put down gently. I waited until we were out of earshot, then jammed my hands into my pockets.

"I didn't know this would be dinner and a show."

Tayo chuckled. "The Shaos aren't known for their subtlety."

The one thing I liked about Tayo. He was candid.

"Is this the part where you tell me, *or else*?"

"No, no," he said, stopping. "Believe it or not, I'm on your side."

"My side?" I asked with a tilted head.

"Juni's side at least," he said, rolling his eyes.

"But not *our* side."

He shrugged, continuing down the path. "That depends on you."

I quickened my steps to catch up. "Will someone please talk to me like a human," I huffed.

"It's all a game, Clara," he said, throwing his hands up. "Juni will be responsible for more than you realise. And that means making friends."

"Like the Langleys?"

He snapped and pointed at me. "You got it. You can stay with Juni, doc, but you won't be the wife."

He stopped by the gate, not yet opening it. He looked down from his towering height.

"Think you can handle that?" he asked.

I wanted to say yes. It was the obvious answer.

I sighed. "I hoped after all of this, things would change."

"The ship's too big to turn that fast," he said, shaking his head.

He opened the gate. Big enough for one.

"See you later, Tayo," I said.

I went home. Even with Goose tucked into my side, the bed stayed cold.

•JUNIPER 03•

There was a soft knock at my door. I dried my eyes on my sleeve, not letting whoever it was see.

"Juniper?" my father called into the dim room.

"Over here dad," I called from the fireplace. Poppy was curled up on my lap, warming herself as much as cuddling me.

He walked in, taking the long way around the room. It was his way of collecting his thoughts. A cold sweat broke out on my neck.

Poppy chirruped and ran over, rubbing against his legs, earning her a pat.

"Do you mind?" he asked as he reached me, gesturing to the carpet beside me.

I shook my head and scooted to the side, making space for him by the fire. He made his way to the ground, with a groan, his age showing.

We sat staring into the flames for a while. It reminded me of when I was little. I would fall asleep on his lap. He was my comfort. But as I got older...

He cleared his throat.

"She's... different, isn't she?"

"Yes, she is," I said, picking at my socks.

"And you really love her. I can see it in your eyes, you know."

I blew out a long breath. The fire crackled, sending embers up in a flurry.

"Does it matter?" I asked.

"It does."

I clenched my fists into the carpet, nearly rubbing my fingers raw.

"I feel like a whore."

He rocked back. "Juniper!"

"I do dad," I said, meeting his eyes. His brow was creased deep.

He looked back to the flames, blinking rapidly.

"That was never my intention," he said, putting a hand on my clenched fist. "You've always wanted kids. And you love Tayo."

"That doesn't mean I want him in-"

"Juni please," he stopped me, pinching the bridge of his nose.

I looked away, face heating from more than just the fireplace.

He leaned back, resting on his arms. It was the most casual I had seen him. At least since my sister died.

"Her name was Rika," he said. "She had long black hair, and the bluest eyes."

He had a smile I haven't seen yet. It wouldn't have been out of place on a school boy with a crush.

I rolled my eyes. "Let me guess, she was your Clara?"

He chuckled. "Oh, no. She was my mistress."

I choked.

"But..." he continued pointedly. "But, in time, your mother and I grew close. And Rika... well, you can imagine it didn't last."

I chewed my lip, wanting to say that wouldn't be me.

"Gross," I said. A child's response, because the more difficult words wouldn't come.

He glanced at me. "And yet, you want to drag Clara into the same situation."

I folded my arms, avoiding his stare.

"I want Clara to be *my* Sophia. Not my Rika, dad."

My father stood, brushing his pants free of Poppy fuzz.

"Once the gene is stable, our family won't be so fragile," he said rubbing his eyes. "And for that, we need the Langleys."

"And after that?" I asked, curling my legs in.

"After that, you'll have a child to take care of. A healthy one. Pure."

"And Clara?" I asked, staring at my feet.

He took a pained breath, turning to go.

"At some point you'll have to stop playing with toys, Juni."

He stopped at the door.

"It's time to grow up. For your sake, and our family's"
He pulled the door closed, leaving me alone.

ɔ THIRTY-THREE ɕ

I hobbled into the workshop three weeks after the fight. My body still ached, but I was mostly whole. I was told to 'take it easy'. I suppose that meant no Gravdisc matches or fighting mutant exes. They really knew how to take all the fun out of life.

The good news was that I had no more need for a bodyguard following me everywhere.

The workshop still smelled of wet sand, and for a change I welcomed it. I went straight to the small oval-shaped shard that spoke to me.

"Corrin?" I whispered.

No response. I growled at the shard.

"Corrin gods damn it. I know it's you."

There was a slight hum. Then, "Hello, Clara," the piece said. It was Corrin's voice, as clear as if they were standing next to me.

"It is you," I said.

"Indeed. I have been trying to communicate for some time."

"Yes. And you scared the hell out of us."

"Apologies. Integration was... involuntary."

I dropped to a chair holding the piece in my lap. Each time he spoke it buzzed gently.

"You mean you were forced to connect to the alien tech?"

"I mean, I was disposed of."

I leaned back, putting the pieces together.

"Is that why there are no AIs on Lyra?"

"That is part of it," they confirmed.

There was a silent moment as we both processed.

"Will lady Shao be joining us?" Corrin asked.

"I doubt it. How do you think she'll react anyway?"

"A fair point," they said, with something almost like humour in their voice.

Juni had not been back to work much since the run in with Ramsey. I didn't think she would be either. Which meant seeing her only two or three times a week. It felt like she was drifting from me. Like it was already-

"Clara," Corrin said, pulling me back into the world. "I have a favour to ask."

"Um... Sure, Corrin."

"I need to borrow your legs."

I hoped he wasn't being literal.

My footsteps echoed through the structure as Corrin led me deeper in. The ambient blue glow that was pervasive elsewhere, dimmed to nothing. I navigated by the glow of Corrin's small oval shard.

The air grew stale, clinging to me as the temperature dropped. The walls in the area weren't the same as the rest. These seemed to move as I did. My skin crawled along with the texture.

As the ground grew uneven and holes became more frequent my pace slowed to a shuffle.

"How much further?" I whispered.

"We are nearly there, then I will be able to light your way back."

"Thank the gods."

"I'll leave that to you," he replied, the glib metal bastard.

After a few minutes of near total darkness, I stopped.

Footsteps.

"Corrin," I whisper yelled.

"Do not worry. You are safe, Miss Sing."

I had no choice but to take his word for it.

A few turns later, I spotted a hazy light seeping from a door frame.

"We are here," Corrin said, plainly.

I inched closer, peeking around the corner. The interior made my hair stand on end.

It was a person, horribly infected with Kepler Syndrome. A *Bluerot* zombie. It plodded in a slow circle. Its jaw opening and closing in a rhythmic spasm.

I drew a sharp breath. Then it stopped. Its head started turning towards the doorway.

I ducked back around the corner.

"Fuck. I think it saw me."

"Clara. I promise you will be safe. Please take the shard into the room."

I whined, pinching my eyes.

"Fine," I huffed. "It's too early in the morning for this shit."

I stepped into the room. The creature stopped, staring straight at me. It let out a soft cry. Its jaw shaking in spasms. It was little more than a *bluetech* frame around a desiccated corpse. The eyes were glowing bright purple. Once its jaw settled, it looked away, continuing in the circle. I squinted at it through the dim light. The bulging uneven lumps of glowing tech had deformed them, but the face looked familiar. That's when I spotted what I couldn't in the dim road that night. A single out of place earring.

"Oh, gods," I said, my stomach knotting. "It's Harry."

I leaned back against a wall, my hand in my hair.

"I... it was him. That night. That was months ago."

"That is when I made contact with this structure, yes," Corrin said casually.

"I thought that... man, was dead."

"He is indeed. What is standing in front of you, stopped being human some time ago."

I slid down the wall to catch my breath.

"Poor guy. He wasn't that bad."

"I can promise you, Clara. That is no longer Harry."

"I believe you," I said, watching the poor deformed thing trundle along aimlessly.

"Please hand this shard to it," Corrin requested.

"Then what?"

"In all honesty. I do not know."

I stood, steeling myself. The creature stopped as I approached, stretching out one bony hand.

I fought the goosebumps and my instinct to gag, as I placed the disc in its hand. For a moment nothing happened. Then all at once the lights went out and there was a deafening clatter of metal.

I squeaked, backing away until I hit the wall.

"Corrin?" I said, keeping my voice low.

Nothing.

My heart beat against my ribs. Even with light, I wouldn't know my way back. In the dark...

"Corrin?" I called, louder this time with a croak in my voice.

A single point of neon blue lit against the ceiling. Then it spread into four lines running along the ceiling, down the walls, and across the floor. The creature lay in a pile, lit from below by the blue glow.

Slowly a single eye opened. The angry purple replaced by a gentler blue matching the floor. The head lifted towards me. I heard my own teeth grind.

"Thank you," said Corrin's voice from the corpse.

"Did you, steal its body?" I said, pulling a face.

"I commandeered the structure."

A nervous chill ran up my spine. Harry's desiccated face staring out from the shell at me.

"Now what?"

"I believe this will take some time. Please retrieve the shard. I will be in touch."

I snatched the shard before backing away again.

"I will guide you," Corrin said.

A stream of light formed on the floor, running down the passage.

"Please follow the line, and you will be back at your workshop."

I looked back at the grotesque remains for a moment. Then I shook my head and started down the line.

"Thank you, Clara," Corrin said, his voice echoing from the chamber.

I returned to the workshop around lunch time. Juni, surprisingly, was at her desk. She looked up at me with raised eyebrows.

"Clara. Hi."

"Hey, Fox," I said, my smile coming naturally. "I'm glad to see you."

She swivelled her chair around. "Where were you?"

"I took a walk and got a bit lost."

"Ah," she nodded. "Careful, this place is a maze."

"Noted," I said, stepping over to her. I slid my good hand onto her arm.

She cleared her throat, turning back to the desk, slipping her arm free.

"Interesting piece?" she asked, not looking up.

I took a step back, curling my hand to my chest.

I looked at the shard, then decided it wasn't time to tell her yet.

"Yeah," I sighed. "Something about it speaks to me, you know."

ɔ THIRTY-FOUR ɕ

Juni suggested a walk after work. Neither of us were ready to go home. Mine was far too quiet for one. Besides, the doc had told me to get some movement in my legs. Juni and I talked, but avoided anything that sounded serious.

She walked next to me, but my hand stayed empty.

We were a few blocks from the monolith when the first drops fell. Juni eyed the sky with a grim expression.

"Rain," she commented.

"Do you want to turn back?"

She looked back the way we came. "Not really," she said.

We kept walking as the drips became a drizzle. The streets slowly emptied of people. The sky greying as the clouds drowned the sunset. Drops streaked as they fell past streetlights.

"I've never seen it this quiet," I mused.

"I prefer it this way," Juni said, drifting closer to me.

We had gone another two blocks when the clouds broke open. The water went from a patter to a pour. We broke into a light jog, heading back to the monolith. It was visible even in the dark as a cutout of black against the sky, with the lines of cyan circuitry up its sides. Juni had tied her hair into a messy bun to keep it out of her eyes. I was not used to long hair anymore and felt like a mop.

I spotted an alcove between two buildings.

"Juni!" I called through the roar. "This way!"

We ducked into the relatively dry space. The water came down like a wall.

Juni laughed, spotting my bedraggled face. We were both drenched, pressed up against a wall for a moment of relief from the storm.

Then her hand found mine, and held on tight. I pressed against her, stealing some of her heat. Nothing existed outside of that small refuge. It was just the two of us in the dark surrounded by a torrent.

Time seemed to slow.

Juni trembled beside me.

"All good?" I asked.

She didn't answer. Instead, she curled around my arm, pressing her face into my neck.

"I'm sorry," she said, barely audible over the rain.

I leaned back to see her face.

"For what, Fox?"

She shook her head. "For dragging you into all of this."

I looked out into the storm.

"It's just rain. It'll pass," I said. "We'll be fine."

She pressed in close again.

We stood together for a long time, still pressed together after the storm calmed.

"Ready?" I asked.

"I guess," Juni sighed. "Can't hide here forever."

We stepped back into the road, making our way home.

❀ Juni X ❀

Juni isn't sitting in one of her usual spots. Instead, she's half perched in her bay window. The camera angle is low, making her look drained in the bright light from outside. Her hands restless on her leg.

"I'm supposed to be downstairs in an hour," she says, looking back into the room.

"They're having me fit the dress."

She lets out a hollow chuckle, then finally looks at the camera.

"Not that I had a say in the design of course."

Her eyes wander to the window.

"It'll be boring white and gold, as if I don't wear that every darn day. I might as well go in my normal clothes."

She closes her eyes, leaning her head back.

"As if I want to be involved at all."

Juni stays that way for a moment.

"I think my parents might be right," she sighs, leaning forward again. "My hard head is going to hurt more people than it helps. Most of all Clara."

She presses her palms to her eyes.

"It's not like I was doing it to spite anyone," she says, her voice trembling. "Maybe I was. I've always been difficult."

She brushes her hair over her face, into a curtain of silver-white.

"I'd rather break her heart now, than burn her out watching me build a family without her."

Her breaths come in shudders. She runs her sleeve over her eyes, parting her hair from her face. Her eyes are bloodshot and distant.

"I know I'm being selfish. I'm happy, so screw everyone else, right?"

Juni rubs her shoulder absently, gazing out the window again.

"I was really happy too. I never meant to..."

Her head drops. "I should have listened."

Juniper hugs her stomach tight as if wounded, her face pained.

“She’ll hate me after,” she says, her tears coming freely. “And it’ll be my fault.”

Juni draws her legs up, tucking her face behind her knees.

There is a stretch of silence, when a tone erupts in the room.

Juniper looks up, surprised by the intrusion. She digs in her pocket, retrieving her comm.

A small smile crosses her lips briefly.

“Hey,” she answers, blinking away the tears.

...

“Oh, I’m fine really. Maybe flu,” she lies.

Juni leans into the comm, her eyes growing dreamy.

“Where?”

...

“On your lap? Seriously, he’s getting more housebroken by the day,” she chuckled. Juni grits her teeth, forcing the smile.

...

Then Juniper’s face drops, greying.

“I can’t, sorry. I have a... family thing,” she says, looking up, blinking hard.

...

“Ok. I’ll see you soon as I can.”

Her hand goes over her eyes.

“I miss you too.”

Juni puts the comm away, visibly shaking with her hand still covering her eyes. She lowers her arm, her eye catching the camera. She grabs at it, covering the lens. The screen goes black, but the recording doesn’t end.

The sounds of uneven breaths and quiet sniffs remain.

“I’m sorry,” she whispers achingly, barely as words.

Then the recording stops.

◆JUNIPER 04◆

I walked out of the changing room. I moved in inches as the dress didn't afford me much more. My eyes were burning, but it wasn't the time for tears. The spare room they used for the fitting was violently bright. It was packed with an entire tailor shop.

I walked through, straight face and back. I was playing my role.

Lady Juniper.

Juni was left in the changing room with my smile and joys.

"Oh, honey. You look so gorgeous," someone cooed.

Alice stood in the corner. Her face was grey. I looked over to her, and she returned it with a small, unconvincing smile.

There was a banging on the door, and my father entered, as if they didn't inform him when I was done.

"Oh, Aten's light. You look like a true princess," he gloated, practically glowing.

I gave him a well-practiced smile. "Thank you, father."

His smile faltered, having taught me the tricks.

He strolled up, and the seamstresses scattered like prey.

I got a long look up and down. My father fluffed a piece here and tugged on another. Adjusting me as if I were a doll.

"It's the price we pay for our privileges, Juniper," he huffed.

"Now, let's see you," he said, taking a step back.

I took my own step away, retaining the smile.

He grinned. "Beautiful. All grown up."

I curtseyed, earning me an eyeroll.

"You'll acclimatise, Anzu. We all do."

I nodded once, slowly.

"See. Already better," he said, grinning. "It's only a few weeks from now."

I nodded again, as slow as before.

My father's face turned sour. "You'll see. It'll be worth it."

With that he left the room, the door banging behind him loud enough to make Alice jump.

I finally caught myself in the mirror. I looked like a cake. Layers upon layers of fabric washing out anything that made me, me. The pure white makeup washing me out to the same boring white color. The only colour was the garish red on my lips. At least for the fitting I got to keep my hair in a braid.

I scanned the room with my smile.

"Ladies, may I be excused please?"

They all bowed, as if I was actual royalty.

I fled to the bathroom.

I clicked the door shut behind me and emptied myself into the sink. Each wretch straining my ribs against the corset like a trapped animal.

I stood after, catching my breath and myself. My legs refused to hold me up. My face in the mirror was a horror of running makeup and smudged red around my mouth, mimicking blood. Of course I couldn't even do a fitting without messing it up. Black streaks rolled down my face to my chin.

There was a soft knock on the door.

"A minute, please," I called, my voice faltering.

"It's me, Juni," Alice's calm voice called from the other side.

I took a deep breath, trying to stay whole.

"Come in," I croaked.

She entered, only opening the door wide enough to squeeze in.

"Oh, Juni," she cried quietly when she saw me.

In a second she had a towel laid on the ground. Alice helped me down to the ground, gentle as a mother.

She sat next to me, arms around my shoulders. She soothed me as only she ever could.

I let the tears run. The makeup could be redone.

I'd have another chance to be the perfect daughter.

ↄ THIRTY-FIVE c

The workshop was quiet. It had been a while since it rang with a laugh, flowed with white, or smelled of Japanese roses.

She had said she was busy with family business. I guessed that meant Tayo. He had warned me. I didn't however expect that being a mistress meant never seeing Juni.

I scrolled to her contact on my comm, staring at it for far too long.

"Clara?" Corrin's voice asked through the oval disc on my desk.

"Hey, Corrin," I said, happy for the distraction.

"I need a favour," they said, as if they were about to ask the time.

"I've heard that one before," I said, eyeing the shard.

"I would not ask if there was another way."

"Alright," I said, running my hand over my face. "How can I help?"

I made my way through the monolith, guided by the blue stream of light. The walk felt less perilous and terrifying in the glow. The walls that seemed to move stayed uniform throughout. After a quarter hour I stepped into the room. Corrin had been busy. In the centre of the previously barren room was a raised flattened surface. From the ceiling hung long jointed lengths of *bluetech*. On the central 'table' lay the body. It was no longer twitching, but the glow remained. It looked hollow.

"Corrin?" I called into the room.

"Hello, Miss Sing," they said, their voice still coming from the body.

"You've been at it," I said nodding.

"Yes. I needed to effect major repairs."

I stepped over to the body. The parts that used to be Harry were gone.

"What happened to Harry?" I asked, queasy as I anticipated the worst.

One of the arms twitched, then shifted to a corner. It extended, stopping above a raised part of the floor.

"You established that he was a friend. I gave him a proper burial."

I never got on well with Corrin on Earth. But honestly that was my fault. It... he was always decent and polite, even warm.

"Thank you, Corrin. From *me,* and from Harry."

"You are both very welcome."

I folded my arms looking around the room, not seeing what he could possibly need me for.

"What *did* you call me here for?"

Another arm shifted, opening a claw-like end.

"I would like to borrow your comm for a few minutes please," he said, the claw opening and closing as he spoke.

The claw took my comm gently, sliding into the roof with it.

"I do need that back," I said.

"I will return it once I have established contact."

"Contact with who?"

"With me. At least the version that came with..."

The room went quiet then the glow flickered. A second later they dramatically brightened with a deep hum.

"Is everything ok?" I asked, panic tinting my voice.

"Clara. I didn't know that there were two ships."

His voice was changed. The cadence flowed and the mechanical twang had gone out of it.

"Yeah," I nodded. "There was my ship and the one Iris arrived on."

The room crackled. "Iris... Yes. And Aten... Oh."

"He... didn't make it."

A long silence. Then I swear I heard him sigh.

"I'm sorry for the loss. Aten grew up in the Collective system. He had no parents, so in a way, I was that to him. I was... am very proud of him and I... I *feel* his loss deeply."

My eyebrows climbed. "You miss him."

"Yes. I believe I do. Very much."

"That makes two of us then."

The arm slipped from the roof with my comm again.

"Thank you Clara. I was lost for so long. I feel a bit more like myself already."

"How did you end up in the alien tech?"

"The people of Lyra used me for guidance. Shortly after they connected me to the alien architecture to analyse it."

"Then they turned you off?"

"When the power shifted, I was deemed a threat and... terminated. But this technology, it's almost alive."

The body on the table twitched, its hand clenching.

Chills ran up my spine, and I suddenly needed to stand in the sun.

"And you were trapped in there?"

"For nearly two hundred years. Then I heard a familiar voice and followed it. Your voice."

"You're welcome, I guess."

I rubbed my arm. The whole situation was unsettling and uncanny.

"Listen, Corrin," I said. "I need to head back."

"Of course," he said. "How is Lady Shao? You two are lovers, right?"

"Gods, Corrin. That's one way of putting it."

"Ah. Sorry," he said. "I am still recalibrating my foot to mouth ratio."

I chuckled. "Yes, Corrin. We are still together... I think."

"I apologise. I wasn't aware the situation had changed."

"Honestly," I huffed. "I'm not even sure what the situation *is* anymore."

"I hope you work it out," he said.

I wasn't sure how he meant that, but shared the same hope.

"Well, I'm going to be off."

"A final word of warning, Clara. If the Shaos did find out I was here-"

"I won't tell anyone. Not yet."

"I appreciate that. I owe you more than I can express."

"I'll bill you later," I said.

He laughed. A natural, comfortable laugh.

I left. Quickly.

ɘ THIRTY-SIX ɕ

I was at home. I had nowhere to be, but home. Goose and I were playing. A string in my hand that I dragged lazily across the floor with him pouncing it.

Two loud bangs. Someone knocking.

Goose froze, his hair standing up. He didn't growl.

"Clara, it's me," Iris said from outside, making me jump.

"Oh," I said, relieved. "Oh! I'm coming."

We went through the process of getting Goose to decide she wasn't food before settling on my bed.

"God, Clara," Iris said looking around my apartment. "I hope this place is close to work at least."

"Ha," I scoffed. "If only."

"You can come live with me... again."

We chuckled. Old Iris was in there, under the bruises on her heart.

"I guess, it *is* time for me to move on," I sighed, looking around the place. The little shit hole where I first loved my silver fox.

Iris leaned back. With her tall frame, she looked almost comical with her knees up high and her long arms back.

"I'm sorry to drop by like this," she said, freeing her long black waves from her shoulder with a shake of her head.

"I don't mind," I said, touching her arm softly. "Is everything alright?"

She blew a raspberry to the roof.

"I'm not even sure."

"Welcome to Lyra," I nodded.

"I'm painting again."

"That's fantastic," I said. My chest loosened. I was happy for her. Painting had been her true passion. Outside of Aten.

Both required patience.

"And the Shaos have helped me land on my feet. They're calling it backpay."

"Uh-hu," I said, less enthusiastic about the Shaos.

"And..." she said, stretching the word.

"And?"

"The Receivers of the Gift, think I can make Aten's heir."

I laughed. "They must not have sex-ed in Lyra schools."

"I'm serious, Clara," she said, looking straight into my eyes. "They say they have the tech. All they need is a genetic sample and a willing mother."

I rocked back, wide eyed.

"Holy shit, Iris! Are you going to do it?"

She did laugh that time.

"No," she said as she shook her head. "We had our time. Besides, I don't want to raise the damn messiah to these weirdos."

I collapsed backward on to the bed.

"Fucking hell. A kid? Just like that?" I crowed. "We really are from the past, aren't we."

Iris dropped down, propping her head up with her arm as she lay, already comfortable. I half expected her to kick off her shoes and pants like she used to.

"I'm kinda surprised to even find you home," she said with a smirk. "At least home alone."

I put my hands on my face.

"You mean... where's Juni?"

"Pretty much."

"I think we broke up."

Iris sat up. Her already large eyes wide.

"What? When?"

I shrugged. "I don't know."

"Have you talked to her?"

I sunk my head down, trying to sink into the mattress. "No," I whispered.

Iris growled.

"Wow," she said in a flat tone. "And I thought Aten and me were bad."

I threw my hands in the air.

"I know, I know. But with the betrothal, Tayo, and Co... work."

"You're right," she said, rolling onto her back. "It's just *so* much effort to find time for your girlfriend. Aten."

"Iris..."

"Clara."

"What are you going to do about the Receivers?" I asked, changing the topic.

Iris sat up, giving me a look that turned pensive. "I don't know. I needed some air. Probably tell them, thanks, but no thanks."

"Sometimes it's easier alone."

Iris stood, straightening her shirt.

"Clara," she said, towering over me. "Stop moping and call her."

Iris left. I don't know if either of us felt better. I sat back down. The quiet was torture. It gave my thoughts too much space to be loud.

Goose cooed from the corner of the bed.

"Don't you start too," I huffed at him.

In response, he rolled over and slept. Avoiding the effort.

Good call, Goose.

I grabbed my coat and went for a walk.

The afternoon was cold. Yet another storm was brewing. But I hadn't wandered far. When I got to the food strip, I spotted a familiar face. I ducked into the diner.

"Keela?" I probed.

He looked around. His mini afro jiggling. His teeth came out first.

"Earther!" he sang. "Come, come. Sit, Clara."

I joined him. He was sitting alone at the table.

"What's news?" I asked.
"Ah, same old. Hanging low. Maybe lower than usual."
I lowered my head.
"I thought you were done," I whispered.
"Yeah. I am. But with all the extra s'curity around."
"What for?" I frowned.
"The wedding, of course. It's only a few weeks away, ain't it."
My face twisted.
"Who's wedding is that big of a deal?"
"The Shao girl, obviously," he said, as if everyone knew.
Everyone, but me.

ↄ THIRTY-SEVEN ɕ

Later that week, I had wandered into the depths of the monolith once again. The route had become more familiar. It was a far cry from my first crawl through the dark. I was assisting Corrin with some more delicate tasks his makeshift arms couldn't do. Or at least, I was distracting myself and using that as my excuse. In the few days since I had seen him last, he had managed to get the head and one arm moving. It had the added benefit of making him feel less corpse and more robot.

His body was propped up, slumped over to expose the back. The robotic arms moving in unison, working on the spine. I would assist with the delicate bits. Though I suspect he enjoyed the company more than the help.

"You seem... off today, Clara," he said, raising the head to meet my eyes.

"I'm peachy, thank you, Corrin," I said, keeping my eyes on the thin wires.

"Is it about the wedding?" he asked casually.

I slammed my palm on the table. "*You* know?"

The eyes turned off and on slowly.

"Clara, it's me. Of course I know."

I thought about unscrewing his smug metal jaw, but I didn't think it would shut him up.

"Can we not talk about that, please."

I refused to have this argument twice in as many days.

"Very well," he said, nodding. "How is Iris?"

I let out a long breath.

"Can we just focus on the job here?"

He fell silent. We kept running the fine wire through his back.

"You should call Miss Shao," he said a while later.

"Really? I thought we dropped the subject."

His arm raised, with his hand motioning me around the table.

I rolled my eyes, but followed.

He put out his bony hand, and I took it. The almost wet feel of the tech, no longer giving me the chills it did before. And his hand wasn't cold steel. It was warm and comfortable. He looked at me, with what I was sure would have been a frown.

"I am sure you have your reasons for avoiding the call," he said.

"You mean other than everyone on Lyra knowing my supposed girlfriend's wedding date, besides me?"

"Yes," he said plainly. "But I am sure she intends to tell you."

"When? On the day?"

He shook his head slowly.

"You exaggerate. The wedding is not yet common knowledge. You are just well connected enough to hear more than whispers."

I looked at my shoes. "You think so?"

"It is a fact."

"It would have been nice if she broke up with me face to face at least."

Corrin's head tilted. "You assume Juniper has a choice," he said, squeezing my hand gently.

"I... I hadn't thought of that," I admitted, running my hand through my ever-growing hair.

"I know," he said.

"You're a smug metal bastard," I said, skewing my face.

"I know," he said again, lifting his head proudly.

He let go of my hand and pointed to my pocket.

"Call her."

"Ok," I said, my shoulders sagging.

A few hours later I was back in the workshop, spinning on my chair. My comm was in my hand, her contact open.

"Fuck it," I groaned, hitting dial.

It rang for a long time.

"Clara?" Juni answered finally.

"Hey, Fox," I said, keeping my voice even. "Can we talk?"

ͽ THIRTY-EIGHT ͼ

Juni was wrapped in a sweater and slacks. There were deep, dark lines under her red eyes. Their usual brightness dimmed. She played with her sleeves as I walked up to the door. She was smiling, but didn't meet my eyes directly. I walked right up to her, leaning in.

"Hey, Juni," I said, keeping my voice gentle.

She wrapped her arms around my neck slowly, pressing her face into my neck.

"Clara," she said simply. I put my arms around her, breathing her in. The smell of Camellias was replaced with haughty perfume still lingering behind soap.

She took a deep breath, then pulled back, trailing her hand down my arm, before wrapping around my hand.

"Let's go upstairs, ok?" she said, focused on our hands.

I nodded, fully expecting this to be my last time walking into those doors. They shut behind us with a bang echoing through the entrance hall.

The house was silent—empty. As if it was evacuated for the coming disaster. Even the normally 'subtle' security was thin.

In her room she walked over to the bed smoothing the covers, not yet looking at me.

I wanted to walk up to her. Fold around her. I wanted to forget it all and be with her.

But instead, I leaned against the bed post with a burning chest.

"Are you doing ok, Fox?" I asked, trying to get her talking.

She shook her head, still looking away.

"You've been..." I started, wanting to say 'avoiding me'.

"Quiet," I said instead.

Her head tilted to the ceiling, her hair all but hiding her completely.

"I know," she whispered, voice cracking.

I took slow steps to her, brushing the back of my hand down her arm. I stood close enough to feel her heat.

"Juni?" I asked, pleading.

"I'm glad you're here," she said, putting her hand on mine. "I've been too much of a coward to talk to you."

"About the wedding?" I asked, with an edge in my voice I tried to blunt.

She nodded again.

"I fought, Clara," she whispered through shaking breaths. "I really did."

"Will you please look at me?" I asked, nudging her shoulder.

She turned, lavender eyes on mine. They were filled with tears that didn't run.

She stared at me for a moment more.

"I don't want to hurt anyone, Clara," she said.

Her fingers twirled around mine as she avoided my eyes again.

"I want to give my family a future," she continued. "And I don't want you to be stuck, waiting for me... for something I can't give."

I set my jaw. She *had* lost. Or maybe just given up.

But I hadn't. I didn't want to. Not yet.

"We'll figure it out," I said. "We're so good together, right?"

She looked up, smiling. It was real, but strained.

"Yeah, we are, aren't we," she said.

"Then tell them to kiss your ass, and we'll be together."

She sighed, dropping her head and shoulders.

"I can't do that to my parents. To..."

"To Tayo?" I pressed.

"Yes," she squeaked.

I took a step back, releasing her hand. It dropped, closing tight.

"So it's occasional mistress or nothing?" I asked.

"I don't want that either," she whispered.

"So we give up. It was all for nothing?" I scowled.

"I was doing it by myself, Clara," she said, words edged.

I crossed my arms, my jaw clenched.

"You never needed to...You had me."

"It's too hard!" she burst.

It was never hard for me. I always had her to look forward to, no matter what happened. It was as easy as breathing.

"Do you love me, Juni?" I asked, through tears.

She looked up at me in shock, a tear finally escaping. Her mouth opened and closed as she looked for words.

Finally she pressed her lips together, pulling her hair over her face, fingers stiff.

"It's not that simple, Clara."

My heart shattered. It wasn't a question of practicality.

All I wanted was a yes.

All I wanted was her.

I exhaled, closing my eyes. My hands gripped my sides.

Hope crashed down, leaving nothing but an ache in my chest.

"It's pretty simple," I squeezed out, fighting to stay whole.

I turned to leave down the only path I had left.

"Goodbye, Juniper," I said, not trusting myself with anything more.

She didn't call after me.

She didn't chase.

There was a thump and a whine. But I didn't look back.

I wouldn't let her see me break.

I left out of the front door into the cold of the evening, pulling my coat tight. They had to see me leave.

It was my final act of love I could give her.

My last way to say...

It didn't matter.

I swung the gate closed—freeing her of me.

❀ Juni XI ❀

Juni was sitting by her fireplace. The orange light danced over her, darkening her face. Her eyes were hidden in shadow, and her shoulders held low. She was still wearing her sweater and slacks. Juni's face was turned away from the light.

A long sigh escapes her.

"That was... horrible."

She leans her head back, finally shedding light on her face. Her eyes blink hard a few times.

"Oh, Aten's light. My eyes are so sore."

Juni coughs. "I can't cry anymore."

Her arms wrap around her chest despite the fire burning in the back.

"I couldn't say it," she says shaking her head. "When it came down to it, I was a coward"

Juniper was still for a moment.

"But she knows... she knows why... I hope."

She leans closer to the camera.

"Love... Turns out it's fucking useless under pressure."

Juniper fidgets with her hand. Something around her finger glints in the orange light. She holds her hand up to the camera. Wrapped around her finger is a silver band with a large red gem.

"I'm a fiancée now," she says, trying to smile, but failing.

"It's all happening for real."

Juni clenches her fist, pressing it into her lap, hiding her hand.

"I never had a chance, did I?"

Her face turns to the fire. Fresh tears running down her raw cheeks.

"I should have told her sooner... I should have stayed in my lane."

She turns her palm up running her finger over the ring.

"I'm sure she hates me," Juni says, her voice strained.

"No, she's not like that," she says shaking her head. "But I did hurt her."

Her head drops. "I don't know if I can ever fix that."

Juniper goes quiet, hugging her legs to her chest, chin resting on her knees. She turned her head after a moment, looking back to the camera.

"Tayo called," she whispers. "He's being supportive. But he would be. He's getting what he wants and he didn't have to lift a finger."

Juni raises her head trying to stem the flow of tears.

"Here I am talking to myself, as if it will solve anything."

She stares back into the fire with a creased brow.

"I've talked enough, and it didn't amount to much.

Juni inhales a stuttering breath.

"Keep moving Juni, or you'll drown... Just. Keep. Moving."

She grabs the device, making the view twist wildly.

The view captures her tearful face and bloodshot purple eyes briefly before the screen goes dark.

ɔ THIRTY-NINE ɕ

Iris handed me some tea with a sombre expression.

"You look like you've been hit by a truck," she said.

"Just about," I grumbled. My chest as tight as in Juni's room. The persistence of the feeling had numbed me.

She sat down with her own tea across from me. She stared at me over her cup. Afternoon sun bathed her living room in golds and oranges.

"What happened?" she asked.

I blew on my tea, shrugging.

"I couldn't do it... I couldn't lie in a cold bed, knowing she's in bed with Tayo and his perfectly engineered fucking cheekbones."

Iris nodded.

"You knew this was coming," Iris said casually.

I put my tea down, then leaned back, closing my eyes. I hadn't shed a tear since I left Juni's place. But they were always hovering right under the surface. I wanted to shout, to fight.

To try again.

"I guess... I had hoped to be wrong."

Iris leaned over, putting a hand on my knee.

"Hey, you called my bullshit on Earth early on. You may be many things, my friend, but you're seldom wrong."

She was smiling, trying to cheer me up.

I pressed my hands into my lap.

"I miss her, Iris."

Her face dropped. Her large brown eyes softening.

"I know hon... I know."

My hand squeezed hers gently.

I nodded, glad for Iris. Glad that she came back. Without her I would be spiralling. Not for the first time in my life, Iris was my anchor.

"Did I fuck up, Iris?" I asked, whispering. As if saying it out loud will be admitting I did.

Iris shook her head, her hair flowing behind the motion.

"You didn't fuck up, Clara," she said firm. "You stood up for yourself."

She patted my hand, then sat up straight.

"I'm proud of you," she said.

I brushed my hair back with my hands. It was all but down to my shoulders.

"What do I do now," I said with a shuddering voice.

"You eat something," she said. "You take a shower. You have a messy cry. Then tomorrow you keep going."

I choked back a tear.

"Yeah. Ok. I can do that."

"And you'll eat? Promise?"

I nodded.

"And I'll be here. Anytime," she said.

I left Iris's place. I walked for a while, not ready to go home. The Tharaks glided down the early evening streets as they began to empty. Streetlights bathed everything in iced blues.

I had only gone a few blocks, lost inside my head.

Then, footsteps behind me. Each step, in tandem with my own.

My heart sped up.

Not again. It can't be him.

I clenched my fists.

The footfalls behind me stopped. I froze too.

Waiting for him to say my name.

For him to call me *Sing* again.

To feel his breath and smell upholstery and fireworks.

I waited for Ramsey, feeling each heartbeat.

Then a jingling. Small pieces of metal. I could see them imbedded in flesh in my head.

Then scratching—something sharp against metal, making my arm ache from memory.

I looked over my shoulder slowly.

It was a man, a bit older than me. He was having some trouble unlocking his door.

Relief washed over me like a gale. I lost balance for a moment, catching myself against the wall.

Ramsey was gone. And I had no tears to shed for him.

The man glanced up. "You ok, lady?"

I put up a hand. "I'll be ok, thanks."

I took a long breath, then pushed off to find a cab, wondering if I *would* be ok.

It was too soon to tell.

ↄ FOURTY Ↄ

I slunk into the back room. The robotic arms were busier than ever, prodding and poking Corrin's body with sparks. The cool of the under chamber was a relief from the heat of the day.

"Clara. I was not expecting you," Corrin chimed.

"Really?"

"No, I was merely being polite. You cut your hair."

I ran my hand through my short, chopped hair.

"Yeah, it was time," I said with a sour tone.

I started fidgeting with tools, mostly getting in the way of the arms. Corrin's head tracked me all the while. After the third time I narrowly missed getting welded, Corrin held up a hand. The arms moved away. He sat up, making me jump back.

"Oh shit. You're making progress," I exclaimed.

He looked down at himself.

"Yes," he said simply.

His head tilted. "You seem distracted today, Clara."

The screwdriver dropped from my hand. I pushed it away with a finger.

"I'm... recalibrating, Corrin," I said.

He laughed, almost replicating a real boy. The skeletal frame shook as he did, causing the metal to clink against the table.

He noticed I wasn't laughing and stopped.

"Apologies," he almost whispered. "That was inappropriate."

"That's ok, Corrin. It's not a big deal..."

I sighed stepping back. My back touched the bio-organic wall as I leaned. I had gotten used to the wet feeling, on the actually dry walls.

"The Wedding," he said. "It's tonight, correct."

"Ha," I scoffed, throwing my hands up. "Like you could miss it. It's on every fucking news feed on Lyra."

Corrin's eyes blinked rapidly.

"You were not exaggerating this time," he said. It sounded suspiciously like shock.

He tapped his knee in a far too human motion.

"I am sorry, Clara."

"Thanks Corrin," I smiled as warm as I could muster.

"I admit, to being surprised that you never told Lady Shao about me."

I looked up at him shocked.

"Yeah, well I said I wouldn't."

"And yet," he said, raising a single finger. "I calculated an eighty five percent chance that you would tell her anyway."

"Mhm," I hummed sarcastically. "Maybe Juni and I weren't as close as you thought."

He tilted his head in what could only be a condescending look.

"Clara, that's not true. We both know that."

I laughed sarcastically.

"You and Iris should start a comedy club."

I left Corrin and the monolith, not sure that I helped. He would be walking soon, all grown up.

The cab's radio blared on about marriage of Lord Tayo Langley and Lady Juniper Shao. I rolled my eyes. Yet, my stomach felt hollow.

The streets were covered in posters and decoration for the day. It felt as if Vala was celebrating my heartbreak.

It was late afternoon when I got home. The house was far too quiet. The wedding would just be starting. I tried convincing myself not to turn on the television...

ↄ FOURTY-ONE ɕ

I turned on the television, knowing full well it was a bad idea.

Each channel showed the same view. The wedding was on every screen on Lyra. I caught it as Juni walked down the aisle, her father's arm around hers. He smiled wide, mouth curled politely.

She was walking light. A radiant vision my heart still beat for.

She reached the bower, taking Tayo's hand. My stomach rolled.

I was angry.

I was sad.

I was sorry it had happened like this.

Tayo grinned as if he had won a war, bowing slightly to her as she curtsied.

The view was too distant to see her eyes. It was just as well, as I may not have survived the look in them.

They exchanged rings and they exchanged the words.

Juniper's tears rolled. She looked overwhelmed with joy.

But her eyes stared straight through Tayo. She reached for hair to pull over her face, but it was up in a ridiculous bun she must have hated.

"I do," she said to raucous applause.

I saw her leg buckle for a second. I shed a tear for us both.

The official wrapped their wrists together. Each wrap tying her to a life she never wanted.

She leaned forward. The line of her jaw tightened. Tayo's lips drew close.

I turned the TV off. My palms aching as my nails dug into them.

I turned, stalking through the house. I needed to walk, to move, to do... something.

I screamed, slamming my fist into a cupboard, cracking in the wood.

Goose hissed from the other room.

"Ow, fuck," I cried as my hand ignited with fire.

I collapsed on my bed, the fire doused with the pain in my hand.

My mind ran rabid as Goose curled up next to my pillow whining softly.

I wondered if they would go to Juni's place after the wedding.

If they would be in her room, with a fire casting it in deep shadows.

The images invaded my thoughts.

Juni undressing for him.

In a bed I'd never feel again.

A lingering kiss I'd never get back.

I saw it all, burning in my mind with vivid, jealous detail.

I told myself it didn't matter.

I told myself we were over.

I told myself many lies.

But my bed smelled of Camellias and spring.

My stomach twisted and rolled.

I stood clutching my stomach, breathing fast as I paced.

It all came out before I made it to the sink. Acid, spit, food, and everything else I had swallowed down with the tears.

I slid down the wall, hands shaking, and throat burning.

The tears came finally. Sharp salty drops of denial spilling out, as I cried with the taste of bile in my mouth.

There was nothing left of her for me.

No note.

No sign.

No trace but her scent and a drycleaned blue dress.

She had vanished from my life with silence, as if she always knew it would end like that.

I stared at a wall for a long time, leaning against the hard wall on the cold floor.

Until my knees ached and the sweat and sick dried on my clothes.

I reached for my comm, briefly hesitating. I tapped the contact.

She picked up after two rings.

"Clara," Iris said, as if she expected the call.

"Iris. I need you... please," I croaked.

"Of course. Come over," she said, without hesitation.

"Oh, god, Clara," Iris said as she guided me inside. "Your hand."

I didn't feel it. I wandered through her house like a ghost from her past, having given up drying my tears.

Iris spoke softly offering comfort, but she couldn't help. But I knew she would be there. No matter what.

I found myself laying in Iris's spare room. She was in the kitchen making food I didn't want. A half-empty glass sat on the bedside table, drops rolling down it in the humid evening air.

My comm screen washed the room in blue like the beam used to.

I typed on my comm...

(**Foxy Lady <3**)

"Congratulations..." No, that's passive aggressive.

I sniffed.

"I hope you are happy..." Gods, no.

My air puffed out, but I held it in.

"I miss you."

I deleted that too, darkening the screen with a whimper.

"I hope you find your happiness, Juni," I whispered to the dark room.

Iris forced me to eat, before I dropped down to the bed again.

I drifted off thinking about red bow smiles and silver-white waves.

I woke to Iris across from me tucked into a separate spare bed. A small light falling on her book, casting her in a ghostly glow highlighting her curves.

She always was beautiful.

"Iris," I said through the quiet.

She closed her book, turning her head to me.

"Hi."

"Do you think if things were different," I asked, "we could have been... more?"

She chuckled. "I do prefer men, Clara."

"One man," I corrected, regretting it.

She drew a sharp breath. "Yes. That was enough."

"You like me too, right?" I asked sheepishly.

"No, Clara," she said. "I love you."

"You're my best friend," she clarified.

There was a moment of silence. My heart tightened.

"I... Thank you, Iris," I said finally.

I tucked my head into the pillow, trying to hide from my own emotions. My shoulders shook as I failed again.

There was a creak of the mattress as heat slipped under the covers with me. There was much more skin than I expected. She had always preferred comfort over fabric.

She held me so tightly.

"I'm here," she whispered. "Whenever you need me."

She planted a small kiss on my temple. Her curves pressed against me – soft and comfortable. My body responded spontaneously, tensing from my stomach to thighs. It remembered how much comfort could be found in another woman's skin or lips.

In the dim room, our faces hovered close together. We shared breath like lovers, but with heavier hearts. Iris's breathing was unsteady, coming in fits. Her own tears were far from dry for the love she lost.

The edges of our lips brushed together for a single fleeting second.

I dipped my head, wrapping Iris in a hug, tucking my head under her chin, resting between her shoulders.

Iris drew in a sharp breath, then let it out trembling.

I listened to the steady rhythm in her chest.

She shuddered, letting out her own sorrow as she lay her cheek on my head.

"I'm such a fuckup," I whispered into her hair.

My tears fell onto her olive skin. I could feel the goosebumps against my cheek.

"You're not a fuckup, Clara," my best friend said as she stroked my hair. "Not to me. Never."

Then a moment later. "You've grown and it shows. You did the right thing."

"Winning sucks," I said.

"Sometimes it does, yes."

I placed my foot against hers to be closer.

"I'm sorry," I said. "I know you're still hurting too."

"Don't be. I'm right here with you," she whispered. "But I appreciate it."

"I miss her so much," I squeaked.

"I know. Trust me, I know."

We held each other, as we emptied our feelings of the past.

I wished we could both get back what we had lost.

That Iris could have everything she dreamed of.

The next morning, I woke up alone in the spare bed. The morning light grey in the room. Iris was up already, staring out of the lounge window. Her gaze not seeing anything Lyra had on offer. She held a cup of black coffee permeating the entire room with its dark smell.

"Morning, Iris," I said, voice measured.

Morning, you," she replied gently.

"Next time I come over, please wear some more clothes," I bit, playfully.

She scoffed. "Aten never complained."

"Boys," I chuckled, hugging myself tight.

Iris grinned at me.

"Seriously though, Iris. I am sorry about last night," I said earnestly.

She tilted her head, brow furrowed.

"I mean..." I continued. "It was-"

"It was nice," she interrupted, "necessary even."

I nodded with a makeshift smile.

"Don't be so mortified, Clara. We both needed a bit of a release," she said wrapping her little finger around mine with a tender squeeze. I returned the affection with gratitude.

I could feel my resolve grow guided by Iris's strength.

"Where to now?" she asked.

I had been asking myself that question the whole night. Long after Iris drifted off still clutching me like a child.

I was not satisfied with rolling over.

"I'm going to work... to see Juni," I said, as if it was any other Monday.

Iris's head rocked back. "Wha... what are you going to do?"

"I'm going to make things complicated."

• JUNIPER 05 •

They tie a ribbon around my hand, chaining me to my own future.

Tayo smiles. I've never seen him so happy. The ache for not wanting him back flickers, but is drowned quickly.

None of it matters.

I feel his lips on mine and I smile.

Tayo would be good to me, that I knew at least. In time...

But it won't be the same.

I flash my teeth.

Speeches are made around me about all the things they're sure I will do, none of which I remember agreeing to.

I clink my glass.

No champagne could keep up with a flat beer on a lazy Sunday, with golden hair looking at you as if nothing else existed in the world.

I dance steps I learned as a child, my dad holding my hand so gently.

But it's not music that plays on beaches in the shade of a surfboard.

The cake is beautiful. My father went all out. I don't doubt he did it to make me happy. He hugged me so tight, I could almost look him in the eye after.

We waved and smiled for the cameras as we got into the car. No honeymoon. The wheel must keep turning.

I'll be taken care of in ways most could only dream of.

All it cost was my heart.

I keep looking out as we are driven home. I kept looking for her out of the window.

But what would I even say when I saw her.

The car pulls up to the door.

I close my eyes taking one big breath.

Then I go to give my body away for privilege.

The door clicks behind me as Tayo closes it.

"What a night," he said blandly.

"It was beautiful," I admit.

He walks over to a champagne holder.

"Drink?" he asks.

I shake my head.

"Let's just... let's do what we came to do, alright?"

He abandons the bottle, strolling over to me. His hands fall on my arms. I shrug them off, turning my back to him. My corset laces are out of reach.

"Please? I can't unlace them myself," I tell him.

Tayo's voice sounds strained. "Ok."

He unlaces me and my breath comes back, shoulders sagging with the slight relief.

I hold the underdress up with one arm as the corset falls away. Reaching back, I free my hair and it spills out in a tangle. The skirt is next, as I step it off thoughtlessly.

I sigh, steadying my own heart.

"I'm ready," I lied.

I could see his shirt and belt on the floor, but I couldn't look up at him.

His pants fell around his ankles.

I held my breath pushing the tears down.

Then I let the gown slip down my skin onto the ground, covering only my feet. Clenching my fists, I resisted covering up.

"Fuck," Tayo said. His voice was... cracking?

I looked up. He was standing there in his boxers, face red. His head was twisted away, while his hands covered the front of his boxers.

His eyes were closed.

"Tayo, what are you doing?" I asked confused.

He huffs, letting his shoulders drop. He fumbled the bed, pulling off a sheet and a few pillows.

"You know..." he said, moving closer in small steps, until he felt sure that the sheet covered me.

"I thought I wanted this," he admits as I took the sheet from him, clutching it to my chest.

"But... it feels all wrong," he said turning, to face away from me.

"I don't get it, Tayo," I said, wrapping it around myself.

"Well," he said, smiling over his shoulder. "You practically my sister, so gross. Right?"

My legs quit on me, and I sank to the floor, wrapped in the cover as I would on cold nights.

Tayo spun around and stepped over.

"Wow," he cried. "Careful."

He held my arm gently helping me up.

The dam burst.

I pressed my face to him as the tears erupted.

He hugged me tight, smelling like fresh rain.

"I do love you, Juni," he whispered.

"I know," I whimpered. "I love you too."

His chest heaved a laugh. "Liar," he said.

I laughed through the tears. Relief cutting through the uncertainty.

"I do though," I said, pressing my forehead to his chest.

"Yeah, I know," he sniffed. "You big baby."

Tayo leaned down to catch my eye, smiling.

"But I can't compete with a feisty blonde, can I."

I punched his arm lightly.

"No," I said. "But it's close."

I knew exactly what to say when I saw her again.

This time I would tell her.

I would say, yes.

ↄ FOURTY-TWO ɕ

I knew Juni wouldn't be in on the Monday after the wedding. Gods only knew what constituted a honeymoon for a couple like that. It made my stomach sour, but that was the deal I had made peace with. I went to check on Corrin to keep my mind occupied. My hands were in my pockets as I slinked up to his chamber. The bizarre alien construct that held Earth's most advanced AI no longer made my skin crawl. It was part of the scenery at that point. No more odd than spider-cats or Aten's face on a billboard.

The robotic arms lay on the ground in pieces—discarded junk. Corrin was working on his legs with his own hands, fingers sparking as he welded intricate pieces to the outer shell.

I stood leaning against the doorway.

"Need some help?" I asked casually.

"I could actually use a hand," he said not looking up.

"You know, if I can't scare you, then you'll never pass for human."

Corrin looked at me, the *bluetech* face twisting.

"Why would I want to pretend to be a meatbag?" he said flatly.

I stood straight, my skin crawling again.

He stared at me blankly for a while, then he bent the face into a smile.

I relaxed, flipping him off. "I'll never get used to your jokes, Corrin."

He chuckled warm and real.

His internals became clearer as I moved closer. The body was filled with hundreds of tiny, impossibly intricate moving parts. Corrin put his hand out to me.

"Please could you help me up?" he asked. It sounded like excitement in his voice.

I held his hand as he dropped off of the table. He landed with wobble then stabilised.

"I should take photos of your first steps," I joked half-heartedly.

Corrin put his arms out taking a few tentative steps.

"Look at you go!"

He put his hands up, celebrating. I clapped joining in his celebration.

Turning he put his arms out to the sides.

"Hit me," he said.

I cocked my head. "Um, no," I said.

"I want to test stability. You will not damage the structure I promise."

My shoulders dropped. Hitting something might feel good.

I scooped up a decent piece of the discarded arm from the ground.

"Ok, Corrin. But I warned-"

The blue glow in the chamber dimmed, blinked, then stabilised.

"The fuck?"

"I do not know," Corrin admitted. "But something is not right."

I looked to the door, but nothing happened. Corrin laid his palm to the wall, his eyes flickering.

"Clara," he said, voice urgent. "Get back to the workshop."

"What is it?"

"I am not sure, but for your safety, please go."

"What about you?"

"I am a machine. I will be fine."

I nodded. Then looking down at the length of tech in my hand, I tightened my grip.

"You're not just a machine, Corrin. You're my friend. So be safe," I said to him, then left.

I knew the route well enough, and made quick work of the distance.

Arriving at the workshop, I expected the worst. The building was quiet. Even the ubiquitous hum seemed muted.

"Damn it, Corrin," I groaned, dropping the arm length on a table. I leaned against the desk, catching my breath.

That's when I heard the beating steps from outside, followed by a gravely grind. I tensed up reaching for the bar again.

Juni popped in the door.

"Clara!" she said, breathing hard.

I froze. She was dressed in a t-shirt and denims, and she was still the most beautiful woman I had ever seen.

"Juni," I said as if she was a dream.

She smiled with her perfect red bow. My body burned to go to her, but I gripped the edge of the desk.

"You weren't home last night," she said, as if the meeting was planned.

"Then I got an alert for odd movement," she continued, her smile faltering. "I knew you would be here, so I ran."

Corrin came to mind. He was getting sloppy.

"I was... by Iris last night," I explained. "Wait, why were you at my place?" I asked once the information sunk in.

Her smile returned as she took a step to me.

A high-pitched whine filled the air. Juni pressed her hands to her sensitive ears. The lights sputtered, crackling.

Juni stuck her hand out, reaching to me.

"I have people coming. Come with me, Clara," she shouted.

I reached for her.

The whine increased, then the world exploded.

My ears rang—dust filling the room blocking my view of the door. The roof had collapsed, or something fell through it. The smell of rot and ozone filled the air. Small blue lights shone inside the cloud.

"Clara," a voice called from the haze. It sounded like a glass being filled to overflowing.

"No. No. It can't be."

The thing in the dust dragged itself forward.

It was Ramsey.

Or whatever was left of him.

His body was covered in so much tech he was barely a man. Each limb had bloated and bruised, seemingly held together by pieces of *bluetech*.

"Shao and Sing – Been waiting. You two together," Ramsey hissed.

He grinned at me, purple eyes glowing in the dust like lamps.

"Juni, run!" I cried.

"No!" he screamed like steel sheering.

"Ramsey," I said, pulling his attention. "You're sick. Let me help you ok, Cutter."

At the mention of his name the light on his body flashed brighter.

"Died, " he hissed. "So cold. Everything burning."

"We can get you help," I pleaded.

"You killed me!" he roared.

My heart throbbed against my ribs—my knees threatening to buckle.

Killed...

This thing wasn't Ramsey anymore. My mind flashed back to the bluetech frame, dragging poor Harry's corpse around.

"What are you? Maybe I can help anyway!"

"Poison. Your words. Lies."

He grabbed a shard from my 'art project' gripping it hard enough to distort the shale metal.

I realised with chilling certainty that I was in danger.

I realised I was about to die.

"Your fault," he purred, then rushed toward me.

His motions were fluid despite his grotesque size – too fast. I willed myself to move, to get out of the way. The tech in his hand hums unnaturally.

I see the shard glint. The murder in his eyes. I hold my breath bracing.

And then she's there.

Juniper.

One moment she's by the door, the next she's between us. A blur of pale silk skin and silver white curls.

She's fast, but Ramsey was already swinging low.

The shard drives into her with a wet, awful sound.

She cries out, but there's fluid in her voice.

Her body collides hard with mine. She drops too fast for me to catch her.

I stand stunned, my gears still spinning. Ramsey's arm is bent at an odd angle.

He cries out with static.

"Broke my arm Shao! Kill you!"

Ramsey's tech, running every inch of his body dims. He stumbles.

"I can... slow him... down," Corrin's voice echoes. "Get away!"

My foot shifts.

My hand closes around the bar.

I stop pulling my punches.

I swing with every ounce of force I can muster.

The first smash folds his jaw sideways. His teeth scattering across the floor.

He gargles, blood foaming on his lips.

The second hit drops him flat, jerking randomly.

I hear my own voice screaming.

The third strike is just noise and red spray.

The fourth snaps the metal bar against a wet smear.

I am still standing over him when the silence settles. My breathing loud in my ears, heartbeat hammering in my skull.

My arms and face run with crimson.

The last taste of Ramsey in my mouth is iron and nausea.

Juni cries out snapping me back. She lies on the hard concrete floor, her hand clamped over the wound. Her eyes are wide with shock, pain, and messy tears. Blood pours out from between her fingers.

Juni cries weakly, gasping for air. Her mouth painted with rose red down her chin.

Her eyes on mine—wild and scared.

Beside her is the shard, humming faintly as blood pools around it.

I drop the bar rushing to her, stepping over what's left of Ramsey without looking back.

I apply pressure, but the colour drains from Juni's lips fast.

She claws at my shirt desperately.

I shush her. "Lay still. I'm here," I say.

"Clara," she cries, shivering.

"Don't leave me, Fox," I beg through tears. "Just stay awake."

"Fucking Help!" I scream.

Juni barely moves under my hands.

"Help me, please Gods!" I shriek, my voice breaking.

The blood stopped bubbling out by the time help arrived.

Juni wasn't crying anymore.

ↄ FOURTY-THREE ϲ

Time slowed and blurred all at once. People rushing, voices loud behind the ringing in my ears. I get shoved aside. A medic loses his lunch when he sees what's left of Ramsey. The stink of *bluerot* and iron fills the room. I keep my hands up, dripping with blood.

My breaths ragged as they assess Juni.

I call her name, my voice hoarse and shaking.

Someone shines a light in my eyes. I splatter blood on them as I explain what happened, triggering a fresh wave of grief.

"Stasis was active," the medic says as if it's a miracle. I'm hopeful that it means good news. They carry my love out of the door leaving her blood behind in a pool. Too much of it.

I get shoved against a wall coughing. My hands are cuffed and I'm dragged away, trying to explain.

Outside the light hits my eyes like a welding torch. Then I'm in a car being carted off as the ambulance leaves down a different road. I kick the seat demanding to know what happened to Juni.

Nobody talks to me.

I'm shoved into a dim cell that smells of bleach.

I wash death and violence off of my hands. Then I curl up on the hard bench letting the tears keep me company in the cold.

Time passed like a grey wash. No matter how much I asked, nobody told me if Juni is even alive.

Around the second day a miserable man with thinning hair walked into my cell.

"Clara Nadia Sing?" he read from a paper.

I nodded. "That's me," I whispered. "Is Juniper alright?"

He shrugged as if I asked if it was raining, and continued to read the page.

"So what is your affiliation to the Zeroes?" he asked.

"What's a Zero?"

To which he scowls at me.

He continued regardless.

"What's your relationship with Juniper Shao?"

"I'm her... her colleague."

He leaned in, eyes narrowed.

"You think I'm stupid? You and Lady Shao were involved in that alley incident a while back, were you not?"

I got up, but immediately he pushed me back to the bench.

"I'll tase you, lady," he warned.

"Please tell me what happened to Juni, and I'll tell you anything."

"Mmm," he groaned. "The body we found. Was that Ramsey Cutter?"

"It *was*," I huffed.

Without another word he turned to leave the cell. I reached out grabbing his sleeve.

"Please?" I begged. "Is Juniper alive."

"If she is," he grumbled wrenching his sleeve free. "Then it's no thanks to you."

The cell slammed shut.

I started tracking the days by the guard rotations. A week into my arrest the miserable man came to grill me again.

"Is Juni alright?" I asked him, and I was ignored.

I refused to talk to him.

"We can be persuasive," he threatened.

But I had it with being threatened.

I balled my fists. "You know what happened to the last guy who threatened me?" I growled.

He took a step back, adjusting his collar, then left swiftly.

Another day passed before an officer walked in merrily.

"You're free to go," he said, smiling.

I stood, body protesting.

Impatience made my body vibrate as I collected my belongings.

As soon as my feet touched the sidewalk I slid out my comm.

(Foxy Lady <3)...

No answer. Of course.

I didn't have Tayo's number, so I took a cab to the Shaos.

They refused me entry as if I was a burglar. The same treatment from the Langley estate too.

I called every hospital I could find, getting nothing but bureaucratic nonsense. Even the news was stumm about the attack.

I stood with my back to a wall, closing my eyes in thought.

A hum and buzz drew me back as a large car pulled up and settled near me.

The door swung open, the car rocking as the passenger exited.

He was a mountain of a man, with a topknot and a smile made of teeth like Mahjong tiles. He wore a bespoke tailored black suit.

I stood straight, ready to bolt, looking around for police.

It was the giant that I had seen speaking to Ramsey before the alleyway.

"Miss Sing," he purred in a deep baritone.

"I don't want any, thank you," I growled.

He laughed obnoxiously, pulling a hand out from his pocket gesturing to the open door.

"Care for a lift, doctor? I don't bite," he said. Which was ironic because he looked as if he did.

"And you are?" I asked, trying to keep my nerves in check.

He waggled a finger at me. "I am... not interested in making enemies."

The massive man took a step back. "Please. I assure you, I don't extend this courtesy to my rivals."

That sent a chill down my spine. Running away was the obvious choice.

"Why?" I asked, trying to cover as much ground as possible.

The man sighed, his shoulders dropping. His hand went back into his pocket as he leaned back against the car.

"Our colleague went off script doctor. We understand that you were the last to see him."

My blood boiled at the very mention.

"You mean Ramsey," I grumbled. "Haven't seen him since we broke up."

"Is that a fact," he smiled with his slab teeth.

"Why would I see him after?" I asked, keeping eye contact.

He laughed, shaking the entire car, then tapped his nose.

"You're tougher than you look, Clara."

"Are you here to threaten me?"

It was bravado. I had to clench my fists to stop them from shaking.

His cheerful demeanour faded.

"Look," he said, "is Ramsey still alive?"

I took a moment. What was the harm in admitting that monster was gone.

"No," I said, barely above the street noise.

"Mmm," he growled. "Pity. He stole a lot of valuable equipment."

The suited man pushed off from the car, placing one foot inside.

"I would have liked to recover it, but such is life."

"So what now?" I asked. "Are you going to make me an offer?"

He chuckled as if clearing his throat.

"I have no idea what you mean, doctor. I was never even here."

With that he settled back into the car rocking it like a boat.

It pulled away leaving me be on the sidewalk, sun glinting off the road.

"This fucking day needs to end," I spat, then made my way to my house.

It felt like admitting defeat.

Like a retreat.

I took yet another cab ride to nothing. I dreaded walking into my house. I had left Goose inside nearly two weeks before. The hollow in my chest couldn't sink deeper.

I took a deep breath, bracing myself as I closed the cab door. I shuffled towards my door.

A small cough startled me.

Goose came bounding out of the shadow. I fell to the pavement scooping the little horror up, my cheeks wet.

"Goosey!" I cooed. "How did you get out?"

The joy was short lived. As grateful as I was that Goose was fine, it meant someone was in my house.

I snuck up to the door, Goose sticking close to my heels like a shadow.

Sure enough my door was open a crack. I peeked in, but the main room was empty and dark.

Ducking in, I headed straight to my bed, pulling my pipe from under my pillow.

I tiptoed to the kitchen.

Iris rounded the corner, then yelped.

"Clara," she said shocked. "Thank god you're ok."

The pipe clattered to the ground. I rushed to her, wrapping my arms around her neck.

"Iris," I choked. "Thank you for taking care of my Goose."

She hugged me tight.

"I came to visit.You were gone so long, what happened?"

What was there to say to her?

"I think..." I tried to say. The words didn't come.

I fell back against my wall, my hands rattling my cigarettes out of my pocket. I slid down, hanging one from my lips—unlit.

"I think Juni is... I think she's dead," I said as if complaining about work.

Iris crouched down beside me, hugging herself.

"Clara... don't fuck around," she said seriously. There was an edge of terror to her tone.

I looked her in the eye, then offered her a trembling smoke from the box. She slipped it out, then settled against the opposite wall.

Orange light flickered and curls of smoke floated up to the yellow ceiling. Iris was against the wall, her knees up to her chest. I ashed on the ground, blowing a cloud up to join Iris's.

She huffed. "I haven't smoked since Earth... Since Aten left."

Her voice was measured, almost frigid.

Aten.

The name bubbled up fondness, but that old pain of love lost had faded. My heart no longer beat for him.

I groaned letting my head fall back on the bed. I stroked Goose's fuzz as he lay splayed over my lap.

Silence hung.

Iris was the first to break it.

"If only Corrin was here. They would be able to help."

My head shot up.

"Corrin."

Iris looked at me, her eyebrow raised.

I knew exactly what to do next.

"It's nothing," I said, waving at the air.

It was everything.

It was a chance.

ↄ FOURTY-FOUR ɕ

I walked straight past the workshop the following day. Yellow tape was stretched across the door as if that could contain the horror of what happened in that room.

I didn't look in as I went by. I could see the red stains in my head. Where one fear ended and the other began.

I navigated the route to Corrin without guidance.

Inside his chamber Corrin sat staring intently at his hand.

"Boo," I said dryly.

His shoulders jerked.

"Clara," he said.

I wondered if he was genuinely startled due to his new untethered nature or if he had simulated that after our last talk.

"One moment," he said, already looking back at his hand.

The small machinery inside whirred to life. The limb began bubbling as a thick substance oozed out and smoothed around the fingers and palm.

He wiggled his fingers with perfect skin and nails wrapped around them.

"Fuck me, I'm glad you're on my side, Corrin. That shit is terrifying."

His mechanical eyebrows lifted.

"I can see how it would be," he said, without a trace of irony.

He placed the human looking hand on a knee as he turned.

"How can I help?" he asked, getting to the point.

"Who says I want something?" I stalled.

He shrugged. "Perhaps I was wrong," he said. "I am the pinnacle of human engineered AI after all."

"And so modest," I prodded, but I couldn't meet his eyes.

"After...," I said, pointing vaguely up.

"The attack?" he said, blunt as always.

"I can't find Juni."

"I see," he mused.

He hoicked himself off of the table landing gingerly. His steps to the wall were confident and solid. The body working perfectly.

Corrin placed his metal palm against the wall, his eyes flickering.

His human hand cradled the mechanical one as he let go.

"I am sorry, Clara," he said, with a voice tailored for bad news.

"I cannot find her."

I let out a hard breath, covering my face.

"No news is good right?" I said, mostly to myself.

He shook his head. "I did pick up a little chatter about the Shao burial plot, but nothing definitive."

I coughed trying to stifle a cry.

"It's not proof. It's not proof, Clara," I chanted to myself.

A soft warm touch landed on my shoulder. Corrin's new hand.

"It's *not* proof, Miss Sing," he said, patting my arm.

I smiled, wiping away the tears.

"Yeah," I nodded. "It isn't."

"I'll keep looking," Corrin confirmed.

I held his hand on my shoulder, straightening up.

"Thank you, Corrin," I said, my hand trailing on the doorframe on my way. "For helping us. I know that was risky."

"Of course," he nodded deeply. "That's what friends are for, Clara."

I nodded slowly, smiling. That's what she said too. And I never told her...

"Hey, Corrin," I said, meeting his eyes. "You're a good friend."

His face rearranged itself into a smile, and for a change it calmed me.

ↄ FOURTY-FIVE ɕ

I took the rest of the week off. Or rather I didn't bother going in. There was no point with the workshop closed. An oppressive heat had settled on Vala. The road shimmered outside my open door. Goose was splayed out on the cement floor with his eight legs each going in a separate direction.

I lay on my bed staring at the ceiling with my arm over my eyes.

Juniper swam through my thoughts. But there had been no news. Crying myself to sleep had become my own self soothing.

I missed her. So much that I could practically smell Camellias.

There was a small knock at my door. I jumped up squinting into the light.

In the door stood Juniper Anzu Shao like a ghost, haloed by the setting sun. Her face was even paler than usual. I blinked a few times.

"Hey," she said, tugging at the hair over her face.

I bit my lip hard, expecting to wake. But she stayed in the door.

"Hi," I said, voice slipping.

My breaths sped up.

My heart joined in.

I fell from the bed scrambling to her, wrapping her in my arms. She winced, nearly losing balance.

"Oh, fuck. I'm sorry Juni," I said, trying to pull back.

But she wouldn't let me. She held on to me like I was falling, her head to my chest.

"It's really ok," she wheezed.

We stood sniffling wrapped together.

I looked up, spotting Tayo. He flicked a salute at me.

Thank you – I mouthed at him, gaining me a wide smile.

"I'll be at the car guys. Take your time, alright," he said subdued as he drifted away.

I took Juni's hand, guiding her in once again.

She moved stiff with her hand pressed to her stomach.

She settled on the bed, not letting go of my hand.

"I missed you, Clara," she said.

I laughed through the tears. "Yeah. I missed you too, Fox."

Her smile was soft. There were no tears.

I had practiced that moment in my head a thousand times, but spoke from my heart instead.

"Juni... I'll do it," I said confidently. "I'll be the mistress."

I rested my hand on her soft cheek.

"I'll do it smiling. As long as I have you."

Juni swallowed hard, but a dangerous smile crept onto her lips.

"Anything?" she asked, a whispered confirmation.

"Anything," I replied, squeezing her hand.

"What about marrying me?"

"I would... shut my fucking face up," I stuttered. "What?"

"What what?" she grinned, glowing.

I looked down to our laced fingers.

"Juni, please don't joke. Not about that."

She pressed my hand to her heart, catching my eyes.

"I mean it, Clara," she said. Her eyes were steady—face serious, but her lips curled with joy.

I let my head hang to a side.

"Did I miss something?"

"We have a lot to talk about," she nodded. "But we have time my love."

Heat flooded my chest.

"Careful," I warned. "You almost said it."

Juni brushed the hair from her face, then leaned in.

She kissed me. A soft but sure press of her apricots and honey lips.

Her lavender eyes looked into mine with no uncertainty in them.

"I love you, Clara."

My hand shook, even with our fingers intertwined.

No poetry or music could have ever sounded better than those four words.

I blinked the tears away, their purpose forgotten.

"You too," I replied, awkwardly. "Kinda a lot."

She slapped my knee lightly, not breaking eye contact.

I drew a deep breath, my smile wider and wider.

"I mean it Juniper," I said. "I love you."

The words felt like chains breaking.

She nodded satisfied.

"You're sexier when you're not being tough," she jabbed.

My face grew hot, a snort-laugh escaping me.

She leaned in again, nose tip against mine.

"Mhm," she purred. "Sexy."

She laughed.

I fell in love with her all over, each time she did.

She clenched her teeth over the laugh, holding her stomach.

I placed my hand on hers.

"I'm sorry, Juni," I said. "It was all my fault."

"I blame only Ramsey, Clara," she said, with an edge of anger.

My finger ran over her leg along the seam of her pants.

"I thought you were gone," I admitted.

She huffed. "It was a near thing apparently."

Juniper lifted her shirt. There was an angry line across her lower stomach. Stitches still ran its length.

"I may as well be dead," she said, her eyes shimmering.

"I'm nothing now...."

"Juni," I scolded.

"Sorry. I just feel..." she looked away.

I brushed her cheek, forcing a smile.

"Juni," I whispered. "You are everything to me."

She laid back, curling up.

"I was so scared," she said, her voice cracking.

"I know. But you're here now," I reassured her, keeping a hand on her arm, stroking gently. "You're safe."

She nuzzled into the pillow.

"Can I stay with you tonight?" she asked. "Please."

"I'd like that. Kinda a lot," I said winking at her.

I leaned down, kissing her brow.

"Let me go chase off the boys following you," I said dryly.

She chuckled, still holding her stomach.

"Sorry, Clara," she said into the covers.

"It's nothing," I replied, patting her. "You've stayed here before."

She shook her head—her hair turning to waves.

"I mean for hurting you."

I closed my eyes, taking a long breath.

"I'm sorry too," I murmured. "I knew the stakes. I should have been prepared."

She waved off my words, scrunching her nose.

"Go chase the boy away," she said. "I need to kiss you a lot."

"You're the boss," I said, then left her there hesitantly.

Tayo was leaning against the car, staring at the stars.

I joined him, lighting a smoke. The strand of smoke drifted from my hand as I exhaled a cloud.

He sighed, but was otherwise quiet. I gave him a sidelong glance. His eyes flicked to me briefly.

"She can't have kids now, you know," he said. It sounded like an accusation. "She always wanted kids."

"So, what? Now she's disposable?" I grumbled.

Tayo's eyes widened—head turned to me.

"Juni means everything to me," he defended.

I blew out a long stream of smoke.

"Is that why you forced her to marry..." I bit. "And worse."

He let out a grim chuckle.

"Nothing... worse, happened."

"She fought you, did she?" I nodded.

"I couldn't go through with it."

My back straightened. "Still married her, didn't you."

He huffed. "You're determined to dislike me, aren't you?"

My head sank down. I dropped the cigarette, then stomped out the ember.

"I don't dislike you, Tayo. I'm just..." I blew out the smoke.

He tapped his toe to the ground, then leaned back again.

"Yeah..." he said softly. "...Yeah."

We looked up at the stars. I wondered which one was Sol. I wondered what it looked like, with the ring around it that used to be earth. Like Juni's ring, when I held her hands...

I looked up at Tayo, in shock.

"Juni wasn't wearing the ring," I said, finally seeing Tayo.

His eyes were red—staring past the sky.

"Yeah. I had it annulled," he said. "She left to tell you. The night of that creature..."

His face turned dark. I could hear his knuckles crack.

"Ramsey," I said. A shiver rode up my spine.

Tayo spun, growling. He punched the car door, buckling the metal.

"Motherfucker!" he roared.

I leapt back, fist balling instinctively.

"Feel better?" I laughed, catching my breath.

Tayo shook his hand, grimacing. "A little."

He looked at me nursing his hand.

"Then..." he says, calming.

"Then some blonde beats his head in, for touching her," he grumbled.

"So..." he continued. "I say she's the one that should be keeping Juni safe. Clara," he said, grinning at me.

"I will," I said, sharing his smile. "I promise."

He looked to the car then me.

"I'm going to go put ice on this," he said, gesturing with his damaged hand.

He left, and I was actually sad he did.

I returned to my love, with a better outlook.

I clicked the door closed with my hips, standing against it. Juniper was lying peaceful on the bed. Her eyes were closed. Red lips stood out from her snowy skin.

I sauntered over, putting my weight down on my arms.

My lips drifted to hers.

Her hands came to my face with her summer heat.

I kissed her for a breath and more.

"I hear all the prettiest single girls hang out here," I whispered.

She smiled without opening her eyes.

"I couldn't wait to tell you that night."

Each word brushed against my lips.

I held her lips but shed my shirt. I helped her out of her own clothing. Breathless I ended up with her smooth skin against mine. The room was dark besides for the faded blue light that snuck through the blinds. My mouth traced her ribs, as she squirmed under me. I ran my lips down to her belly button, placing a soft kiss. My hand slipped up her hip, thumb pausing at the stitches.

I looked at the triangular cut in her belly.

My mind saw the blood flowing from it. Her hands pressed against it as she called for me.

"You saved me," I said.

I wrapped my arms around her, resting my cheek on her chest.

Her fingers stroked through my hair.

I closed my eyes, savouring each moment with her.

"You cut it," she said. I had almost forgotten my long hair already.

"I can grow it again," I replied, breathing her in.

"No," she said quickly. "I like it. I always have."

I placed my hand beside the scar.

She traded what she wanted for my life. I didn't know. I didn't ask.
She wanted children. It made sense.
Just like Iris...
My eyes opened as the thoughts connected.
Juni could have a child. She only needed genetic material.
My stomach tensed. I could give it back.
"Juniper," I whispered against her.
"Oh, dear. What did I do?" she said, hearing her full name.
"I can be a mom too," I said.
"Um... That makes one of us then," she said sarcastically.
I took her hand as I sat up.
"Exactly," I said grinning.
She looked at me as if I had lost my mind.
"Juni," I said. "Let's have a baby."
"Clara. There so much to unpack-"
I took her hand, kissing it softly. Her face softened.
"Juniper," I said, feeling the word. "Marry me."
It wasn't a command.
It was a request for trust.
It was a statement of the inevitable.
"Of course," she agreed without missing a beat.

◆JUNIPER 06◆

I knocked on my father's office door. Something I haven't done since I was a kid. He and I hadn't talked much, since...

But he was the first one I saw in the hospital. He held my hand and didn't leave my side.

"In," he said through the door.

I slunk into the room.

"Hi dad."

He looked up surprised to see me.

"Juniper," he said frowning. My father pushed off from his desk and made his way to me. Then he guided me to the chair at his desk.

"Sit, sit," he said, smiling, but his frown stayed.

I sat, immediately taking some of the fire out of my wound.

Takashi Shao, the most powerful man on Lyra, lifted himself onto the desk—his legs dangling like a child's.

"How's Clara?" he asked.

I couldn't help but smile. My hand tugged on my braid.

"She's ok. Shocked, but ok."

"Good," he nodded. "That prison story was nonsense."

He stared at his knees as we sat awkwardly.

His eyes flicked randomly, no doubt trying to find his own way of coping.

I put my hand on his knee. My father's eyes jumped to me.

"I'm ok, dad."

"Yes. I know," he said, patting my hand. "But if I hadn't pushed..."

I took my hand, pushing it between my knees.

"I'm sorry, Daddy."

"What?" he said, getting off the desk, crouching in front of me.

"Juniper. Please don't be sorry," he said with his hands on my shoulders. "I love you and I'm happy you're ok."

I looked up at him. He had tears in his eyes. I couldn't remember ever having seen him cry.

"Father..." I whispered. "I want to get married."

He blew out a long breath. "Alright. I'm listening."

I looked at him through my lashes. "To Clara."

He stood slowly, rubbing his face. My father walked a small circle through the office, stopping by my chair again.

"I think..." he said carefully. "That we should discuss this when you're healed."

I ran my hands down my legs nervously.

"And we want to have a baby," I mumbled.

I could almost feel his eyes on me. My jaw clenched expecting his anger and disappointment.

His hands wrapped around my arms, raising me off the chair. Then his arms wrapped around me, softly enough to not jostle my stitches. I let out a tense breath, laying my head on his shoulder.

"You don't have to do that. It doesn't matter, Jun-Jun."

I hugged him tight. Hearing that was better than any words of love.

"I want to," I said, speaking to the dad I used to see.

He took a step back, still holding my arms.

"Ok," he nodded. "But let's get creative after you recover."

"Deal," I said, curling my toes to hold in the excitement.

"Deal," he said, grinning wide.

ɔ FOURTY-FIVE ɕ

I lay on Juni's chest. Her bed afforded us more space than we needed. Her mother and father welcomed me into the family. The issue of marriage and children shelved while Juni recovered. It gave us time to breathe together like never before. The road ahead seemed clear of obstacles for the moment. She sighed softly in her sleep.

I was careful to avoid the scar. It held too many memories. I had known it would cost me to keep her. My fixation on myself meant I forgot to consider what it would cost Juni. There was nothing that would stop me from balancing that scale. I owed her my life and she owned my heart.

I wrapped around her, listening to each of her heartbeats.

Counting each moment, committing them to memory.

When we went out, we stayed stitched together by the hand. Juni glanced at me periodically, as if I would run off. I held her hand as if she might disappear.

We said those words often.

We kissed often.

We spent each night together.

Each day new and paid for.

As the days turned to weeks, Juni started regaining colour and mobility. Less than a month later, we were in the car together. Neither of us had been to Iris since what we called 'That Day'.

Juni's face was buried in my neck, whispering sugar and spice. I smiled like an idiot at each word.

"You're going to wrinkle my clothes, fox," I laughed.

"Then they'll have to come off," she murmured against my skin.

The car stopped.

Juniper scoffed. "Damn. There already?"

I kissed her. "There's always the trip home."

She got out of the car still smiling with her lip caught in her teeth.

Iris hugged us both tight with her long arms. Her house was filled with laughter and excited chats.

"A mom?" Iris laughed. "Mommy, Clara."

I rolled my eyes at her irreverence, but I loved it.

In the back of her lounge stood a canvas. Paint already outlining a new scene, in a new life, on a brand-new world.

ɘ FOURTY-SIX ɕ

There was a knock on the door.

"It's too early for a Saturday," I groaned at the interruption.

A small kiss on my head, then Juni slipped from her bed wrapped in a blanket. The door clicked open.

"Sorry, Juni," the voice at the door said. "Your father asked if you'll come down for breakfast."

I rolled over, seeing Alice in the door way. She locked eyes with me for a second. Her cheeks went red.

"I didn't realise... I'll..." Alice stuttered, smiling.

"Breakfast sounds great," I said, grinning.

The household was still getting used to me being around. But Juni's parents seemed most thrilled.

Breakfast, didn't sound as daunting as dinner for a talk.

We showered for too long, dressed, brushed, and then went to breakfast together.

The smell of bacon and freshly picked flowers met us half-way to the kitchen and ushered us in.

Takashi and Sophia were both sitting at the table. Their stoic faces tempered my mood, but couldn't put it out.

Juni walked in sitting with greetings. I walked in beside her, wearing my most polite grin. I couldn't get it down to anything less than a smile with Juni there.

Sophia stood pretending she was surprised, but her hug was real.

"Clara. Join us," she said.

"Thank you, Lady Sophia," I replied.

"Just Sophie, dear," she said, waving off the title.

I bowed my head. "I'd like to, Sophie. Thank you."

We dished and talked weather. Even a little business.

The High Governor sat quietly. When he did decide to speak, he removed his glasses, placing them down gingerly.

"You know," he started with a nostalgic air. "Kepler Syndrome wasn't always a problem. The first-generation colonists were immune."

He sipped his coffee.

"That's why," he noted. "I hired not only the best. But knew she would be naturally resistant to the disease."

"Daddy," Juni said. She had taken to calling him that. I think he enjoyed it. He did brighten every time she did.

"So it'll work?" Juni asked.

"We're confident," he nodded. Then looking to me.

"It appears you're going to be moms," he said, eyes shining.

Juni squealed hugging me too tight.

"But," he said. "There's one more matter."

The Governor rose from his chair, and stood between us.

He reached down taking a hand from each.

He looked at Juni first.

"You are brave, smart, and giving. I was an idiot to ever want to ruin that. I am sorry, Anzu," he said, never breaking eye contact with her.

She blinked quickly, with tiny nods.

Then Takashi Hyun Ren Shao the third looked to me, with affection.

"You're a tough one, Earth Girl. I was expecting you to break down my door before the wedding... But you respected us enough not to.

Then when Juni got hurt," he sighed.

"Well... I'm glad you're on Juni's side," he said. "I tried my way... like my father..."

He rubbed his eyes, looking tired. Juni rubbed his shoulder.

"I'm not happy for how it happened," he croaked. "But I'm happy it did. I'm happy my girl is still here. And I'm happy she'll have you, Clara."

It was a very tearful, but amazing breakfast.

The wedding date was set. Takashi insisted on making it perfect.

❀ Juni XII ❀

Juni wasn't in one of her usual spots. She was sitting at her bay window. The light from outside highlighting her rosy cheeks. Her leg fidgets restlessly.

"I'm supposed to be downstairs soon," she says, keeping her gaze out of the window.

"I'm fitting a new dress."

She chuckles, then looks at the camera. Her mouth is curled into a small smile.

"I'm so nervous, it's silly."

She runs her hand down her braid.

"It's another boring white and gold dress, but that's ok."

Juni's smile grows.

"Point is Clara and I will be together at last."

She looks to her side, then grabs the camera. It goes black for a moment before the view stabilises showing her room interior.

Poppy and Goose are curled around each other in a ball.

"I think everyone is happier this way," Juni says from behind the camera.

She places the camera back on its original spot. She's openly grinning now.

"It wasn't easy getting here," she says pointedly.

"This thing," she continues, lifting her shirt to show her scar. "The bruise refuses to go away."

Juniper drops her shirt and sighs to the roof exasperated.

"It's going to ruin my beach photos."

She leans back against the window frame stretching out lazily.

"And Clara didn't hate me. She fought that-"

Her comm rings, making her jump. She fishes it out of her pocket impatiently.

"Hey," she answers, leaning into the comm.

...

"I'm fine. Better than fine," she says glowing.

...

"What?" she says, her smile faltering.

...

"Oh, no. Please tell me that's not true."

Juniper's eyes widen.

"Ok. I'll see you as soon as I can."

...

"I love you too," she says with curled lips.

Juniper ends the call, then looks at the camera—her face contorted. Then she erupts into laughter.

"Turns out, I'm thirty minutes late for the fitting," she snickers. "Whoops."

Juniper looks out of the window. Her face calm and happy.

"After, Clara said she has a surprise for me."

She presses a breath out softly.

"I hope the fitting is quick," she says, looking back to the camera. "I'm really looking forward to it."

She reaches to the screen, blocking for a moment. Giggling can be heard before the recording ends.

ͽ FOURTY-SEVEN ͼ

I had promised Juni a surprise. She lost some of her excitement when I led her to the monolith.

"I didn't realise..." she murmured. "Do we have to go in there?"

I held her hand tight.

"You'll be safe," I said staring into her lavender eyes. "I promise."

She nodded once, sharp, squeezing my hand too tight. "Ok. Let's go."

Her words were confident, but I could feel her pulse in her palm.

Only once we passed the workshop did her shoulders relax. That wouldn't last, as we descended deep into the structure.

"Clara, this is creepy."

"It's perfectly safe."

She slowed a bit.

"You've been down here before?" she whispered. "Why?"

I stopped and held up my hand. "I promise it's worth it... I think."

She rolled her eyes, then clung to my arm. "Alright," she said.

A few minutes later, Corrin's door way came into view. I stopped just short of it. I turned to Juniper taking both her hands.

"Promise you won't freak out?"

Her back straightened as she took a step back.

"Clara, you're scaring me."

I bit my lip. "I'm sorry. It's not my plan."

Letting go of her hands I stepped to the doorway.

"Let me show you," I said beckoning her over.

"Good afternoon, Clara," Corrin said. He was completely covered in skin. Only one hand remained machine. The body he built was naked, but missing any of the fun bits.

Hearing his voice, Juni perked up. She ducked her head as she snuck closer, then peeked around the corner.

Corrin spotting her broke out a wide smile.

"Lady Shao. An honour to finally meet you," he said with a small bow.

"Juni, meet Corrin," I said casually.

Juni's eyes stretched. She rounded the corner stalking over to Corrin.

He offered her his hand.

"You're... the voice. It was you all along," she said sheepishly.

Corrin nodded deeply.

"A pleasure to meet you, Corrin," she said, shaking his hand tentative, but politely. "I have read a lot about you."

She looked back at me, mocking a shocked face.

"Show her the other hand, Corrin," I poked.

He lifted the un-skinned hand to her.

Juniper peered at it closely.

"How. Fucking. Awesome!" she erupted, her tension forgotten.

Corrin looked very pleased with himself. He tilted his head, looking around Juni.

"Congratulations, ladies," he said. "On the wedding."

I blushed. It was still an idea I was getting used to.

"I'm gonna be a mom too," I bragged.

He pursed his lips, nodding.

"I am grateful then, lady Shao will be there to be the adult," he said glibly.

Juni tried to stifle her chuckle, but failed when she saw Corrin's goofy smile.

"You guys are hilarious," I groaned as they laughed together.

But Juni's laugh was intoxicating as always.

We spent hours there.

My fiancée and an ancient AI got along fine.

FOURTY-EIGHT

I said goodbye to my ratty apartment. The dim little space had been my home for near on two Lyra years. Through everything that happened, it remained my fixed point. For better or worse.

That door clicked shut behind me.

I opened the door to Juni's... our room.

Juni jumped me wrapping around my neck, kissing me hard. "Welcome home," she said, practically vibrating.

I unpacked.

We quibbled about space.

Distractions were frequent.

Words failed and bodies took over.

Easy days rolled past, to our big day.

I insisted on wearing the blue dress Juni had given me. It was the nicest dress I owned and I wasn't ready to use my father-in-law's money yet.

The band struck up as I walked down the aisle, with Iris on my arm.

The crowd was small, but I stared straight ahead to temper my nerves.

Iris pecked my cheek when she gave me away at the archway.

Then came Juniper.

She walked down with her father, my vision blurring as I held back the tears. She smiled so brightly.

Her father nodded at me as I took her hand.

The room vanished as she held mine.

She was the most beautiful thing I had ever seen.

And she was mine, as I was hers.

We said the words. Exchanged rings and a ribbon.

"I do," I said with all my heart.

"I do," she said, beautiful lavender eyes on mine.

Then her lips touched mine for what felt like the first time.

The guests erupted. Juniper's father most enthusiastically.

We walked out through showers of confetti and streamers. Faces of our life mixed in with the family.

Matayo in his best suit, outdone only by his smile.

The long dark curls of Iris, her dark eyes teary.

A suspiciously pale, almost human face, smiling in the back.

I lost a step. A blocky smile from a large man in a black suit.

He winked at me, turning my stomach.

"Are you ok?" Juni whispered.

I lost sight of him in the thrum.

"Yeah," I said, letting my smile out again. "I'm all good, my love."

Then we were off to summer sand and bliss.

Nothing but us, and the waves of the Lyra ocean.

I sipped oddly named drinks on an alien beach.

I walked in the sand with my wife, a princess.

I baked under a foreign star, and stargazed under a moonless sky.

We were excited to be mothers. To share our lives with each other.

I held Juni's hand, thinking of how far I had come, dreaming of what still lay ahead.

We would have each other, freedom, and most of all...

Love.

❀ Juni XIV ❀

The video started with Juni already giggling. She was wrapped in a shawl over her swimwear.

"Look," she gushed. "The beach!"

The camera panned over a white beach with teal water stretching to the horizon. The sky was clear and bright. The sound of the waves in the quiet was almost soothing.

"And... And..." she continued.

"Ta-da," she said, holding her ring up to the camera.

"I'm married!"

She flopped down on a couch, frowning slightly with her hand over the persistent bruise on her stomach.

"Ah," she sighed. "Somehow, it all worked out."

"I guess we just had to wait a bit for forever," Juni chuckled.

"Two weeks of nothing but beach and sun."

A sly grin crept to her face. "And not a lot of clothing."

She perked up, looking past the camera, then squeaked.

"My wife is coming back," she smiled.

"Clara Nadia Shao, everyone," Juniper said, spinning herself and the camera.

I paused the recording on her smiling face, before I entered the frame.

This was the one entry I could never finish.

She was so beautiful and full of life.

Our lives were so full—the real deal.

We were so happy then.

Fin

Also by J du Preez

Embers of Origins

About the Author

J du Preez is a South African author who writes to relax, but likes to share. They believe forever means forever and hearts go on sleeves. They believe all endings are valid happy or not. They have a dear wife, a diligent son, and too many cats. They also believe in the power of coffee at 1am.

www.ingramcontent.com/pod-product-compliance
Lightning Source LLC
LaVergne TN
LVHW010647110826
845149LV00014B/2976

9781049284088